Praise for **Kate Bateman**

A RECKLESS MATCH

"Bateman launches a Regency trilogy with this pitch-perfect enemies-to-lovers romance centered on the feuding Montgomery and Davies families . . . Brimming with intrigue, passion, and humor, this is sure to win the author new fans."
—*Publishers Weekly* (starred review)

"*A Reckless Match* is sexy, sassy and distinctly divine. Explosive!"
—*Romance Junkies*

THIS EARL OF MINE

"Bateman's scintillating first Bow Street Bachelors Regency is full of intense emotions and dramatic twists. Intelligent, affable characters make this fast-paced novel shine, especially for fans of clever women and the men who sincerely admire them. Future installments will be eagerly anticipated by Regency readers."
—*Publishers Weekly* (starred review)

"A book that begins with a Regency heiress seeking a bridegroom in Newgate Prison promises daring adventure, and Kate Bateman gives readers just what they're looking for in *This Earl of Mine*. . . . Pure fun."
—*BookPage*

"Genuine romance that shines through . . . delightful leads and sexy capers."
—*Kirkus Reviews*

"*To Catch an Earl* is a fun, fast-paced read with lots of sexual tension and capers a-plenty. It's been one of my favorite books so far this year and I highly recommend it."

—*Smart Bitches, Trashy Books*

THE PRINCESS AND THE ROGUE

"This smart Regency romance and its resilient heroine are sure to win over readers."   —*Publishers Weekly*
(starred review)

"*The Princess and the Rogue* is a sweet, steamy, romantic, humorous, yet slightly angsty Regency/historical romance deftly balanced with bits of mystery, royal intrigue, and action that readers will find hard to put down."

—Affair de Coeur

"What's not to enjoy about a roguish former soldier and a Russian princess in disguise? . . . [A] thoroughly entertaining read."   —*BookPage*

"*The Princess and the Rogue* is a delightful Regency romance that'll leave readers with a smile."   —*Fresh Fiction*

"An excellent story with delightful characters, including Seb's partners, *The Princess and the Rogue* is the perfect conclusion to this terrific series."   —*Romance Reviews Today*

A Daring Pursuit

Kate Bateman

St. Martin's Paperbacks

This is a work of fiction. All of the characters, organizations, and events portrayed in this novel are either products of the author's imagination or are used fictitiously.

First published in the United States by St. Martin's Paperbacks, an imprint of St. Martin's Publishing Group

A DARING PURSUIT

For information, address St. Martin's Publishing Group, 120 Broadway, New York, NY 10271.

www.stmartins.com

ISBN: 978-1-250-80160-9

Our books may be purchased in bulk for promotional, educational, or business use. Please contact your local bookseller or the Macmillan Corporate and Premium Sales Department at 1-800-221-7945, ext. 5442, or by email at MacmillanSpecialMarkets@macmillan.com.

Printed in the United States of America

St. Martin's Paperbacks edition / June 2022

10 9 8 7 6 5 4 3 2 1

Wrth gicio a brathu mae carida yn magu.
(While kicking and biting, love develops.)

—OLD WELSH PROVERB

Chapter 1

Lady Carys Davies dressed to meet her blackmailer in the same way she dressed for every other social occasion: scandalously.

Her clothes were both her armor and her weapons, and although outright murder—however justified—was out of the question, there was still a slim hope that her outfit would induce a fatal apoplexy in her tormentor, Christopher Howe.

If the sight of her near-naked figure *also* managed to spur a reaction from the terminally laconic Tristan Montgomery . . . well, that would be a delightful, if unlikely, bonus.

Tongues were already wagging as she and Rhys paused at the top of the steps leading into the ballroom.

"You're causing a sensation." Her brother sent her a cheeky sideways grin.

His tone was amused, indulgent, and Carys felt a familiar flash of gratitude for her easygoing sibling.

"That's the plan," she whispered back, smiling through her teeth. "What's the point in going to a party and being ignored?"

Exhale. Calm. Smile.

This was the Carys Davies who appeared in public: carefree and delightful, a girl who cared for nobody's opinion but her own. No one could guess that on the inside she was besieged by panic and uncertainty. Not even her brothers.

Especially not them.

The three of them thought she relished setting the fashionable world on its heels, but that wasn't entirely true. Tonight's outfit—indeed, every outfit she'd worn for the past two seasons—had been carefully calculated to provide a distraction. If she could keep people talking about her dress, or *un*dress, in this case, then nobody would start asking awkward questions like, *Why haven't you chosen a husband yet?*

Carys spied her best friend, Frances Roque, and tugged at Rhys's arm. "There's Frances. Come on."

The room was a rainbow swirl of costumes. Nuns and friars squashed up against shepherdesses and chimney sweeps. Several people, like herself, had come dressed as characters from classical antiquity. Three vestal virgins giggled in a corner with a knight in full armor, and a man she recognized as Lord Burlington was Bacchus, with a wreath of vine leaves circling his head.

Her own outfit was still the most remarkable. The sheer white fabric left one shoulder bare and draped, Grecianstyle, diagonally across her body before flowing in liquid pleats to the floor. The wide silver belt encircling her waist matched the quiver of arrows on her back, and the crescent

moon that nestled in her hair surrounded by a galaxy of bob-
bing silvery stars.

It was the transparency of the material that had everyone whispering behind their fans; was that *naked skin* they
glimpsed whenever she moved? Was that a *nipple*?

In truth, her outfit was a masterpiece of tease and innuendo. Madame de Tourville, her dressmaker, had fashioned
a skin-toned underdress; Carys was more fully clothed than
almost every other woman in the room, but the dress gave
the appearance of being scandalously translucent. She could
already see several men squinting in a vain attempt to see
through the fabric.

Her smile widened as she and Rhys made their way
through the crowd.

"Looking ravishing, Aphrodite!" Lord Caseby brayed,
bowing low over her hand.

Carys extricated herself with a trilling laugh before he
could kiss her bare knuckles.

"What a delightful Athena." Colonel Brant smiled, his
monocle fogging up as he lifted it to his bloodshot eye.

Carys gave him her best eyelash flutter and deftly escaped.

Frances was dressed as a flower seller, with a wooden
tray filled with posies suspended from a ribbon around her
neck. Her forehead wrinkled as she greeted Carys. "Are you
supposed to be Minerva?"

"Diana. Goddess of the hunt and the moon."

"Ah. That explains the stars." Frances eyed her elaborate
coiffeur with a smile. "How have you got them to bounce
around like that?"

"Each one's on a wire, pinned into my hair." Carys shook

her head, and the halo of metallic spots shimmered like a shoal of silvery fish.

"Clever. But *please* tell me you have something on under that dress."

"Perfume?" Carys teased.

Rhys chuckled at her side. "I'm off to the cardroom. Try and stay out of trouble. And if you can't be good, be careful."

"I think that's the unofficial Davies motto." Carys laughed, waving him off.

"You know what I mean." Frances dropped her voice. *"Unmentionables."*

Carys lowered her own voice to the same theatrical whisper. "If you mean, am I wearing a corset, and a chemise, and drawers, then yes, of course I am."

Frances exhaled. "Oh, thank goodness. You're treading very close to the line, you know."

"Pfft. There are plenty of other risqué outfits here."

"Not on single women. It's all very well for married ladies and widows to wear something so provocative, but you don't have the protection of a husband's name."

"Nor do I want one," Carys said stoutly. "Hence my choice of Diana. She, too, swore never to wed."

Frances shook her head. "I don't understand why you've developed this aversion to marriage. At school we used to giggle about the men we'd choose. What changed?"

"I actually met some men," Carys said drily.

Frances rolled her eyes. "They're not all bad. You can't still be peeved because Christopher Howe proposed to Victoria Jennings? That was almost two years ago."

Carys hid her instinctive grimace. "I promise you, I'm not. Victoria's welcome to him."

That was the truth. She'd thought Howe handsome once, but now the idea of meeting him left her nauseous. Unfortunately, his summons tonight was one she couldn't refuse.

"What about Lord Ellington?" Frances murmured. "He's nice."

"He *is* nice. I'm just not ready to marry yet."

Maybe not ever, thanks to Howe.

"Your perfect match is out there somewhere," Frances said confidently. "You'll find him, just like I found James."

Frances was head over heels in love with a cavalry officer named James Sinclair. They'd been courting for almost three months, and everyone expected a proposal very soon.

"Who knows?" Frances smiled dreamily. "Maybe your future husband's here, at this very party."

"And maybe pigs will fly."

Frances shrugged, and the two of them turned to scrutinize the dance floor. Carys suppressed a little sigh as she spied her eldest brother, Gryff, and his new wife, Maddie, waltzing together, oblivious to everyone else in the room.

Frances followed the direction of her gaze. "Now that Gryff's married a Montgomery, do you think that'll be the end of the Davies-Montgomery feud?"

Carys snorted. "I doubt it. Five hundred years of adversity isn't going to be smoothed over by one little wedding. It's like the Wars of the Roses, only worse."

"I thought a wedding *ended* the Wars of the Roses? Wasn't Henry Tudor's mother a Lancastrian? When he married a York princess it united the families and stopped all the bloodshed."

"Nothing wrong with a bit of bloodshed. It keeps things interesting."

"Maybe Gryff marrying Maddie will heal the rift?"

Carys sent her a pitying glance. "That's what I love about you, Frances. You're such an optimist. *I* predict things will only get worse."

"Why?"

"Because now there are even more opportunities for Davieses and Montgomerys to be in close proximity. Gryff and Maddie's house party at the end of the month is a case in point. It's bad enough when we're miles apart with a river between us. But Gryff's invited all the Montgomerys to Trellech Court every day for a whole week, to take part in the activities."

"Isn't that a good thing? An olive branch?"

"It's a naked flame to a keg of gunpowder."

Frances took a delicate sniff at one of the posies from her tray and slid her a sideways glance. "I expect Tristan will be there."

Carys frowned at her carefully innocent tone. Frances might be blissfully unaware of her problems with Christopher Howe, but she knew all about Carys's long-standing obsession with her sardonic country neighbor. "I suppose he will. What of it?"

"I always thought you and he would make a good couple. If you weren't sworn enemies, of course."

Carys couldn't contain her splutter. "Me? And Tristan? Are you mad? Where did you come up with that idea?"

"I've seen you with him," Frances said simply. "You smile at other men, but with Tristan you *glow*. It's like you come alive in his presence. You're the fire to his ice."

"That's awfully poetic," Carys managed, trying to hide her shock at being so suddenly exposed. She'd forgotten how perceptive her old friend could be. "But nothing will ever happen between Tristan and me. He just likes having someone to disapprove of, that's all. After Bonaparte, I'm his next favorite opponent."

Frances shrugged. "Well, maybe there will be some *other* nice single men at the house party?"

Carys opened her mouth to protest, but Frances spoke again before she could interrupt.

"Oh, I know you flirt with every man between the ages of seven and seventy, but you don't take any of them *seriously*. There are some good men out there, Carys. Promise you'll try to find one you could be happy with. As I am with James."

Frances was looking at her with such starry-eyed enthusiasm that Carys didn't have the heart to disillusion her by revealing the ugliness of her situation with Howe. She sent her dear friend a bright smile instead.

"All right. For you, my love, I'll try. Although I strongly suspect you've bagged the only decent man in England."

Frances glanced across the room and her face creased into a smile. "Oh, look, there he is! With Tristan Montgomery."

Carys's heart began to pound, but she forced herself not to swirl around and look. She turned slowly, bracing herself for her first glance. Looking at Tristan was like leaping into a frigid Welsh stream: One had to prepare.

Her pulse gave an irregular little flutter as she located his imposing figure standing alongside Frances's beau. The two men were complete opposites. James was unfailingly jolly, with a ready smile and floppy brown hair that was always getting in his eyes. He reminded her of a spaniel: ever pleased to see you, full of bounding energy. His ruddy complexion spoke of exhausting outdoor pursuits like riding and cricket.

Tristan, in contrast, was stillness, calm control. His cynical blue eyes missed nothing but gave little hint as to what he might be thinking.

As ever, he looked faintly bored, as if all this unnecessary exuberance was keeping him from doing something more important, like redesigning the world into a more orderly place. His tall frame was relaxed and elegant, but the power in the muscles beneath his dark evening jacket was unmistakable.

He was a paradox of a man: harsh, rigid features, lips made for sin. Glacial eyes that somehow made her burn.

Quite *why* she was so desperate for Tristan's approval was a mystery. As Rhys said, she should content herself with her scores of other admirers, but there was something so deliciously *unattainable* about Tristan. His cool reserve was a challenge she couldn't ignore.

It was probably because everyone else thought she was charming and witty and he was the sole anomaly. The idea of getting him to smile, or to look at her with anything other than slightly sardonic amusement, occupied far too much of her time.

She had to admit she enjoyed their long-standing adversity. Goading him had always been her favorite thing to do. If, as Frances had always maintained, the world required balance, then surely Tristan's cool, logical existence was needed to counteract her own hotheaded frivolity. Who knew what might happen if the two of them ever agreed on something? The sky would probably fall down.

She studied him covertly. Tristan's hands, with their long

fingers and broad palms, had always held a particular fascination. She could well imagine them holding a pencil to sketch out one of his architectural wonders. *Or sliding over her skin . . .*

No!

He'd barely spoken to her during last month's wedding, when his sister had married Gryff. He'd never touched her with anything but the most impersonal contact. A steadying hand on her arm when she'd "accidentally" bumped into him at a soiree a few weeks ago. The briefest brush of his shoulder against hers as they'd walked down the aisle—before they'd peeled off to sit on opposite sides of the pews.

Carys had worn a sage-green gown for the wedding, the most demure thing she'd worn for ages, but demure Carys clearly hadn't appealed to Tristan. She was beginning to think that *no* version of herself would tempt him.

Still, perhaps brazen Carys would have more luck in piercing his displeasure tonight?

Chapter 2

Tristan Montgomery tried very hard to keep his attention on his best friend, James Sinclair, and not on the scandalous appearance of Lady Carys Davies on the opposite side of the ballroom.

The merest glimpse of her, standing like some semi-clad goddess at the top of the stairs, had been enough to stop his heart and send a hot flare of outrage—it *was definitely* outrage—sweeping through his body.

He'd spent a large part of his twenty-seven years perfecting the art of ignoring her, of appearing cool and indifferent to her inflammatory presence when his entire being prickled with awareness whenever they were in the same room.

He gave in to the temptation to look again.

Who was she supposed to be, for God's sake? Lady Godiva?

Her dress was as sheer as a whisper, as if Botticelli's Venus had stepped out of her giant shell and donned a che-

mise made of spiderwebs. She might as well have been naked, for all the coverage the material provided. Her breasts,
shimmering with silver-flecked powder, rose above the dar-
ingly low neckline like an offering to the gods.

*What were her brothers thinking, to allow her to expose
herself in public like this?* There wasn't a man in the entire
ballroom who wasn't wondering what it would be like to inspect those incredible curves at closer range.

Tristan fought the urge to push his way through her
throng of admirers, throw a cloak around her near-naked
shoulders, and bundle her out into his carriage.

Quite what he'd do with her then, he didn't know.

*Spank her for her foolishness, probably. Someone needed
to take the girl in hand.*

Heat rose on his skin and he curled his fingers into a fist.

No. No spanking. Bad idea. Touching her would be a terrible mistake. He wouldn't lay a hand on her. He would simply give her a strongly worded dressing down.

That was such a stupid phrase. *Dressing down.* What did
it even mean? She was only wearing a few scraps of muslin.
If she dressed down any further she'd be naked—

"Tristan, are you even listening to me?"

James's amused tones finally penetrated his racing brain.
"Sorry. I was just marveling at that red-haired hellion's
nerve." He made a disapproving clucking sound with his
tongue. "Her brothers give her far too much leeway."

"Yes, it amazes me that she and Frances are such friends.
They're complete opposites."

Tristan frowned. Carys's deep-red hair was decorated
with what looked like a swarm of metallic bees. Her freck-
led nose was too small to balance out the generous width of

her smile, and her green eyes flashed as she tossed her head
back and laughed at something Frances said.

His chest tightened unpleasantly.

"I'd like some time alone with Frances," James murmured. "Can you keep Carys company while we're gone?
I'll meet you back in the cardroom in fifteen minutes."

Tristan suppressed a groan. Dear God, the last thing he
wanted was increased exposure to the woman. It was hard
enough pretending he wasn't aware of the precise moment
she walked into a room. Hard enough to keep his hands by
his sides, or holding a glass, when all he wanted to do was
touch that glorious molten hair to see if it would singe him
as much as the clash of their gazes did.

He knew it would and playing with fire was such a mistake.

He sent James a resigned smile. "Of course."

Carys gazed across the crowded ballroom, trying to locate
Howe, and found him deep in conversation with Lord Holland, a Whig politician known for his radical political views.
The sight of him turned her stomach, but she wasn't due to
meet him until just after midnight, so she still had a little
time to enjoy herself.

Frances excused herself to go to the powder room, and
Carys scanned the room again, looking for Tristan. She'd
lost sight of him in the crush. She spotted his aunts, Constance and Prudence, seated near the entrance to the cardroom, but Tristan wasn't with them.

And then her heart leapt into her throat as his deep voice
rumbled directly behind her.

"The cost of your wardrobe is legendary, Lady Carys, but

I can't imagine you paid much for *that* outfit. There's hardly enough material there to make a handkerchief."

How on earth had he managed to sneak up on her, the devil?

She turned and found him half hidden behind a pillar, one eyebrow raised in question, and willed her heart rate to calm to a healthy level.

"As a matter of fact, this is the most expensive dress I've ever worn."

"That cannot possibly be true."

"Oh, it is." Wickedness seized her. She stroked the fabric that ran over her shoulder and watched in delight as his eyes followed the movement. She slid her fingers down, skating over the dangerously low neckline of the dress.

He swallowed.

"This is one of the most costly materials ever made," she purred. "It comes from Bengal. Most muslin has three or four hundred threads per inch, but this has over a thousand. It's so fine, a bolt of it can be pulled through a wedding ring."

She leaned a little closer. "I heard a story that a Mughal emperor once berated his daughter for appearing naked in public when she was, in fact, wearing *seven* layers of this."

Tristan lifted his gaze and his eyes clashed with hers. Her heart missed a beat.

"How many layers are you wearing?"

She opened her eyes wide in faux innocence. "Me? Only five."

A muscle twitched in the side of his jaw and she bit the inside of her lip to stop herself from laughing. Seeing how far she could push him was so much fun.

"You are determined to be scandalous, Lady Carys," he growled.

"Pfft. If I'd *really* wanted to shock I'd have taken a leaf out of the Duchess of Kingston's book. She attended the Venetian Ambassador's masque sixty years ago as Iphigenia, with one breast completely bare, and her modesty only partly covered by some artfully draped fig leaves. The King was enchanted."

Tristan leaned sideways and eyed the quiver of arrows on her back. "I suppose you're Diana?"

She nodded. Trust him to be the only one to correctly guess her outfit. "Yes. Or Artemis, depending on whether you're Roman or Greek."

She'd chosen the outfit with deliberate irony. Diana the huntress was skilled with her bow, capable of defending herself and inflicting pain on her enemies. Carys only wished she had such power. And of course, Diana was a virgin goddess; a claim *she* could no longer make, thanks to her youthful misadventure with Howe. Still, that was the nature of a costume party, was it not? Everyone dressed as they wished to be, not as they were.

Pushing back such serious thoughts, she allowed herself the sinful pleasure of inspecting Tristan at close range, just as he'd done to her.

He, too, was wearing a toga, although his was secured at each shoulder with a gold-colored clasp. His arms were bare, and her mouth went dry as she took in his long, muscled limbs. His skin was unusually tanned—a remnant of his months spent traveling the Continent on his Grand Tour—and something about the sinews in his forearms made her feel a little light-headed.

She slid her gaze lower, to the leather belt fastened around his hips, then lower still, to where the pleated material of his chiton ended just above his knees. Who'd have thought *knees* could be attractive? And what was he wearing underneath?

She forced her tongue to work. "It seems you're also someone from an ancient civilization."

"Yes. But no one's guessed who I am."

"Well, you're not Zeus, with a lightning bolt. Nor one of those dull philosophers like Plato or Socrates." Carys racked her brain for inspiration. Tristan would never come as someone frivolous. He would be a man of brilliance, of talent. Someone he admired . . .

"An architect," she hazarded.

His brows rose a tiny amount—which could have been surprise. Or possibly just indigestion. It was difficult to tell, with him.

"Palladio," she said confidently.

His lips curled up. "I am indeed. How did you know?"

To indicate that she was intrigued by every aspect of his life would be fatal, so she tried to look bored instead.

"You're so *predictable*, Montgomery. You'd never come as someone fun. And since you're so interested in all this architectural stuff"—she waved a hand dismissively at the pillars and pediments surrounding them, a gesture guaranteed to annoy—"I knew you'd come as someone like that."

He didn't rise to her baiting. "You're rather predictable too."

"I am not!"

His lips quivered at her outraged gasp. "Oh, yes, you are. I could have guessed you'd be wearing something to make all the other unmarried girls despair."

"What do you mean?"

"What chance do any of them have of catching a husband
when you're dressed like that? The gentlemen are hanging
on your every word. You should marry one of them and put
the rest out of their misery."

Carys bit back a snort at the irony. Her outrageous dresses
were supposed to *deter* potential suitors, but they seemed to
have the opposite effect. An alarming number of men found
her rebelliousness fascinating. She'd already turned down
three proposals this season.

"*You're* not hanging on my every word," she said, keen to
steer the conversation away from the dangerous topic of marriage.

Tristan sent her a mocking bow. "On the contrary. I always find whatever you have to say vastly entertaining. The
last time we met we discussed courtesans, I recall."

A flash of heat spread through her at the reminder. She'd
brought up that scandalous topic to goad a reaction out of
him. The ploy had failed—as usual.

She managed a careless shrug. "Well, you already have
an incredibly low opinion of me, so it doesn't matter if we
talk of scandalous things."

She held her breath, hoping he'd demur, but he did not.
Her spirits sank.

"Is there some particularly indecent topic you think we
should visit tonight?" he asked.

His expression was polite, as cool and as composed as ever,
but she thought she could detect a hint of teasing in his cool
blue eyes. No, it was probably just wishful thinking on her
part.

"Perhaps you'd like me to describe the outfits of the

courtesans in Venice, so you can emulate them?" His gaze
flicked downward for a split second. "Although I have to say,
that dress is a fine approximation."

He *was* teasing her! A thrill shot through her at the unexpectedly naughty turn in the conversation, and she tried not
to show that she was overheating.

"You've had much experience with Venetian courtesans?"
she managed.

"Some. Enough to be of service."

The double meaning of his words made her stomach
swoop. Did he mean "be of service" in describing their
gowns? Or "be of service" in other, more scandalous ways?

*Surely not the latter. Tristan Montgomery wouldn't flirt
with her if she were the last woman in England.*

She was still searching for a suitable retort when his attention was caught by a group of guests nearby, and a frown
creased his handsome features.

"Now there's an outfit even more disgraceful than yours!"
he growled.

She followed his gaze. Lord Holland was wearing the
uniform of a French officer. Lady Holland, his wife, was
dressed to match, in a high-waisted gown, the kind favored
by the former Empress Josephine.

The couple had caused a minor scandal some years ago
when Lady Holland had remarried two days after her first
husband divorced her on grounds of adultery. Now they
hosted elite gatherings at Holland House, their mansion in
Kensington.

"Lord and Lady Holland have been openly sympathetic
to Bonaparte's cause for some time," she murmured.

"So I understand. They were great friends with Napoleon's

sister and her husband when I was in Italy last year. But to support him now is an insult to every man who's given his life or risked his limbs to protect this country."

The quiet anger in his tone made Carys wince in sympathy. Tristan had fought against the French for two years; he must have lost friends and acquaintances in battle. Seeing someone like Lord Holland flaunt his unpatriotic leanings so openly must be a bitter pill to swallow.

A nearby clock struck midnight and her enjoyment of sparring vanished as she recalled her upcoming meeting with Howe. She opened her mouth to tell Tristan she needed to find Frances, but it seemed he was suddenly as keen to part company as she was. He sent her a brief, stilted bow.

"If you'll excuse me, Lady Carys, I promised to meet James in the cardroom. I'll bid you good evening."

Carys wasn't sure whether to be relieved or disappointed.

Chapter 3

"Tristan, did you hear what Caseby just said?"

The room slid back into focus and Tristan realized he'd been glaring at a potted fern. "Sorry, what?"

James sent him an exasperated look. "Mentally redesigning Lady Banbury's ballroom, were you?"

Tristan cursed the heat of embarrassment that crept up his neck. "Something like that."

It wasn't the imperfect proportions of their hostess's ballroom that bothered him; it was the perfect proportions of one of her guests. Not that he'd admit it to James.

He glanced at the group seated at the baize-topped card table behind them. "What did Caseby say? Something stupid, I suppose. The man's an ass."

"He said he'd be the one to 'bring Carys Davies to heel' this season."

Tristan grimaced. "Good God. She's not a wild animal to be tamed."

It was easy enough to make the comparison, though. She was a flame-haired vixen, leading them all on a merry chase, far too clever to be caught by a bumbling bunch of hounds. And the way she snapped her fingers at convention reminded him of the wild white horses he'd encountered in his travels in southern France, tossing their heads at the idea of being corralled.

In Italy, or France, her spirit would be celebrated, but here in England they frowned on young ladies with opinions of their own. He disapproved of her rebelliousness himself, but there was still a small part of him that found her wildness entertaining.

And thoroughly arousing.

He shook his head to dislodge that supremely unhelpful thought. She was a Davies. The worst of the worst.

Without conscious thought he glanced back into the ballroom, to where she was now dancing with the suave, silver-haired politician Lord Ellington—another of her many admirers.

"There's more chance of a meteorite streaking out of the sky and hitting me on the head than of Carys Davies getting leg-shackled," he murmured.

She'd turned down numerous proposals. The woman was clearly impossible to please. Or else she had some mysterious criteria to which none of her previous suitors conformed. Maybe she was holding out for a duke. Or a prince.

"Caseby should save himself the aggravation," he continued. "That woman is chaos. Disorder. Ruinously expensive." He ticked off her "attributes" on his fingers, keeping his voice low so they wouldn't be overheard. "Not to mention disobedient, reckless, and likely to cause a scandal on a weekly basis. Any man who marries her will need deep pockets and an even deeper reserve of patience."

James followed his gaze. "I heard she might actually be considering Ellington."

Tristan suppressed an amused snort. "Not likely. He's even less inclined to wed than she is."

"Well, you can't deny she's gorgeous enough to make a man reconsider," James said evenly.

Cheers and groans from the card table behind them saved Tristan from having to answer that provocative statement. Caseby and his bosom friend Colonel Brant were congratulating Lord Holland on winning a hand. Tristan frowned again at the man's French uniform, then raised his brows as he identified the fourth occupant of the table.

Two years ago Christopher Howe had been the golden boy of the *ton*, feted for his good looks and smooth manners. He'd been a great favorite with the matchmaking mamas, despite having only a modest income and a fondness for gaming, and he'd pursued Carys with such ardency that many had assumed the announcement of their engagement was imminent.

But Howe had instead married Victoria Jennings, the only child of wealthy industrialist Obediah Jennings. Their wedding—according to the letter Maddie had sent to Tristan in Venice—had been the talk of the town.

Tristan hadn't examined too closely the relief he'd felt on hearing that Howe had transferred his affections to Victoria. It wasn't as if he'd ever consider marrying Carys *himself*.

It was, without doubt, time for him to wed. After two

years battling Bonaparte, followed by a Grand Tour of the Continent, he'd returned to London with that express goal in mind. He'd been mentally cataloging possible candidates for the past few months.

Carys Davies was definitely *not* one of them.

The most logical choice for a wife was Lavinia Purser. The daughter of a viscount, she had impeccable breeding and a cool competence Tristan found quite admirable. Her father was a noted patron of the arts, and his support would be invaluable for garnering further architectural commissions.

Tristan turned his head and found Lavinia in the crowd. He didn't have to brace himself to do it, since the sight of Lavinia aroused none of the inner turmoil that looking at Carys Davies did. Which was precisely why she would be the ideal partner. Lavinia was calm and pragmatic. She would make an excellent hostess and mother to his children. There would be no messy emotions to contend with. She was sensible, levelheaded, and drama-free.

All the things Carys Davies was not.

Almost without volition, his gaze strayed to where Carys now stood talking with Frances at the edge of the ballroom. Compared to Lavinia's understated elegance, Carys was almost offensively vibrant. Her beauty dimmed that of every other woman in the room, but disaster trailed her like iron filings after a magnet. If it wasn't racing horses along Rotten Row, it was scandalizing the *ton* with outrageous outfits like the one tonight.

Howe's petulant tones came from the gaming table behind him.

"Curse you, Holland. You have the devil's own luck."

The older man accepted the pile of coins Howe pushed toward him with a thin smile. "And what of the remaining two hundred?"

Howe slouched lower in his seat. "You can take my carriage. It's worth at least double that."

"I have enough carriages," Holland drawled coolly. "You may call on me later in the week to discuss more appropriate payment."

Howe's face flushed, and he took a gulp of brandy from the tumbler before him. "Very well."

Holland nodded and walked away. Howe glared after him, then seemed to shake off his frustration. He pulled a pocket watch from his waistcoat, glanced at it briefly, then put it away.

"Another quick game?" He lifted his brows at Caseby and Brant, who both nodded. "We need a fourth." He looked up and spied Tristan. "Ah. Montgomery! Haven't seen you in an age. Fancy a hand?"

Tristan sent him a polite smile. He'd always been skilled at cards, and his talent had only increased during his time in the army. Beating Howe would be a pleasure—what kind of idiot chose Victoria Jennings over Carys Davies?—and relieving a letch like Caseby of his money was equally irresistible.

He took the vacant seat between Caseby and Howe.

Howe grinned. "Excellent. My luck's bound to change sometime, eh? I'll wager my carriage against your two hundred pounds. What say you?"

Tristan nodded. "I'll take that bet."

Chapter 4

Carys slipped through Lady Banbury's garden gate and hurried along the shadowed alley that linked the stable mews to the front of the house. She'd already reclaimed her evening cloak from inside, and she drew the hood over her ridiculous hair, cursing the impractical stars-on-wires.

A line of carriages stretched down the street, dipping in and out of the circular pools of illumination afforded by the gaslights. Horses stamped and snorted in impatience, while coachmen huddled beneath their greatcoats atop each box or stood chatting in pairs.

She glanced up and down, searching for Howe's carriage, and her heart gave a jolt of relief when she identified his crest on the door of one of the nearest conveyances, half hidden in shadow.

Two years ago, when she'd been a naïve debutante, Howe had sought her out, charming and flattering at every func-

tion she'd attended. She'd encouraged his advances, impressed by his handsome face and faultless manners—and
childishly proud that the season's most eligible bachelor had
chosen *her* over all the other girls.

Of course, the one man she'd secretly dreamed of lav-
ishing her with such attention, Tristan Montgomery, hadn't
even been there to witness her triumph. He'd been off fighting
Bonaparte in France.

She'd long ago given up hope that Tristan would, *mi-
raculously*, overcome a lifetime of disdain, discover he was
actually in love with her (despite all evidence to the contrary), and demand her hand in marriage. Such dreams were
far beyond the realm of possibility. She could only hope
that news of her success would reach his ears and that he'd
realize—alas, too late!—what a terrible mistake he'd made
in ignoring her for all these years.

Certain that a proposal from Christopher was imminent,
Carys had allowed her natural curiosity to override her
good sense and had agreed to meet him in the gardens "for
a kiss." When his embraces had turned more ardent, she'd
been a willing, if naïve, participant in her own seduction;
recklessly impatient to experience the fiery passion the poets
were always describing in their sonnets.

When he'd thrust his tongue into her mouth she'd been
surprised, and a little repelled. He'd tasted of wine and tobacco, but she'd tried to kiss him back, inexpertly, waiting
for the same bubbles of excitement she always felt when she
thought of Tristan.

They hadn't materialized.

When Christopher slid his hands over her dress, squeez-
ing her breasts, she'd tried to squirm away, but he'd tumbled

her down onto the grass in a blur of limbs and coaxing words. He'd levered his full weight on top of her and rucked up her skirts, and as his hand slid up her thigh he'd pressed his face into her shoulder and groaned her name.

"Carys. I'm mad for you! Say you'll be mine."

"Oh, yes! Yes please." She'd thrown her arms around his neck, certain that the enjoyment others experienced from lovemaking would soon be hers. She couldn't wait to discover what all the fuss was about.

He'd fumbled with the fall of his breeches, and then he'd been between her legs, a surprising contact of flesh at the juncture of her thighs. He pushed forward, and discomfort turned to a flash of pain. Carys gasped. He thrust forward a few times, breathing heavily, then collapsed in a groaning, shuddering heap.

Carys had stared blankly at the stars overhead, at the way the moonlight filtered through the trees, distinctly underwhelmed by the whole experience.

This was the big secret? *This?* It hardly seemed worthy of a limerick, let alone an entire sonnet. Dear God, if this was what the physical side of marriage was all about, perhaps she was making a terrible mistake . . .

Just as Christopher's weight became intolerable, he pushed off her and righted his breeches. She'd straightened her clothing in a state of numb disbelief.

"I'll return to the house now," he said briskly. "Wait five minutes, then do the same. Don't speak to me once we're inside. Nobody can know what we've done."

"You'll speak to my father in the morning?" She'd tried to sound enthusiastic.

"Of course."

Carys suppressed a derisive snort at the memory. *Liar!* While she'd been wondering how to cry off, she'd never considered that Christopher would be the one to do the jilting. When he hadn't called the following day she'd been relieved, as if she'd been spared the hangman's noose . . . but she'd been as shocked as everyone else when he announced his engagement to Victoria Jennings not three days later.

The fact that pique and indignation had been her strongest emotions, instead of heartbreak, only confirmed what she'd suspected. She'd been infatuated with Christopher, taken in by his handsome face and easy charm. More in love with the *idea* of being in love than with the actual man. In hindsight, she'd a lucky escape, and she felt nothing but pity for poor Victoria, saddled with such an awful husband.

Unfortunately, her recklessness had placed her in a rather difficult position. As far as the *ton* and her brothers were concerned, she was still an untouched, eligible heiress, expected to wed. Any prospective suitor would expect her to be a virgin. How could she enter a marriage based on such a lie?

If she failed to disclose her nonvirginal state before the ceremony, she'd face the poor dupe's anger and disappointment on their wedding night. What chance would a union have after such a deceptive start? Even worse, by that point her new husband would have complete control over her person and her finances. He'd be quite within his rights to lock her away forever, if he chose. Carys suppressed an instinctive shudder.

And yet how could she trust a man enough to confess her lack of virginity *before* the wedding? What if he cried off, and exposed her secret to the world? She'd be ostracized, and her family and friends would all suffer in her downfall.

No, it was too risky. Staying single was clearly the best option, and after such a miserable experience with Howe, she wasn't sure she even *wanted* to marry, anyway. Love-making was vastly overrated.

Howe's perfidy, however, hadn't ended at her ruination. A few months after his marriage, he'd started to blackmail her, threatening to expose their liaison to the world. The envelope beneath her evening cloak contained the infuriating cost of his monthly silence: fifty pounds in banknotes.

She could see no end in sight.

His carriage was empty. The horses stood calmly, their heads bowed, and the coachman had dismounted to chat with another driver farther up the street. With one last look to be sure she wouldn't be seen by any other guests, she dashed forward and jumped up into the carriage, careful not to rip her fragile skirts. She settled on the velvet seat and pulled the shades down over the windows; she wanted no witnesses to her shame.

She didn't have long to wait. After a few minutes she heard footsteps and a dark figure swung open the door. The sudden lamplight illuminated the man stepping up into the carriage, and a gasp of pure horror escaped her.

Oh, dear God, no!

Tristan Montgomery paused on the step, half in, half out of the doorway, and for an instant the world simply stopped.

A flurry of unguarded emotions raced across his face: surprise, disbelief, shock. And then his features settled into an attitude of cynical disdain.

Carys prayed that he'd apologize for getting into the wrong carriage and leave, but he shouldered his way in instead. The coach rocked on its springs as he closed the narrow door behind him, plunging them into near darkness.

He settled onto the bench across from her and Carys shrank back against her seat, her pulse thumping uncomfortably in her throat. The scent of him, overwhelmingly male, filled the small space as a thousand explanations—excuses—tumbled through her brain.

His deep, cold tones filled the awful silence. "I'd ask what you're doing in Howe's carriage, but it seems rather obvious."

He held up a gloved hand to forestall her instinctive denial. Now that her eyes had adjusted to the shadows she could make out his broad shape, sprawled across the squabs.

"You're having an affair with him." He shook his head, almost in wonderment, like a boxer who'd taken a blow to the head.

What could she say? To have him believe she was having a liaison with Howe was awful, but the truth was even more humiliating.

His eyes glittered in the darkness. "He's a married man, for God's sake. If you were going to have an affair, couldn't you have chosen someone single?" His voice held the diamond-hard edge of disapproval. "And Howe, of all men? The man's an ass."

Carys tugged the edges of her cloak around her, a pathetic shield against the cold fury emanating from him. "You're in the wrong carriage," she managed hoarsely. The envelope of banknotes rustled in her hand as she clenched it against her skirts.

"I am not," he growled. "This is my carriage now. I just won it from Howe in the cardroom."

Dear God, what horrible luck.

He sat forward abruptly, resting his elbows on his knees, and Carys stilled, uncertain of his mood.

"Do you go to a hotel? Or does he have a little town house set aside?"

"What? No! It's not like that."

His brows lowered. "Oh, drop the innocent act. Why else would you be in his carriage alone?"

The need to defend herself was almost overwhelming, but Carys swallowed down the denial and the silence stretched to an excruciating level as they stared at each other across the narrow confines of the coach. She could feel the heat of his knees, so close to her own, through the fabric of her cloak.

Unable to bear any more of his soul-stripping scrutiny, she put her hand to the door handle, but his low voice stopped her.

"Do you deny that you've given yourself to Howe?"

She bit her lip. Would he believe her if she said no? Unlikely. In his mind she was already a fallen woman, a liar who'd hoodwinked society, pretending to be chaste when she was really a soiled dove.

Which was entirely true.

A strange, angry part of her rose to the surface. She was so tired of keeping it a secret. His opinion of her couldn't get any lower. It might almost be a relief to tell someone.

She turned back and met his stare. "No, I don't deny it." She raised her brows in a faint *what are you going to do about it?* challenge.

His own brows rose too. In disgust? Disappointment? She couldn't tell.

The silence stretched taut.

And then he leaned back, the epitome of masculine grace, and a flush raced across her skin at his intense regard. Even with her cloak wrapped around her she felt the heat of his look all the way down to her bones.

"Lucky Howe," he said softly.

Her heart missed a beat.

"It seems I've ruined your evening." His tone was cool, mocking; his previous anger seemed to have dissipated. "You were clearly expecting a little amour. Maybe I should make amends by inviting you home with me instead?"

Carys couldn't have been more shocked if he'd suddenly sprouted wings. "What?"

His broad shoulders lifted in a shrug. "I can't decide if that's the most honorable thing to do . . . or the most *dis*honorable."

"You're propositioning me?" she croaked. *Was this some kind of a test? Or a joke?* "Don't be ridiculous. You don't want me, Montgomery. You don't even *like* me."

He tilted his head, as if she were a puzzle he had to solve. "You don't need to like someone to be physically attracted to them, or to have a satisfying sexual encounter."

Carys could scarcely draw a breath. He couldn't possibly be serious. "But . . . what about Lavinia Purser?"

"What about her?"

"I thought you were on the verge of offering for her?"

"What if I am?"

Her heart was slamming uncomfortably hard against her ribs.

"The thought of bedding an almost fiancé shouldn't bother you if you're already sneaking around with someone's husband," he said reasonably.

She suppressed a grimace. He'd have a valid point if she really *were* sleeping with Howe. Still, he didn't truly desire her, despite what he'd just implied; he'd made his lack of interest in her perfectly clear for months.

"*You'd* make love to *me*?" She tried to sound amused, and not simply incredulous.

"I would, in fact." He made it sound like a point of theoretical interest, but the intensity of his gaze brought a flush to her skin. "Most thoroughly."

The contrast between his scandalous words and the cool manner in which he said them made her head spin. *What on earth was happening?*

She managed a scornful snort. "You're very sure of your abilities."

He shrugged again. "If I do something, I like to do it well—whether it's architecture, garden design, or pleasing a woman."

Holy hell. What would it be like to be on the receiving end of Tristan's expertise? She could just imagine the intense look on his face as he dedicated himself to achieving his goal. She'd always teased him about being single-minded in his pursuit of perfection, but for the first time it didn't sound like a flaw.

Quite the opposite.

He crossed one leg casually over the other. "I've always found you attractive. I stayed away because I assumed you were saving yourself for marriage. It's intriguing to have been proved wrong."

Chapter 5

Intriguing.

Carys swallowed down a bitter lump of disappointment at the word. Tristan might be joking with her now, but his was a telling glimpse of the reaction she'd get from every man in the *ton* if they discovered her secret. She'd be fair game, endlessly propositioned. The same "gentlemen" clamoring for her hand would abandon that path with alacrity if they thought they could get her into bed without the benefit of marriage.

For the briefest of moments she wondered what would happen if she called Tristan's bluff and said yes. Her experience with Howe had been bad, it was true, but logically she understood that making love couldn't be unpleasant for *everyone*. Having listened to her brothers' ribald comments on the subject, she was quite sure men enjoyed it. Then again, men seemed to enjoy plenty of *un*pleasant things, like

chasing foxes and bludgeoning fish on the head, and getting
so drunk they vomited in flowerpots, so their opinion hardly
seemed reliable.

For the past year, however, she'd closely observed a
number of married women, and eavesdropped on several
private conversations, and several of *them* had hinted at enjoying, even encouraging, the amorous attentions of their
husbands.

Tristan was so different from Howe. He elicited a whole
range of hot flushes and bothersome tinglings that she'd
never experienced with anyone else. Perhaps making love
with him would be an entirely different experience.

Perhaps she might even enjoy it . . .

No.

It was one thing to have given up her virginity through
youthful curiosity and ignorance. It was quite another to
knowingly agree to sleep with a man who would never offer
her marriage.

Not even for one night.

Tristan was still watching her calmly. "You seem lost
for words, Lady Carys. I never thought I'd see the day." He
stretched one arm across the back of the seat and studied
her with a look that made her feel like an insect under a
microscope. "At least now I understand why you've shown
no interest in accepting any of your suitors. You don't want
them to discover you're not a virgin on the wedding night."

She cursed the way he cut to the very heart of her problem.

He tilted his head, as if considering the idea. "You might
still be able to risk it, you know. I doubt many of them would
notice."

Carys frowned. This was new information.

For someone who was technically "ruined," she was woefully lacking in actual carnal knowledge. She hadn't been able to discuss her experience with any of the married women of her acquaintance, so she knew next to nothing about the whole damnable business.

"What do you mean? Surely a man can tell?"

How, though? Had Howe been able to tell? She had no idea.

Was she truly having such an intimate conversation with Tristan Montgomery? It seemed unreal, but perhaps he was the perfect person with whom to discuss such scandalous things. He'd already judged her and found her wanting; she had nothing to lose and everything—including vital information she couldn't get from anywhere else—to gain.

"Have you ever . . . ?" she ventured.

He raised his brows. "Slept with a virgin? God, no. Never."

She bit back a snort of amusement at his apparent disgust. Of course he hadn't. When would he have encountered a virgin? His mistresses would have been women of equal, or greater, experience. He'd probably bedded all manner of gorgeous, sophisticated European women on his Grand Tour. Like those barely dressed Italian courtesans.

Yet another reason she couldn't accept his outrageous offer. How could she possibly compete with that level of expertise?

"I've heard it's sometimes difficult for a man to tell if he's the first, though," he continued evenly.

But how? she wanted to scream. Was it because the woman bled the first time, as she had? Or did that happen every time?

"I suppose you'll find out if you marry Lavinia Purser," she said tersely.

There was no doubt that proud, perfect Lavinia was still unsullied. She'd never have allowed herself to be debauched in the shrubbery.

Tristan sent her a reproachful frown. "For your information, I haven't proposed to Lavinia Purser, despite what the gossips are saying."

A knot of something loosened inside her, even though he hadn't actually said that he *wouldn't* be asking her in the future. Just that he hadn't yet. Still, she was inexplicably buoyed by the news.

"Well, whoever you eventually marry, she'll be a virgin, won't she?" she pressed.

"Probably. It's a practical way of ensuring one's fiancée isn't carrying another man's bastard. And of knowing she doesn't have the pox."

Carys felt her cheeks heat with anger. "Isn't the man far more likely to be the poxy one? What protection does a woman have against that?"

"None, unless she can find a virginal man. And they're fairly thin on the ground." His bright gaze met hers, as if he'd just received enlightenment. "Ahh. Is *that* what you're looking for in a husband? I've been wondering about your criteria. You're after someone too inexperienced to tell if he's your first? Someone you can dupe, and then instruct?"

Now her cheeks flushed with more than anger. "Don't be ridiculous."

The idea that Tristan obviously saw her as some kind of highly experienced femme fatale was ludicrous. As if *she* were in a position to instruct anyone.

"Or maybe you're hoping the poor sod will fall so much in love with you that he won't even *care* you're not a virgin?"

Carys didn't even bother to hide her skepticism. "You think there's such a man?"

His gaze lingered on her face. "Oh, I think you'd be surprised. Inexperience can be quite tedious, I'd imagine."

"Well, it's a moot point, because I'm not looking to get married."

"Yes, I can see how a husband might get in the way of your string of lovers."

She glared at his sarcasm. "Despite what you might think, Montgomery, I didn't come out here tonight expecting to go home with Howe."

"You were planning a quickie in the carriage? Not my personal favorite, but I suppose if time is of the essence—"

"No!" Her cheeks flamed even hotter at the mental image of uptight Tristan losing control enough to make love to a woman in a carriage. Surely he'd never—"No!" she repeated more firmly. "Not that either. I merely needed to speak with him. A business matter. That's all."

Tristan straightened, his expression cynical. "Business. Of course. Well, as you can see, he's not here. Nor will he be. So if you don't require me as a substitute, I'll be on my way home."

Her rejection of his "offer" clearly didn't bother him in the slightest, and she quashed a perverse sting of pique. He *had* been joking.

"Can I give you a ride?" His lips twitched. "No pun intended."

Carys cast an anxious glance at the door. How long had

she been in here, sparring with him? "I should get back to the ballroom."

"Make sure you're not seen getting out of the carriage. We wouldn't want to cause a scandal, now would we?"

She ground her teeth at his mockery. "You think *you* would be ruined, Montgomery? Your prestige would only increase if your friends thought you'd seduced me. My reputation would be the one to suffer. The rules don't apply to you men."

"Ah, but you're forgetting those brothers of yours. They'd kill me if they thought I'd dishonored you."

She tilted her head in wry acknowledgment. "Well, that's true. Hell hath no fury like an overprotective brother. Or three."

"And yet it seems they weren't protective enough."

His tone was deadly soft, but she didn't miss the underlying accusation, and she bristled at the criticism. Her brothers hadn't been at fault; she'd been the architect of her own downfall.

She fixed him with an icy stare. "Swear to me that you won't mention this to anyone."

"Howe doesn't deserve your loyalty."

That was true.

"It's not for him. I'm protecting my stupid, impetuous brothers· from being charged with murder. And Howe's sweet wife, Victoria, from a very public scandal."

"Perhaps you should have thought about her *before* you started sleeping with her husband?"

Carys flinched. Another direct hit, and she couldn't even defend herself. She'd slept with Howe weeks before he'd married his bloody wife. Her ruination had been over so quickly—she'd been naively flattered by his speed. She'd imagined it signaled an undeniable passion . . . and not merely the need for haste. What an impetuous, trusting fool she'd been.

Never again.

"You don't need to worry," he said suddenly. "I hate drama and gossip. Your secret's safe with me."

Carys exhaled, still a little dazed by the unexpected turn the night had taken. When Tristan leaned forward she stiffened in alarm, but he only reached across her and swung open the door of the carriage. He glanced up and down the street, then glanced back.

"The coast is clear."

He extended his hand to help her down, and a jolt shot through her as she put her hand in his. The heat of his palm warmed her, even through his gloves, and his long fingers engulfed hers in a strong squeeze that made her heart beat faster.

"I'll bid you good night, Lady Carys."

Carys made good her escape.

Chapter 6

Tristan dropped his head back against the seat of his newly acquired carriage and let out a slow, incredulous exhale. *Bloody hell! Carys and Christopher Howe?*

Disbelief warred with fury at the thought of the two of them together. Howe might have been one of her more persistent suitors, but when he'd married Victoria, Tristan had thought it the end of the matter.

How wrong he'd been.

The other man clearly regretted his choice now. Victoria was nice enough, but she was nothing compared to Carys.

No one compared with Carys.

Tristan clenched his jaw, annoyed at his own bitter sense of disappointment. Carys had always been reckless, even as a child, and she clearly relished bending society's rules now, but he'd never thought her so lacking in morals as to sleep with another woman's husband.

He prided himself on being a good judge of character, and she'd just proved him a gullible fool.

He closed his eyes and thought back over the past few months, trying to recall occasions when he'd seen the two of them together. He could barely recall any—and he'd certainly spent enough time watching her. They'd obviously agreed to avoid each other in public so as not to arouse suspicion.

Now that the initial shock of her confession had faded, he could admit that his anger was partly self-directed.

He was envious of Howe.

He let out another deep sigh. Despite his attraction to Carys, he'd always kept his distance, believing her untouched—and therefore untouchable. She was out of bounds, not someone with whom he could contemplate having an affair.

He'd never considered her in the role of wife either. Aside from the reasons he'd given James, he needed to marry someone who would support him in his architectural endeavors. A sensible, cultured woman who would be an asset when it came to convincing aristocratic patrons to employ him for their building projects.

Carys was not that woman. He couldn't envisage her being anything but a beautiful, infuriating distraction.

Besides, even if she *had* possessed the temperament he required in a wife, the enmity between their two families had always been an invisible barrier between them. His sister's recent marriage to Gryff, the head of the Davies clan, had gone partway to dissolving that particular obstacle, but centuries of mutual mistrust were not so easily set aside.

Added to that, he'd only recently discovered how close his father had been to plunging the family into bankruptcy.

While he'd been away in Europe, his father's stock investments had suffered catastrophic losses and it was only the fortuitous discovery of a new seam of gold in the Welsh valley they shared with the Davieses that had saved them from disaster.

As someone who hated to be at the mercy of the fates, Tristan was determined to become financially secure. He would one day inherit the title and estates from his father, but he hoped not for many years to come. He would make his own way before then, by accepting architectural commissions.

Carys was almost as wealthy as Victoria Jennings; she could well afford her outrageous extravagances, but Tristan had no desire to be deemed a fortune hunter. Unlike Howe, he would never marry a woman for her money.

Lucky Howe.

What was it about the other man that attracted Carys enough to risk society's censure? Howe was good-looking, in a suave, blond, boyish way, but he was supremely self-obsessed. He was also an inveterate gambler who seemed to prefer cards to women; the man hadn't done an honest day's work in his life. He'd stayed safely at home while Tristan and his men had risked life and limb fighting Bonaparte in Portugal and France.

Was he a particularly skilled lover? Maybe that was the reason Carys was carrying on with him? God knows, if *Tristan* ever had Carys in his bed he'd love her so thoroughly she'd never want to leave.

His pulse began to pound at the mere thought. Carys had taken a lover. Did that mean she could be seduced away from Howe?

He swallowed. Their shocking flirtations had always left him hard and aching, but until now he'd barely allowed himself to imagine it. It would have been worse than torture, when nothing could come of it. She was out of bounds. Untouchable, except in his dreams.

But now?

He couldn't remember a time when he hadn't wanted her. But ever since he'd been old enough to identify the sensation, as a youth back in Wales, he'd known that Carys Davies not only spelled desire, but also trouble. And danger. Because whenever she was near, he was tempted to be as reckless and as passionate as she was.

It had happened tonight. His semi-sarcastic suggestion that she come home with him had surprised *him*, as well as her. The words had been out of his mouth before he'd even considered what he was saying. His tongue had moved without consulting his brain.

Thank God she hadn't taken him seriously. What would he have done if she's said yes?

His cock throbbed.

Taking her to bed, even for one night, would be a monumentally bad idea. No matter the spark that always fizzed between them. She was still a Davies, still a siren who would leave him smashed on the rocks of his own desire.

Tristan stared blankly out of the carriage window.

God help the poor bastard who eventually won her hand. He wouldn't know what had hit him until it was far too late.

Chapter 7

"Ready?"

Carys tied the ribbons of her bonnet under her chin and smiled at Frances's excitement. "Absolutely. Gryff says this one isn't as big as the Bartholomew Fair, but I can't wait!"

She stepped up into the carriage and settled on the seat opposite Rhys and Morgan.

The three youngest Davies had elected to stay in the town house on Hanover Square when Gryff had bought a new home just around the corner for himself and his new wife, Maddie. *Close enough to keep an eye on you,* Gryff had joked, *far enough away for my sanity.*

Since Carys was effectively living in bachelor lodgings with her two unmarried brothers, Gryff had arranged for a nominal chaperone to live with them—their ancient spinster aunt Judith—to add a necessary veneer of respectability.

Judith was a wonderfully lax caretaker. Vague and short-

sighted, she always had her nose in a book and rarely noticed or cared what Carys was up to. She'd refused today's
outing on the grounds that she "didn't want to see people."

"We're following Gryff and Maddie's carriage to Hampstead so we don't lose them," Morgan explained, stretching
his long legs out in front of him. He let out a jaw-cracking
yawn and Carys sent him an amused look.

"I'm impressed to see you out of bed before noon," she
teased. She pretended to study him like some strange new
species of animal. "Look, Frances! The elusive, nocturnal
Morgan-beast. It's said to be grouchy and extremely hard to
tame. Few have ever seen one in daylight."

Morgan sent her a good-natured growl.

Rhys elbowed him in the ribs. "*Somebody* didn't get
home until just before dawn." He chuckled. "You must have
had a good night."

Morgan shot him an evil look. "I did, actually. I won a
hundred pounds at faro, got drunk at White's, and ended the
night with a charming young lady from Drury Lane who
did the most amazing thing with—" He noticed Carys's and
Frances's rapt attention. "Never mind what she could do," he
finished quickly.

Carys laughed. "Oh, don't stop there. It was just getting
interesting."

Rhys shook his head. "Definitely not, minx. Some things
are not for a lady's ears."

Carys's heart clenched in her chest at his brotherly teasing. It was sweet, but also a little poignant that they still
thought to shield her from such bawdy topics. She would
never be their unsullied little sister ever again.

That thought flashed her back to another carriage, and her

conversation with Tristan, and her face heated. She hadn't been able to think of anything else for days. He'd implied that he found her attractive. She didn't know whether to believe it or not, but her sinful imagination kept wondering what would have happened if he'd been serious.

And what would have happened if she'd said yes . . .

"I've arranged to meet James," Frances sighed happily. "At the hot-air balloon ride at one o'clock. It should be easy to find."

Rhys and Morgan both rolled their eyes at her besotted expression. Since Frances had been their London neighbor and Carys's best friend for most of their lives, they considered her an honorary, extra sister.

The two girls had both attended Miss Wickerstone's School for Young Ladies, and their friendship had been the only good thing to come out of the whole miserable experience; Carys had had no desire to learn embroidery, flower arranging, or household management.

Perhaps if Miss Wickerstone had offered instruction on *interesting* subjects, like the care of exotic animals, or piracy, or treasure hunting, then she might have applied herself to her studies more diligently, but as it was she could only look back on her two years at the academy with profound dislike.

"James said he was bringing Tristan Montgomery."

Frances's sunny expression belied the sly sideways smile she slid at Carys.

Rhys groaned. "Ugh. Not just a Montgomery, but a *cavalryman* too. Those boys are insufferable. They think they're single-handedly responsible for winning every battle they've ever been in."

Morgan chuckled. "Said like a true fusilier. But you can't blame Tristan if he prefers horses to blowing things up."

"I happen to like both." Rhys sniffed haughtily. "Just not at the same time."

Carys bit back a smile. Gryff and Rhys had both seen action in the Royal Welsh Fusiliers, an infantry regiment. Morgan, just to be perverse, had joined the navy. Tristan and James, on the other hand, had both been dragoons: mounted cavalry.

Considering the terrifying number of battles they'd all been involved in, it was a miracle that none of them had been killed or seriously wounded. She'd prayed every night for their safe return. Now, with Bonaparte on the rampage in Europe again, the possibility that they might be called upon to fight once more was a looming specter she didn't want to contemplate.

Not today. Today was a day to have fun.

Was that even possible with Tristan Montgomery in the vicinity?

The thought of seeing him again had her stomach in knots. How should she act when she saw him?

She'd spent an unusually long time trying to decide what to wear. The fair was being held on the notoriously windy Hampstead Heath, but the weather was mild, the perfect spring day, so she'd settled for a pretty sprigged muslin and a matching spencer jacket. Nothing too expensive that would make her an easy target for the gangs of thieves and cutpurses who abounded wherever there were crowds.

When the carriage pulled up at the entrance to the fair they all jumped down, and Carys grinned with anticipation as they joined the throng heading toward the maze of covered stalls and sideshows. Fairs like this were popular with people from all walks of life, from aristocrats to slum dwellers, all glad of a distraction from their daily lives.

A cacophony of conflicting musical tunes floated over the laughter and conversation. There was an air of palpable excitement as friends hailed one another and vendors hawked their wares.

"Oysters! Get your fresh oysters 'ere!"

"Step this way, ladies! See the Tall Dutchwoman!"

"Baby crocodiles hatched from their eggs by steam!"

A miasma of roast pork and spiced wine enveloped them as sellers of beer and tobacco shouted for custom. Stalls selling everything from mousetraps to puppies, purses to singing birds, lined the temporary "streets."

Rhys pointed toward a brightly painted hot-air balloon that was rising majestically over the top of the stalls. "That way."

They skirted around a fire-eater but paused to watch a Scaramouche on a rope, who somehow managed to push a wheelbarrow containing two children and a dog along before him.

Frances tugged at her sleeve. "There's James and Tristan!"

Carys's heart gave a foolish jolt. Tristan in daylight was just as attractive as Tristan in a candlelit ballroom. He was dressed with his usual precision, in tight buckskin breeches, shiny black leather top boots that seemed to scorn the very idea of mud, a white shirt, and a perfectly fitted dark-navy jacket.

He would probably look just as good if it were streaming with rain and the field was a muddy quagmire.

As always, she was seized by the urge to grab his cravat and muss up his hair. To see him all scruffy and befuddled. She clenched the handle of her parasol. *Stop it.*

He acknowledged their approach with a bow, and as he greeted her brothers she decided to behave as though their conversation in the carriage had never happened. The group started forward, with Rhys and Morgan at the front followed by Frances and James, so she and Tristan fell into step together.

"I suppose the tightness of your coat is an antitheft measure," she mocked, by way of greeting. "So you'd feel if someone tried to slide a hand into your pocket to relieve you of your watch."

His amused glance liquefied her insides. "I'm gratified you're paying such attention to my tailoring. Would you care to test your theory? Try and rob me. I'll say if I can feel your touch."

The thought of sliding her hand over the silky satin of his waistcoat, or inside the lining of his jacket, made her feel faint.

"No thank you." She cleared her throat and took a cooling step away from him. "I'm surprised to see you here, actually. All this rowdy frivolity is hardly your style. Wouldn't you rather be designing an orangery or something?"

"You don't think I know how to have fun? I assure you I do. If you'd taken me up on my offer the other evening, you'd have been left in no doubt."

His gaze dropped to her lips and a fizzle of excitement shimmered through her blood. *The devil!* Why was it that she could flirt with a hundred other men and feel nothing but faint enjoyment, but every interaction with Tristan left her singed? It made no sense. *She* was the flame-haired, passionate one. He was as calm and collected as a glacier.

Except for the heat in his eyes when he looked at her.

She bit her lip.

"What offer's that?" Frances asked brightly. She'd been eavesdropping shamelessly.

Carys's heart pounded in alarm, but Tristan sent Frances an easy smile. "Oh, nothing really. I . . . just offered to help Carys find a husband."

Carys's mouth dropped open in shock at his unexpected improvisation.

Frances looked no less surprised. "You did?"

Tristan nodded, completely unruffled by his monstrous falsehood. "I offered my services in vetting potential suitors. To provide a gentleman's perspective."

Carys glared at him, but he met her look with a bland smile. She ground her teeth. Oh, he was thoroughly enjoying her discomfort.

Frances beamed, oblivious to the scalding undercurrents. "Why, that's a marvelous idea. How kind."

"Indeed!" Carys growled. "Almost *unbelievably* so."

Tristan nodded graciously. "It makes sense, if you think about it. I'm about the only man in the *ton* who doesn't want to marry her. Which means I can be completely impartial."

Carys laughed to cover her mortification. Hearing him reject her so clearly was like a knife to the heart. "I told him how ludicrous it is! How could *he* be impartial? Our families have been enemies for centuries. He'd shackle me to someone dreadful just for his own amusement."

Tristan had the gall to look offended. "You don't trust me?"

"No! And I certainly don't require your dubious help. I'll find my own husband, thank you."

Frances shook her head, as if Carys was being unreasonable, and Carys feigned interest in the stalls and sideshows, glad of the distraction.

A glassblower in a glass wig was blowing teacups for three pence apiece. Vendors of miraculous medicines promised to cure everything from baldness to "love fever." They stopped to buy some still-warm gingerbread, then watched a troupe of acrobats tumble and balance to riotous applause.

"Look at that!" Morgan laughed, pointing to a sign that advertised "Wallace the learned pig." "It says he can tell the time to the minute, and pick out any specified card in a pack, *while blindfolded*!"

He was interrupted by another cry. "Step up, step up, ladies and gents! Come see Wombwell's famous traveling menagerie! See the fearsome lions and leopards! Gaze in wonder at the mighty rhinoceros—the true unicorn of scripture!"

The jolly music of a brass band was coming from within a huge cloth tent, beyond which a semicircle of fifteen or so wagons was arranged, the cages filled with dark shapes.

"Oh, I've always wanted to see a rhinoceros!" Frances clapped her hands, her face aglow with excitement. "Even you don't have one of *those*, Carys."

"Come see the zebra that once belonged to Louis the Sixteenth!" the man shouted. "Taken from Versailles in the revolution. Rescued from Paris last year!"

"I'm not sure I believe that," Carys muttered. "I heard all the poor King's animals died of starvation, like half the populace of Paris."

Tristan sent her an amused glance. "Oh, come. Let's take a look. I've never seen a rhinoceros either. Unless you count my friend Seb's aunt, the Dread Dowager Duchess of Winwick; she's terrifying and impossibly thick-skinned too."

Chapter 8

Carys disliked seeing big animals in small cages, but the others had already disappeared through the tent flap, so she followed them into the darkened interior with a resigned sigh.

The sickly-sweet smell of fresh manure and sawdust greeted her. The scents were familiar—she was personally responsible for maintaining the motley assortment of animals known as the Davies Menagerie back at their house in Wales—but her charges had huge, airy enclosures. Here in the warm tent the odors were almost overpowering. She fumbled for her handkerchief and pressed it to her nose, gratefully inhaling the perfume of rosewater.

The sun shone more brightly through the white stripes of the tent than the red, banding the interior like the bars of a cage. The crowd sucked her forward, steering her inexorably toward several barred pens that contained a zebra, a llama, and a kangaroo respectively.

Carys strained her neck, trying to catch sight of Frances or James, but they'd been swallowed by the crowd.

The crush of warm bodies became increasingly oppressive. A burly man in a flat cap shoved her aside; then a small child stepped on her skirts as he pushed past her to see the boa constrictor. Her chest began to feel tight. The combination of sweaty, unwashed bodies, beer, and silage was starting to make her feel nauseous.

A strong hand caught her elbow and she glanced up at Tristan's face with an inexpressible feeling of relief. The crowd surged, jostling them even closer together, and she sucked in a gasp as his strong thighs pressed the back of her skirts. When she swayed, he slid his arm easily around her waist and drew her back into the protection of his body. The full length of him imprinted against her back.

Heat flashed through her. He was so strong, so solid. She felt like Odysseus, lashed to a mast in a storm. How tempting it would be to melt against him, to surrender to the siren song of sensation. The darkened tent was full of people, but awareness of him obliterated everything else. He smelled of vetiver and spice, masculine and delicious. She wanted to turn around and press her nose into his shirtfront, to sniff at him like a truffle-hunting pig.

Madness!

His deep voice rumbled in her ear as he leaned over her. "Stay close. You don't want to get trampled."

Carys managed to nod, grateful for the darkness that concealed her sudden blush. Of all the people in England, why did it have to be Tristan Montgomery who made her react this way? It wasn't fair.

Thankfully, the crowd eased. Tristan released her and moved to inspect a bored-looking giant tortoise as if nothing unusual had happened, and Carys let out a long exhale. *Ugh.* If only she could affect him as much as he affected her.

They made it to the end of the display without further mishap and ventured back outside, blinking in the sudden brightness. Frances and James stood near one of the circus wagons chatting with a tall, sandy-haired man, and Carys rushed to join them, hotly aware of Tristan close behind her.

She recognized the newcomer as one of her long-term admirers, Charles Ashton, whose overabundance of side-whiskers made him look like a friendly walrus. He smiled broadly when he caught sight of her.

"Lady Carys! What a delightful surprise. Have you been enjoying the animals?"

She prayed her heated flush had subsided. She'd been enjoying one particular male animal a little *too* much. "I have indeed."

Ashton nodded. "You must visit the Royal Menagerie at the Tower of London, then. The leopard there destroyed my sister Lucy's parasol."

"How?"

"She poked it through the bars."

"Perhaps Lucy should have left the poor leopard alone?" she said pointedly.

"That's what I told her. Do you know, the cost of admission used to be either three halfpence, or the gift of a cat or a dog to be fed to the lions?"

Carys shuddered. "That's horrid."

"Yes, well, they don't do it now, of course," Ashton assured her quickly. "We live in more civilized times."

Frances stepped in before Carys could argue that point.

"We have been to the Tower, actually, but Carys doesn't approve of the conditions."

"None of the animals have enough space," Carys said. "It's as much a prison for them as it was for the humans who were held there long ago."

Rhys joined them in time to hear that, and he sent Ashton a droll look. "Oh, you've done it now. Our Carys is quite zealous about the subject of animal welfare. She petitioned parliament last year to have the Tower zoo closed down, and the animals moved to more humane quarters."

"So you're not a fan of the famous Tower ravens then?" Ashton ventured.

Carys shook her head. "I'm not. Their flight feathers are trimmed so the poor things can't fly any distance. And for what? Because of some stupid superstition that Britain will fall if the ravens ever leave the Tower. What nonsense."

Her anger rose, as it always did when she thought about animals being mistreated. Perhaps it was because she found it all too easy to sympathize; she, too, was trapped by circumstance, held hostage by a pack of well-intentioned but outdated traditions.

"What about fox hunting?" Ashton persisted.

Rhys laughed. "Definitely not. Carys hates any kind of hunting."

"Good God."

Poor Ashton clearly didn't know what to make of such radical ideas, and Carys suppressed a smile. She had no doubt that he would find such opinionated meddling unattractive in a female, and she fought the urge to send Tristan a gloating look over her shoulder.

Another candidate successfully deterred. Good luck in finding me a husband!

Why was needling him her favorite occupation? It was like poking a tiger with a stick—or a leopard with a parasol. One day the big cat would pounce.

Quite what would happen when—*if*—Tristan Montgomery ever did pounce was a mystery. But a wicked, perverse part of her *really* wanted to find out. She had a suspicion it would be thrilling, and probably dangerous too. At best it would be wounding to her pride. At worst it could be fatal to her heart.

Still, she couldn't seem to stop.

A commotion a little farther on diverted everyone's attention. The furious snarl of an enraged bear and the clang of metallic chains echoed from the last wagon. A crowd had gathered in an awed semicircle around a thin man in a tattered top hat who stood at a safe distance from the barred cage.

"Stay well clear o' the bars, ladies and gents. This brute's got teef an' claws wot'll shred a man to pieces."

An impressed, "Ooohh!" echoed from the crowd.

"That's right. This bear's a killer! Maimed three dogs last month, 'e did, in Shoreditch."

Carys's stomach clenched. The bear inside the cage was a fearsome-looking beast. Even as they watched, he took a swipe at the showman through the bars and roared his displeasure, then reared up on his hind legs, revealing a terrifying set of jaws.

"Does he mean the bear was forced to fight the dogs?" Frances whispered.

"I'm afraid so," Morgan replied grimly. "Bearbaiting's still a popular sport with some."

"It's not a *sport* at all," Carys snapped. "It's barbaric."

"Carys has a pet bear," Rhys explained to Ashton. "Back at Trellech. She rescued him as a cub."

"Buttercup would have ended up like that poor creature if I hadn't intervened," Carys said tersely. "Or worse. He could have been killed and made into bear grease for dressing people's wigs."

"Your male bear's called Buttercup?" Tristan queried from behind her, a laugh in his voice.

Carys glared at him over her shoulder. "I didn't know he was a boy when I named him. I was only eight."

"Right."

She nodded toward the angry bear in the cage. "That animal's known nothing but being bitten and baited. You'd be equally cross if you'd been provoked and chained in a cage hardly big enough for you to turn around in."

She turned to Rhys. "Have a word with the owner and see if we can buy him."

Tristan stepped forward. "You can't do that. The creature's dangerous. I admire the sentiment, Carys, but he's too far gone to be rehabilitated."

"I don't believe that. Every creature deserves a second chance." She sent Rhys a pleading look. "Please, Rhys? Do it for your favorite sister."

"You're my *only* sister." Rhys chuckled.

Morgan rolled his eyes. "Here we go again. This is exactly how we ended up with Buttercup. Street performer.

Dancing bear. And Carys Davies, champion of all things feathered and furred."

Carys shot him an embarrassed glare.

"You have a kind heart." Tristan somehow made that sound like a flaw, not a compliment.

Rhys, however, sighed in good-natured capitulation. "Oh, all right. Wait here. I'll go and see if the owner's willing to sell."

He trudged over and held a low-voiced conversation with the circus owner, but from the defeated slump of his shoulders and the owner's repeated head shaking, Carys could see that the man had refused.

"He says it's not for sale," Rhys confirmed when he returned. "I told him we'd give the beast a good new home in the famous Davies Menagerie, but he wasn't impressed."

"Did you tell him it was for Gryff, the Earl of Powys?" she pressed. "How much did you offer? Whatever it was, double it."

Rhys raked a hand through his hair. "Give it up, Carys. The man's not interested."

She opened her mouth to argue, but Rhys raised his hand to forestall her. "He did, however, say that the circus would be touring after this. He said to find him in a month or so and ask him again."

Carys frowned, dissatisfied with the answer but knowing there was little else she could do. She would be going to Trellech Court for Gryff's house party soon. But when she returned, she would track that bear down and badger the owner until he relented.

She was nothing if not persistent.

Chapter 9

"Come on," Frances said. "I want to see the rhinoceros."

James, Rhys, and Morgan all trotted after her, but Carys drifted over to admire a pair of bright macaws in another cage. Tristan lingered by her side.

"I think we can safely exclude Ashton from your list of potential suitors," he said drily. "You managed to horrify him with your opinions on hunting."

Carys tossed her head. "I'm not even going to *pretend* to be interested in a boor like that. Don't tell me you're a fan of it too?"

"I'm not. I love to ride cross-country, but I've seen enough senseless killing during the war. It's not as if we eat the fox, or the badger, is it?"

"Quite so. And for those who say they're pests—they should meet my brothers. They're pests too, but nobody suggests shooting *them*. Not often, anyway."

Tristan smiled. "Ashton isn't right for you. He's too slow and stupid. You need someone with sharp wits and an even sharper rapier."

"Oh, really. Why?"

"Because the poor sod will spend most of his time dealing with scandals and fighting off cuckolds. That's what husbands *do*. They defend their lady's honor."

Carys rolled her eyes, even though the idea of having someone fighting on her side was a very appealing prospect. "I don't expect anyone to win my battles for me. Besides, what makes you think I would continue being scandalous once I marry? I might settle down and become the perfect wife."

"You might," Tristan said with a snort. "But I doubt it. A leopard doesn't change his spots. You've always been a hellion, ever since you were a girl. Remember that time you cut off all your hair and tried to run away to sea? Or the time you and Morgan decided to be highwaymen and held up poor Doctor Williams's coach?"

Carys glared at him. "That was years ago. And we were trying to stop *your* coach, as it happens. You were late."

He laughed at her aggrieved tone. "I was the target? I didn't know that. What were you going to do? Tie me up and rob me? Toss me in a ditch? 'Your-money-or-your-life' kind of thing?"

"I believe I suggested your money *and* your life," Carys muttered darkly.

He sent her a wicked sideways glance. "Did you wear breeches? I'm sure you made a very fetching highwayman. I'm sorry I missed it."

Carys felt her cheeks heat at the unexpected compliment. "Yes, well, I'm past all that now."

"Of course you are." He looked unconvinced. "You wouldn't have killed me, anyway. A dead enemy's no fun."

She inclined her head in grudging acknowledgment of that, and gifted him with a kernel of truth in return. "True. I'm glad Napoleon didn't finish you off in France."

"So am I." He chuckled. "Although he got close a few times." He shot her another teasing look. "Sometimes the only thing that got me through was wondering what new and scandalous things you were getting up to in my absence."

Carys blinked in surprise.

"Maddie sent me regular letters detailing your adventures," he explained.

"Oh." She didn't know whether to be pleased or mortified.

They rejoined the rest of the group and duly marveled at the rhinoceros, but Carys couldn't resist a glance back at the poor caged bear.

The man Rhys had spoken to was now talking to another gentleman, and she blinked in surprise as she recognized Christopher Howe. His wife, Victoria, stood a few paces away, idly twirling her parasol as she studied some ring-tailed lemurs in another cage.

Carys frowned. Howe and the bear handler seemed deep in conversation. Did they know each other? She couldn't imagine Howe being altruistic enough to be trying to rescue the bear—he cared as little for animals as Ashton did—but it wouldn't surprise her if he'd attended the poor creature's fight against the dogs. Wherever there were games of chance or bets to be made, Howe was certain to be there.

The temptation to sneak over and try to eavesdrop on

their conversation was almost overwhelming. If she could get some information on Howe, something unsavory with which to counter his blackmail, she wouldn't hesitate to give him a taste of his own medicine. Perhaps then she wouldn't be paying for his silence forever.

Unfortunately, there was no way for her to head in that direction without attracting attention, and even as she watched, Howe gave the circus man a brief handshake and returned to his wife's side. Carys let out a huff of disappointment.

The sight of him was an unwelcome reminder that she still hadn't managed to give him his fifty pounds of hush money. He'd sent her a terse note after last week's failed attempt to make the exchange in his carriage, telling her to meet him at the opera instead.

Frances and James ambled over.

"Is that Victoria Howe and her husband? It is! Carys and I went to school with her," Frances explained for James's benefit. "She was a year older than us, so we didn't really know her that well, but she always seemed nice."

Carys's spirits sank even lower. Poor Victoria. Howe might not be carrying on with *her* behind his wife's back, but she'd bet he was being unfaithful with other women. She found herself hoping that Victoria had taken a lover too, but it was doubtful. She and Howe had yet to have any children, and it was an unwritten rule of the *ton* that a married woman wasn't expected to take a lover for herself until she'd produced the requisite "heir and a spare" to continue the family line.

"To tell you the truth," Frances murmured, "I don't think theirs is a very happy marriage. Caroline Appleby told me

Victoria *knew* Howe was more interested in her fortune than her person, but she married him anyway, because her father wanted her to have a title."

"Howe's a gamester." James frowned. "And even with her money he's always short of funds. My father plays bridge with Obediah Jennings. He says Jennings was so concerned about Howe's gaming that he only gave the two of them a fraction of his money as Victoria's dowry. He put the rest in a trust for her and any future children, administered by himself."

Carys raised her brows. That certainly explained why Howe felt the need to relieve *her* of fifty pounds every month.

"He lost a fortune at Lady Banbury's ball last week," James continued. "First to Lord Holland, and then to Tristan. He had to pay Tristan with his *carriage*!"

Tristan appeared soundlessly at her shoulder. "I've already had his crest removed from the side panels. It's a definite improvement."

Carys felt her face flame. She was sure Tristan was watching her to gauge her reaction to Howe. He probably thought she was jealous of Victoria, and pining for her lover.

Nothing could be further from the truth.

The rest of the afternoon passed pleasantly, except for an awkward moment when they encountered Lavinia Purser.

The other woman was dressed in a spencer the color of lemon sorbet, with matching silk flowers on her bonnet. She looked cool and composed, not a blond hair out of place, moving gracefully over the uneven ground like an iceberg.

Carys tamped down a tiny stab of jealousy. Her own pale skin—the curse of redheads everywhere—flushed easily in

the sun and she was plagued with childish freckles no cos-
metics could conceal.

She sent a resentful look at Lavinia's fashionably slim
frame. The girl was like a sparrow, so slender she barely had
enough bosom to bounce. *She probably didn't even have
a crease beneath her breasts to get sweaty. And she was
doubtless too well-bred to perspire.*

Carys glanced down at her own bosom and noticed a
crumb of gingerbread lodged in the lace of her décolletage.
She brushed it off, praying nobody had noticed.

Sparrows like Lavinia probably didn't even eat cake.
That's how they stayed so slim. And so miserable.

Tristan excused himself and went to greet Lavinia, bowing low over her hand. Carys feigned disinterest, but ground
her teeth when Tristan bought the other woman a posy of
hyacinths from a stall. Lavinia's vapid smile raised her pulse
even more.

Flustered, she stormed over to a stall holder who was selling songbirds in little wooden cages. She scrabbled around
in her reticule and pulled out a handful of guineas.

The man's eyes lit up at the sight of the gold coins.

"'Ow many d'you want, love?"

Carys lifted her chin. "All of them."

"*All* of 'em?" he repeated, dumbfounded.

"That's what I said." She thrust a handful of coins at him
and started to unlatch the little wooden doors. A procession
of flustered songbirds escaped into the sky, reveling in their
newfound freedom in a blur of tiny, fluttering wings. One
swooped low over Lavinia's bonnet, lured by the false
yellow flowers, but quickly realized its mistake. It soared off
toward the trees.

The stall holder shook his head, eyeing Carys as if she ought to be incarcerated in Bedlam.

Rhys laughed at the bemused man's expression. "Eccentric," he explained brightly, pointing at Carys. "More money than sense, you know."

"I should say so," the other man marveled. "Wot's the point in letting 'em go? I'll 'ave caught another bunch by next week."

"But not these particular birds," Carys said firmly. "*These* ones—hopefully—will have learned their lesson. They won't be caught again."

Tristan raised his eyebrows as he rejoined them, but Carys tossed her head. She was the only one who understood the symbolism of her quixotic gesture, the only one who saw the parallels between the birds and herself. He, like her brothers, probably thought she'd just done it for attention.

She told herself she didn't care.

Chapter 10

Carys usually adored the opera, but the knowledge that she had to sneak out and hand over fifty pounds to Howe dimmed her anticipation of the evening.

Gryff and Maddie were already in the box when she entered through the rear curtain; she greeted them, then leaned out over the low balcony and cast her eye over the assembly.

The discordant tuning up of the orchestra was almost drowned out by the excited chatter of the crowd down in the pit. Fans fluttered and dresses rustled like the whisper of the wind through the trees, and the ladies' high-pitched laughter provided a soprano counterpoint to the men's deeper bass tones.

Movement in one of the boxes opposite caught her eye and she stiffened as she saw Howe enter with his wife and another gentleman Carys recognized as Lord Prowse. Howe sauntered to the front of the box, then raked the boxes that circled the stage.

Her skin prickled unpleasantly as he caught her eye and tilted his chin subtly to indicate that she should meet him outside, in the corridor. She sent him a hard stare and an almost imperceptible shake of the head. As a protest it was petty, but the tiny rebellion was her way of wresting some small amount of control over the situation. She would meet him, but at a time convenient for *her*.

The opera was Mozart's *Così fan tutte*, and Carys had dressed accordingly, in the Italian style more suited to the last century. Her deep-red watered-silk gown had an exceedingly low-cut front and a dizzying series of ruffles and bows. The color should have clashed horribly with her red hair, but instead the jewel tone was wonderfully flattering.

She looked exotic and ridiculously theatrical—just as she'd planned. The fuller style suited her curvaceous figure far better than the Empire-line dresses worn by every other woman in the room. Tall, slim girls like Frances might look elegant in those high-waisted gowns, but for someone like herself, who possessed hips and a bust, the style wasn't the least flattering. Why not wear something that made her look good?

Several more people had entered her box while she'd been looking for Howe, and she turned to greet them with a bright smile. It became more genuine as she saw one of her favorite acquaintances, the suave silver-haired peer Lord Ellington.

He took her extended hands and bowed low to kiss them in an elaborate flourish that brought a smile to her lips.

"Good evening, my lovely. You look like you just stepped out of a Fragonard painting."

Carys bobbed a mocking curtsey. "Why, thank you, my lord. You're looking rather handsome yourself."

"Are you looking forward to tonight's performance?"

"I confess it's my least favorite of Mozart's operas. Not because of the music, but because of the plot."

Ellington's gray eyes sparkled with anticipation. He loved discussions such as this. His ability to debate a whole range of subjects was the reason he was such a successful member of the House of Lords. "Interesting. Do tell me your objections."

"Well, the two 'heroes' bet between themselves that their fiancées can't remain faithful, so each agrees to don a disguise and try to seduce the other's woman, as a test. The foolish women actually give in, and even get to the point of agreeing to marry the wrong fiancé!" Carys shook her head in despair. "Even worse, when they realize they've been tricked, the women are stupidly forgiving, and the men just shrug and laugh, because '*così fan tutte*'—women are all like that."

Ellington chuckled at her ire. "Oh, come, it's a joke. Mere entertainment."

"I fear it's a sad reflection of current male beliefs."

Ellington regarded her with fascination. "You think women are capable of remaining faithful to the man they love?"

"Absolutely."

A shadow fell over them, and her heart leapt as she glanced up into Tristan's face. What was *he* doing here? She hadn't expected to see him this evening.

"How charming to hear you defending fidelity so passionately, Lady Carys." His tone held the razor edge of sarcasm. "Your eventual husband will be a lucky man."

She ground her teeth at his mockery. He looked irritatingly

gorgeous in his dark evening clothes, and she was acutely aware of heat rising in her cheeks as he took in her finery.

Damn him. He always managed to discompose her so effortlessly.

"I'm still hoping *to be* that lucky man," Ellington said smoothly. "I pray she'll say yes to one of my proposals eventually."

Carys smiled at him. "Perhaps I will."

"Lady Carys is so much more interesting than most of the other young ladies of the *ton*," Lord Ellington continued, turning to Tristan. "She never lacks an opinion."

"Some people would say I'm overeducated." Carys shot Tristan a defiant glance. He'd said as much to her on several occasions. She might not have learned anything at Miss Wickerstone's academy, but she'd badgered her father to allow her the same tutors as her brothers, and she had excelled. She was far from the empty-headed miss she pretended to be.

She put her hand on Ellington's arm and leaned in. "I'm sure I'll enjoy tonight's opera in your company, my lord. Despite the contentious subject matter."

Tristan lifted his brows in a sardonic amusement—as if he knew exactly what she was doing and was amused at her maneuvering.

Was she trying to make him jealous?

Maybe. She certainly wanted to remind him that he was the only one who didn't find her thoroughly fascinating.

The orchestra launched into the lively opening bars, and Ellington sent her a regretful look. "I must return to my box, but I hope to see you next week at your brother's house party? He was kind enough to invite me."

"I look forward to seeing you there, my lord."

When Ellington left she turned an impatient glare on Tristan. "What are you doing here?"

"Maddie invited me." He nodded toward his sister, who'd already taken her seat next to Gryff at the front corner of the balcony.

Carys sank into one of the velvet chairs near the back of the box and spread her fan. Tristan, undeterred, took the seat next to her.

"As fun as it was watching you work your charms on Ellington," he murmured, "you're wasting your time with him."

"Oh, really? He's asked me to marry him three times. I'm considering accepting."

"He only asks because he's sure you'll say no. Marrying him would be a grave mistake. He's not the man for you."

Carys tossed her head. "And why not?"

Tristan lowered his voice even more, and his gravelly whisper brushed along her nerve endings like velvet stroked against the grain.

"He is—how can I put this?—incapable of enjoying your abundant charms."

His gaze flicked down to her breasts, squashed together like two perfect peaches by her dress, and a swooping sensation fluttered low in her belly.

"You don't believe he desires me?"

"He desires you from an intellectual and aesthetic perspective," he conceded. "As a beautiful object to look at, but not touch. Like his collection of Venetian glass." His warm breath raised goose bumps on her skin as he leaned even closer. "But I'm afraid from a *physical* standpoint, I have some bad news for you. He prefers members of his own sex."

Carys's heart started to pound. "How do you know this?"

"I ran into him in Venice, at a masquerade, and he introduced me to his lover. His male lover."

He glanced at her face, but she kept her expression deliberately bland.

"Ellington works extremely hard to keep his preference a secret," he continued. "Here in England it's a crime punishable by death, but on the Continent, they take a more liberal view. I've assured him of my discretion, of course, but that's the reason he's never married. Any wife of his would share in his public disgrace and downfall if he was ever exposed."

When Carys still said nothing, his gaze sharpened. "You don't seem surprised." His tone changed to a note of wonder, and accusation. "You already knew!"

"I'd heard a rumor," she conceded.

In fact, Ellington had told her of his preferences himself. He'd called on her the day after Howe announced his engagement to Victoria and confessed that he'd seen the two of them emerge from the gardens after their tryst.

Ever discreet, he hadn't mentioned it to anyone, since he'd assumed their engagement would shortly be announced, but when it became clear that Howe had no intention of marrying Carys, he'd made his own surprising proposition: a marriage of convenience, to protect them both from social disgrace.

Not wanting there to be any misunderstanding, he'd baldly admitted that theirs would not be a physical relationship, since he preferred men, but that if Carys found herself pregnant by Howe, he would gladly claim the child as his own and give them both the protection of his name. She would, of course, be welcome to take lovers of her own once they were wed, provided she was discreet.

Carys had found his offer incredibly sweet, despite the humiliating circumstances. She'd told him that if she *was* carrying Howe's child, then she would accept his offer—because what other choice did she have? The thought of admitting her disgrace to her father and brothers was horrifying.

Thankfully, her monthly courses had arrived the following week, and she'd breathed an enormous sigh of relief. She'd declined Ellington's offer, but to her surprise he'd told her it would remain open indefinitely.

When Howe had started to blackmail her, she'd seriously considered accepting once again. The threat of exposure would lose its sting if she were married, and Ellington already knew she'd been compromised. He was probably the only man in London who wouldn't care.

Ellington might be nearly twenty years her senior, but he was charming and clever, and his dry wit and irreverent comments on the *ton* always made her laugh. He was truly interested in her opinions, which was more than most men she knew, and he possessed a level of maturity and pragmatism that most of her other suitors lacked.

They also had a lot in common. He, like her, was well versed in keeping secrets. And she knew all about desiring someone you couldn't have; the man responsible for *that* was sitting right beside her.

She glanced sideways at Tristan. He would doubtless say she was searching for a father figure, and perhaps there was some truth to that. Her own father, the Earl of Powys, had been cold and distant, more interested in running his mines and his estates than in conversing with his own children, least of all a girl.

Ellington represented safety, security. Roots.

And yet. If she married him, theirs would be a celibate union. Her experience with Howe had been so uncomfortable that the thought of never doing it again truly hadn't felt like a sacrifice, and she hadn't given serious thought to taking a lover . . . until Tristan's scandalous proposal in the carriage had forced her to question everything.

What if there *was* more to making love than Howe had shown her?

Was she missing out on a vital, pleasurable aspect of life?

Tristan was so close that she could feel the warmth of his body against the bare skin of her shoulder, and she realized he was waiting for her to expand on her thoughts on Ellington.

"I might still marry him," she said coolly. "There's more to a marriage than physical fulfillment. There's humor and companionship and stability. Ellington's private preferences needn't affect the union at all."

Tristan's mouth thinned. "You mean you'll keep Howe as your lover to satisfy you, since Ellington won't. Will he provide you with heirs too?"

Carys tried to keep her expression level. She hadn't considered either of *those* things as a possibility, but she'd be damned if she'd tell Tristan that. It was none of his business. "Ellington would give me his blessing," she said stubbornly.

Tristan shook his head, apparently disgusted. "Well, if you want my advice—"

"I don't."

He ignored her interruption. "I think you'd be making a big mistake."

Onstage, Dorabella was complaining that her lover had sailed off for war, and Carys let out a defeated sigh. Tristan was probably right. However mutually beneficial an arrangement with Ellington might be, it would still be a lie, and her life had quite enough of those already.

That dismal thought reminded her of her assignation with Howe—a quick glance over at his box showed he wasn't there.

Blast.

She rose, and Tristan, ever the gentleman, did the same.

"It's hot in here tonight, don't you think?" she murmured. "I'm going to get some air."

Tristan instantly looked concerned. "Are you unwell? Would you like me to accompany you?'

"No, thank you. I'll only be a moment." Without giving him time to follow her, she pushed through the velvet curtain.

Chapter 11

Carys hastened along the near-deserted corridor. As she passed one of the decorative alcoves lining the walls a gloved hand caught her elbow and she was unceremoniously hauled behind the velvet drapery into a dimly lit passageway reserved for the opera servants and staff.

"Shhh." Howe chuckled at her outraged gasp.

Carys glared at him. "Let go of me." She shook herself free of his hold and pressed back against the wall, as far away from him as the narrow passageway allowed.

He probably thought he looked handsome in his evening clothes, but the past few years of dissipation were starting to show on his face. His blond hair had lost its golden luster and there were dark circles beneath his bloodshot blue eyes.

How on earth had she ever thought him attractive?

He sent her a chiding, amused glance. "Tsk. Don't be like that, Carys. We were good together. Don't you remember?"

He stroked his finger down her arm in a casual caress. "We could be again."

She shuddered in revulsion. "Never."

"Is it because of Victoria?" he murmured. "You needn't feel guilty on her account. She and I have an understanding. She's not interested in what I do."

"Neither am I."

He snorted. "You would have married me in a heartbeat two years ago."

Her blood ran cold at the reminder. It was true. She'd been a besotted idiot two years ago, flattered by his attention. Thank God the scales had fallen from her eyes. The charm she'd once found so attractive now struck her as practiced and insincere.

"Get your hands off me," she hissed, struggling to keep her voice low so they wouldn't be overheard.

He dropped his hand and the seductive façade fell away with it. His eyes hardened. "Fine. Do you have my money?"

She snapped open her reticule, withdrew the folded notes, and thrust them at him with a look of loathing. The sly satisfaction on his face made her feel nauseous. How had it come to this? Being blackmailed by this snake.

"This is the last time, Howe. I'm not doing this anymore."

His low laugh made her grind her teeth. "Oh, we both know that's not true. We'll keep doing this until I say we stop, and this little arrangement is working perfectly well for me."

"But not for me."

"You don't get a say in the matter, my love. You know what will happen if you don't pay up. I'll tell everyone you're used goods, no better than those tarts out there on the stage." He smirked. "I'll say you threw yourself at me, begged me for it."

His smile was so sweetly mocking that she curled her fingers into her palm and fought the urge to punch him. God, if she were a man she'd break his nose.

"Let's not forget the words of the minister James Fordyce," he said with mock piety. "From his *Sermons for Young Women*. 'Remember how tender a thing a woman's reputation is; how hard to preserve, and when lost how impossible to recover.'"

Carys glared at him in disbelief. "You hypocrite! God, you disgust me."

Anger burned a hot ball in her chest: fury at her own impotence, her own youthful stupidity. Tears threatened, but she forced them back. She would *not* give him the satisfaction of seeing her cry.

"Just take your money and go!" she growled.

Howe plucked the banknotes deftly from her fingers and slipped them into his jacket.

"I don't *like* doing this, you know. But I have debts of my own that I need to repay."

"To Lord Holland?" she hazarded, recalling what James had said at the fair.

Howe narrowed his eyes. "Among others. But yes, he's my most pressing creditor. And believe me, he's far more unpleasant to deal with than I am."

Carys curled her lip. "You expect me to feel sorry for you?"

Howe shrugged. "A pleasure, as always." He pretended to tip his hat to her, then slipped back through the curtain and out into the corridor.

Carys expelled an unsteady breath and sagged back against the wall. She was perilously close to tears. A cauldron of simmering resentment bubbled inside her, a combination of self-recrimination and hatred.

She closed her eyes. The sound of the orchestra was muffled, but the joyous trills only served to mock her own black misery. She tried to take a deep breath, but her stays were too tight to allow any real relief and she was beginning to get a headache from all the pins that had been jabbed into her scalp to create her elaborate hairstyle.

God, she wished she were back in her bedroom at home, or—even better—back in Wales, far from the problems of her life here in London. At Trellech she could go corsetless and barefoot. Here she was confined in an elegant cage of pins and combs, whalebone and lacing, rules and regulations.

Howe had likened her to the actresses out there on the stage. He'd meant, of course, to imply that her morals were as loose as those of the opera singers, who were infamous for their affairs. But that was not where the similarity lay. Carys was like them because she, too, was capable of putting on an extraordinary performance. But whereas the opera on the stage concluded neatly in the space of three hours, her own performance had to last the entire social season.

Would it have to last her entire life?

She tried to gather herself, but she felt brittle, as if she would snap at any moment. Her life was a charade and she was so *tired* of having to deal with it alone.

With her eyes still closed, she inhaled a shaky breath. She couldn't fall apart here. Not in public. "Polite" society had a thousand inquisitive eyes; her upset would be noted—then gossiped over and speculated about ad infinitum. She didn't need that kind of scrutiny.

She would return to her box and smile. Even if she was breaking inside.

Chapter 12

Carys had been gone a suspiciously long time.

Tristan poked his head out of the box and scanned the deserted corridor. Where the devil was she? She was dressed like a sultry shepherdess; God only knew the trouble she could get into.

A door clicked, and Christopher Howe emerged from behind a drapery, glancing furtively up and down the corridor. Disbelief, then fury scalded Tristan's blood. He'd bet his entire fortune that Carys had sneaked out to meet him. They were shameless, carrying on their blatant affair right under the nose of Howe's poor wife.

He waited until Howe disappeared around the corner, then sprinted to the concealed service door. The panel swung open silently to reveal a dimly lit passageway and Carys, half sagging against the wall.

A flash of jealousy pierced his gut. Was she weak from

a passionate kiss? Howe was a gaming-obsessed charmer. What the hell did she see in him?

Carys didn't even look up to acknowledge him. "God, what now?" There was a touch of anger, of weary asperity, in her tone. "You've got your money, Christopher. Leave me alone."

Her voice was shaky, as if she were on the verge of tears, and the way she leaned her head back against the wall now looked more like an attitude of frustration than an excess of passion.

"Lovers' tiff?" Tristan drawled.

Her reaction was instantaneous. She jolted upright off the wall as if she'd been shot, and her hand flew to her chest to cover her heart.

"Montgomery!" she screeched.

Her previous words finally penetrated his anger. "Wait. Money? *What* money?"

A panicked, guilty look flashed over her face before she hid it behind a shuttered expression. "Nothing. I don't know what you're talking about."

"You thought I was Howe returning," he said slowly. "I saw him leave, so don't bother to deny it. You said, 'You've got your money.'"

She looked hunted. Trapped. She waved her hand in an airy gesture that was entirely unconvincing. "You must have misheard. Excuse me." She stepped toward him and made as if to push past, but he stood his ground.

"I don't think so. Why are you giving a weasel like Howe money?"

"None of your business. Leave me be."

"You're upset. I'm not leaving you here alone."

She gave a humorless laugh. "What, do you think I'll be accosted by unwelcome company?"

Carys sucked in another bitter laugh.

Oh, God. Could the evening get any worse? Why couldn't Tristan just leave?

It would be the ultimate humiliation to break down in front of him, and she was perilously close to crumbling.

She never cried. Why would her poise desert her now, when she needed it most? It was so unfair.

Ha! But life was never fair, was it? Nanny Maude, her old nursemaid back at Trellech, was always reminding her of that.

She put her arms in front of her to fend him off. "Just go." She could hear the watery desperation in her voice.

The bloody man ignored her. He took a step closer, his breathing deep and even in the enclosed space. She backed up, into the darkness. Her heart was pounding, but she was relieved to feel her tears recede.

"I'll ask you again. Why were you giving him money? God knows, the entire *ton* knows he's up to his ears in debt—that's why I ended up with his carriage last week—but a man's supposed to buy things for his mistress, not the other way around. Surely you haven't been lending him money?"

Carys barely concealed her snort. "Ha! A loan would be paid back."

Too late, she realized what she'd just admitted and she froze as understanding dawned on his face. His jaw hardened.

"My God, you're not having an affair with Howe. He's *blackmailing* you."

"Don't be ridiculous. You must be foxed." Even to her own ears she sounded unconvincing.

He took another step toward her. "Jesus, Carys. What's going on between you? Tell me."

She pressed her spine against the wall to keep herself upright. Her knees felt like jelly. "Nothing! Go away. This has nothing to do with you, Montgomery."

"Bollocks. Stop lying to me."

Her nerves were fizzing like bath salts as he pressed ever closer.

"Tell me." The command was low, spellbinding in the darkness.

A maelstrom of thoughts tumbled over one another in her brain and all her old recklessness resurfaced. Why *not* tell him the truth? He'd hardly be disillusioned. And she was so bloody tired of shouldering it alone.

"Fine. You really want to know?" She lifted her chin. "Yes. He's blackmailing me."

There was a pregnant pause. She half hoped he'd assume she was joking, but his silence said otherwise.

"Why? What have you done that you need to hide?"

She tried for a flippant tone. "Oh, any number of things. You know me. I'm a walking scandal." Her weak attempt at humor fell flat, but she forged on. "I laugh too loudly, talk too much, dress like this." She made a vague gesture at her outlandish dress.

"That's hardly a secret," he growled. "There's something more. Something worse."

Oh, yes. Worse indeed.

"You accused me of conducting an affair with Howe. Very well, he and I were lovers—briefly—but it was before he married his wife." Carys's heart was in her throat, but she felt compelled to fill the silence. "I thought we'd be wed."

What a fool she'd been.

"I waited three days for his proposal. And then the *Gazette* announced his engagement to Victoria Jennings."

"He seduced you and then left you."

Tristan's voice was without inflection. Was he incredulous? Angry on her behalf? Contemptuous of her foolishness? She couldn't tell.

"To be fair," she said, "I let myself be seduced. I wanted to see what all the fuss was about."

There was a beat of silence as he digested the information.

"When did this happen? He's been married for almost two years."

"Before that. I was just out for my first season. I was too ashamed to tell my father, too scared to tell my brothers. They'd only have done something stupid, like challenge Howe to a duel, and made everything worse."

"He took advantage of your innocence."

"Maybe. But some of the blame must lie with me. I thought I was in love." She gave a derisive snort. "It hardly matters now, does it? I'm still ruined." She met his eyes with a hint of defiance. "Which is perfectly fine. I have money of my own. Friends and family. My animals. And if I *do* decide to marry, for companionship, I can always accept Ellington."

Her heart leapt as he rested his hand on the wall by her head, enclosing her in the masculine cage of his body.

"Companionship's all very well, but what about your physical needs? If Howe's not your lover, you'll need to find a replacement. You can't mean to live the rest of your life without sex."

Heat flashed across her skin. "I can and I do. Why should I care about missing something so overrated?"

She actually heard him suck in a breath, as if he'd received a blow.

"Wait. *What?* You think sex is so bad you *never want to do it again?*"

The mix of anger and incredulity in his tone was almost enough to make her smile. He sounded like someone had just proved the earth was flat—and made of cheese. "Dear God, I always knew Howe was an idiot, but . . . didn't he show you a good time?"

"He did not."

"How brief was your affair?"

"Very."

His forehead furrowed. "A few weeks? Months?"

"One night."

His lips parted in shock. "One *night*?"

Heat stained her cheeks, but there was no point in hiding the truth now. "Our 'affair' lasted approximately five minutes. And it was entirely forgettable."

"And you haven't had another lover since?"

"I have not."

"Ohhh, Carys." His slow exhale tickled her neck. Goose bumps pebbled her skin. "My God. What an ass. I could kill him just for *that*, let alone for the blackmail."

Without thinking, she caught the front of his evening jacket and gave him a desperate shake. "No! Swear to me you won't do anything to Howe. Or tell my brothers. Swear it."

He glanced down at her fists and then back up to her face. One of his perfect brows lifted in polite inquiry. Presumably nobody had ever handled his evening wear so roughly. She loosened her grip, but didn't release him entirely.

"I swear I won't tell your brothers," he said levelly. "But I can't promise not to hurt Howe. What he's done is unforgivable."

Panic swamped her. "I'm not your responsibility. It's not up to you to defend my long-lost honor. Just forget it. Please."

The space between them crackled with tension. His face was only inches away from hers and his hands had moved to grip her arms, just above the elbows. His exhale fanned the fine hairs at her temple, and the scent of him, so delicious and forbidden, coiled in her belly like a snake.

"I'm not sure I can."

His tone conveyed both apology and anger, and her stomach somersaulted.

"You have to. You'll ruin my life if you don't."

He glanced away, tension evident in the harsh line of his jaw. "What you're asking is impossible. He can't be allowed to—"

"Please." The need to silence him, to distract him, overwhelmed her, and she did the only thing she could think of to do. She tugged hard on his lapels, rose up on tiptoe, and pressed her mouth to his.

Realization of what she'd done came a split second too late.

Dear God in heaven, she was kissing Tristan Montgomery!

Chapter 13

Carys stilled, expecting him to thrust her away from him in disgust, but Tristan's fingers tightened on her arms. And then his lips returned the pressure of her own with an urgency that almost made her swoon.

He was kissing *her back*?

There was no time to process the astonishing reversal; when she gave a shocked gasp, his tongue swept inside her mouth to tangle with her own.

Darkness and wicked heat consumed her. This was no tentative exploration; it was hot and wet and hungry, and Carys clutched the front of his jacket, drowning in a sea of sensation. One of his hands slid to her waist and he leaned into her, holding her against the wall with a delicious pressure that made her stomach swirl. And then he cupped her jaw, his long fingers angling her head to taste her more fully. Her senses reeled.

Good God, she'd had no idea kissing could be so pleasurable!

Howe had kissed her with slobbery insistence, grinding her lips against her teeth.

Tristan reached inside her and stole her soul.

How had she ever thought him cold? The taste of him was enough to melt her into a puddle on the floor. Heat flashed from the tips of her breasts to the juncture of her thighs. She flattened her hands against his chest and slid them up over the hard slope of his shoulders, but the moment her fingers touched the warm skin above his cravat he seemed to come to his senses. He jolted back with a stifled curse.

"Bloody hell."

Carys sucked in a breath, bereft at the sudden loss of contact. Her chest was rising and falling in agitated gusts and she opened her eyes wide, trying to gauge his reaction in the semidarkness.

What the *hell* had just happened?

They were *enemies*. He didn't even like her. And yet her blood was like magma, her limbs liquid and shaky.

Tristan took another step back, jerking his coat from her grip. "That . . . shouldn't have happened."

His voice was lower, rougher than she'd ever heard it, like a bear awakened from a nap. "You need to go back to the box."

She managed to nod.

"I won't follow you. Tell Maddie I've gone to my club." Without looking at her, he straightened his coat, pulled on his cuffs, and raked his hand through his hair, even though it was still perfectly unruffled.

Carys smoothed her own skirts, amazed that the fabric hadn't burst into flames. Her cheeks were still burning, her blood surging in her veins. This, clearly, was the lust the poets talked about. Dear God, she'd had no idea! In less than three minutes he'd shown her the narrow range of her experience—and given her a desperate craving for more.

When Tristan took yet another step back she pushed off the wall and rushed past him, desperate to escape.

There was no one in the corridor. She tripped back to the box on unsteady legs and sank onto a velvet chair. Gryff sent her an absentminded nod over his shoulder, then returned his attention to the stage.

Oh, God, what a disaster!

The frustration of dealing with Howe combined with the humiliation of having Tristan find her at her lowest ebb had pushed her into another rash, impetuous act. She snapped open her fan and tried to cool her flaming cheeks. *She was an idiot.*

But he'd kissed her back.

Why on earth had he done that? He wasn't the kind of man to get swept away with passion. Had he just been taking advantage of the opportunity she'd so shamelessly given him? Or had he somehow known that she'd needed the distraction, the comfort—even when her mind rebelled against taking such things from him?

It didn't matter why.

It had been a mistake of epic proportions. A moment of idiocy that would never be repeated. He was probably trying to forget it. It would be best if she did the same.

That would be a great deal easier if she never had to see him again, of course, but the universe clearly had a perverse sense of humor, because they were both expected to attend Gryff and Maddie's country house party in Wales next week.

Facing him would be excruciating, but at least if he was

in Wales he would be far away from Howe, which would prevent him from doing anything stupid, like challenging him to a duel.

Carys's heart gave a strange twist. Of all the men in London, Tristan Montgomery was the last man she'd have expected to want to defend her nonexistent virtue. It wasn't like him to become embroiled in such drama. He was always so cool, so unemotional. His love affairs probably all ended with perfect civility. He was probably desperate to wash his hands of this whole sordid affair.

It would be the height of foolishness to imagine him in the role of savior. He wasn't her knight in shining armor. She just had to remind *him* of that fact when next she saw him. If she could bear to look him in the eye.

Tristan forced his shaking hands into his pockets and tried to calm his raging pulse.

Had he completely lost his mind?

Carys Davies had the worst effect on his self-control. He only needed to get close to her and every ounce of willpower disappeared, snuffed out like a candle in a gale.

Dear God, he'd never kissed a woman—any woman—as thoroughly as he'd just kissed her, and the unexpected passion of her response had almost brought him to his knees.

The scent of her lingered in the air and his erection throbbed painfully in his breeches. What had he been thinking?

He hadn't been thinking. At least not with his head. He'd been moments away from taking her up against the wall, blinded by the hazy need to block out the misery he'd heard in her voice. He'd wanted to take it into himself, to give her something else to focus on, something a hundred times more enjoyable.

The impulsive gesture was so unlike him. He never did anything without thoroughly weighing the pros and cons, but whenever he was near her logic and reason abandoned him. He'd acted purely on instinct. And that instinct had been to take her in his arms and shelter her from the world. To make her forget everything except pleasure.

"Bollocks."

It wasn't his place to protect her. She'd said it herself.

He scowled into the darkness. Desire hadn't been the only emotion driving him. The rush of fury he'd felt when she'd revealed what Howe had done was like nothing he'd ever experienced, even in wartime. He wanted to tear the bastard limb from limb.

Carys might believe herself equally to blame, but Howe was older and more experienced. He'd taken advantage of a naïve, passionate girl, and then ruthlessly abandoned her. And now, to compound his wickedness, he held the threat of ruination over her head like the sword of Damocles.

The bastard didn't deserve to live.

Tristan ached with the need to avenge her. If someone had done that to Maddie, his sister, he would have killed him without a second thought. He doubted he'd even have bothered to challenge the man to an official duel first.

He hissed out a frustrated whoosh of air. Carys's brothers would no doubt react in exactly the same way if they learned the truth. Her desire to keep it a secret from them was entirely understandable, given the circumstances.

God, how had he ended up tangled in such a mess?

There would be no avoiding her; he'd see her in Wales next week. They might not be sleeping under the same roof—the Davieses would be staying in their monstrous eyesore of a castle, Trellech Court, whereas he'd be at the Montgomerys' neighboring Newstead Park—but Maddie had a whole week of mingling planned. Picnics and excursions to the coast, trips to see her archaeological digs, visits to the cave where she and Gryff had found the gold that had restored the Montgomery fortunes.

He was bound to see Carys at some point in the proceedings. The question was, where on earth would they go from here?

Chapter 14

It was so good to be back in Wales.

Carys lifted her face to the morning sun and let the rays warm her cheeks, even though it would increase her freckles. Her skirts swung loose around her legs and she reveled in the luxury of being able to leave her hair unpinned.

Guests had been arriving at Trellech Court for the past couple of days, but it was too early for most of them to be up and about, and the menagerie was a good distance from the house, so she'd tied the heavy mass up with a simple ribbon to keep it out of the way while she tended to her animals.

Geoffrey, one of the peacocks that freely roamed the grounds, greeted her with a piercing shriek.

"You're not making any friends, you know, making that racket this early," she scolded. "You watch, Rhys'll pluck your feathers and send them to London to make fans."

Geoffrey clearly knew this was an empty threat. He gave

a scornful caw and disappeared behind a bank of rhododendrons with a dismissive shake of his long tail.

"Are your brother's guests all so dull you need to converse with the animals?"

Carys almost dropped her bucket of kitchen scraps. Her heart lodged in her throat as Tristan emerged from the same bank of shrubbery, looking tall and unnervingly gorgeous in a dark riding jacket, buff breeches, and boots.

Ugh. She wasn't ready to face him yet. Not like this. She needed an amazing outfit with which to dazzle him.

"Montgomery," she panted. "I didn't expect to see you—anyone—so early."

His gaze traveled over her from head to toe and she fought the rising tide of heat that accompanied it. Her simple cotton day dress was plain and practical, and while it was perfectly modest it was so different from the outfits she wore in London that she felt defenseless, especially in the face of his sartorial perfection. Her scuffed ankle boots were probably a mortal affront.

"So I gather." His lips twitched in amusement. "What would the *ton* say if it could see you now? Carys Davies, doyenne of fashion, with a pail of vegetable peelings. You look like Marie Antoinette playing at being a dairymaid."

Irritation returned in a rush. "I'm not *playing* at anything. My animals don't care if I'm wearing satin or sackcloth. They just want their breakfast."

She fought to keep her hands steady and the embarrassment out of her voice. This was the first time she'd seen him since the opera over a week ago, and despite her best efforts she'd been unable to stop thinking about *that kiss*. Memories of his touch had haunted her day and night.

In the cold light of day it seemed like a fever dream, some dark fantasy she'd only imagined. Had she really kissed those stern lips?

Flustered, she started toward one of the nearest enclosures, cursing silently when he fell into step behind her.

"I like you better like this."

She glanced back at him, startled. "Like *this*?"

He nodded. "Back in town you're like a gilded lily. All shimmering color to dazzle the eye. Your dresses are the architectural equivalent of the rococo: far too ornamental."

Carys bit back a laugh, torn between amusement and offense. "I don't think I've ever been likened to an architectural style before. Is this a strategy you've found successful with the ladies? Did you tell Lavinia Purser she looks like a Grecian pillar?"

He narrowed his eyes at her levity. "I just hate to see a perfectly good structure hidden beneath ivy and trellis. Or frills and bows, in your case. That dress you wore to the opera was a monstrosity." He gestured at her simple skirts. "Here there's only . . . you. Without artifice."

Carys didn't know how to answer that. The fact that he saw through the illusion of her London self, that he might actually prefer the real, unadorned version, made her distinctly uncomfortable.

"My grandfather started this menagerie," she said, to cover her nerves. "It began as a friendly rivalry with his friend the Duke of Richmond, who had his own at Goodwood House in Sussex. Exotic pets used to be all the rage back then. Sir Robert Walpole had a flamingo that warmed itself by the kitchen fire. The Earl of Shelburne kept an orangutan and a tame leopard in his orangery.

"We even had a moose, all the way from Canada. Grandfather had some idea of getting a breeding pair and introducing the animals to Britain for domestication, but the scheme came to nothing."

"He couldn't find a lady moose?" Tristan asked drily.

"Oh, no, there was a lady moose, but she rebuffed the male's advances. She didn't want anything to do with him."

"That sounds rather familiar." His amused chuckle sounded at her shoulder and she felt her own lips curl up in response.

"Well, just as in the *ton*, arranged matches seldom lead to success. The lady moose was lucky; she kept the male at bay."

"As you've been keeping the gentlemen of London at bay for the past few seasons."

She waved at the nearest enclosure and tried to infuse a teasing note into her voice. "Why would I add to my menagerie? A husband would be less loyal than a dog, less affectionate than a cat, and less amusing than a monkey. Not to mention less obedient."

Tristan let out a bark of laughter. "I feel I should be offended on behalf of men everywhere."

"Animals are cheaper than husbands too. If I marry— even someone like Ellington—I'll lose the right to manage my own money. I'll become a possession, thanks to the laws of couverture. *I'd* be the one in a cage. Why put myself in that position?"

"Good point," he conceded. "But women have found ways around that particular issue. Just look at Victoria Howe. Her money's tied up in a trust so her husband can't get at it."

She didn't want to talk about Victoria Howe. Or her pig of a husband.

Thankfully, her two ravens provided a distraction. Carys opened the door to their enclosure and whistled. Both birds immediately came and settled on her shoulders.

"Meet Huginn and Muninn," she said fondly. "Named after Odin's ravens in Norse mythology."

Huginn playfully nibbled her earlobe, while Muninn hopped onto her head and pecked at the ribbon that held her hair.

"Leave me alone, you naughty boys! Go!" She shooed them off with a laugh and the two of them flapped away to settle on the branches of a nearby tree.

"Considering your views on the ravens at the Tower, I assume you haven't clipped their wings?"

Carys hid her surprise that Tristan recalled the conversation. She hadn't thought he'd been paying much attention.

"No. They're free to fly wherever they please. They come back each night because they trust me to care for them. But it's up to them if they want to stay or leave."

Wasn't that the true measure of love? Entrusting something with its freedom, and having it return to you through choice? Keeping it with kindness, not restraint?

"They're incredibly intelligent," she continued, keeping her eyes on the birds rather than glancing over at Tristan. "They're especially good at mimicking sounds. One summer, a few years ago, I decided to practice shooting Rhys's pistols in that field over there." She waved vaguely to the north.

It had been the summer after Howe had ruined her. She'd

imagined his perfidious heart as her target every time she fired. She'd become an excellent shot.

"I heard the sound of a pistol cocking in the trees behind me. At first I thought it was Rhys, playing tricks, but when I shouted a challenge, no one came out. *Then* I thought it was poachers. I was about to fire, when Huginn flew out of the trees." Carys smiled in memory. "He landed on a branch next to me and made the exact sound of a pistol being cocked and fired."

"Can you get him to make the sound?"

"Sometimes, if I nudge him and click my tongue. But usually it's random. Muninn can do it too. And I'm fairly sure they both mimic Geoffrey the peacock, as well. It drives Morgan mad. Geoffrey's lucky none of us have strangled him by now."

Tristan's low chuckle sent a frisson of awareness through her. She could see his broad shoulder and sleeve from the corner of her eye.

"One time, Huginn pretended to play dead. Another crow, Colin, really had died, and Thomas, our keeper, put him in a box lined with cloth, ready for burial. Huginn, seeing all the attention Colin was getting, decided *he* would try it. He lay on his back and curled up his claws and stayed completely still. He was so convincing that Thomas got a box for him too, but when he went to pick him up, Huginn bit his finger and flapped off, croaking evil raven laughs."

Carys snorted in memory, then clapped her hand over her nose and mouth, horrified that she'd made such an unlady-like sound. Tristan, however, only laughed, and when she glanced over at him her heart missed a beat at the unexpected warmth in his eyes.

A strange, weightless feeling came over her. Who'd have thought she'd be able to relax like this in *Tristan's* company?

His gaze settled on her face and her self-consciousness returned in a rush. She put her hand up to her hair, grimly certain the birds had mussed it beyond repair, and sure enough, the ribbon that had fastened it fell free.

Thank you, Muninn, you wretch.

Her hair tumbled loose over her shoulders and her heart started to pound as Tristan's gaze flicked from her hair to her lips. He looked as if he wanted to kiss her, but she must be misreading the signs. He was probably just disgusted at her state of deshabille.

She glanced away, more unsure than she'd ever been in her life, and could have kissed Geoffrey for choosing that moment to reappear from behind the bushes, tail fanned majestically as he tried to impress one of the peahens farther along the walk.

I will never let anyone turn you into peacock pie, she promised him silently.

She glanced back over at Tristan and allowed herself to admire the perfect cut of his jacket and waistcoat. They fitted him like a second skin, and it was clear that he was in no need of cheap tricks like padding or sawdust to improve his form. If one of the Greek heroes like Achilles or Hector has been born in this century, in England, he'd have looked exactly like Tristan in those clothes. Power and grace constrained beneath the flimsiest of layers.

To distract herself, Carys lifted her brows and adopted the wry, amused expression she used in the ballrooms of the *ton*. "Isn't it funny that in the animal kingdom it always seems to be the *men* who have the bright, exotic plumage."

She gestured at Geoffrey's magnificent blues and greens. "Look at the peacock, or the cockerel. The females are all brown and nondescript. Yet for us humans, it's the opposite. We women are expected to be the ones smothered in jewels and frills to attract a mate." She forced a laugh. "Sometimes I wish we lived in the last century, when you men dressed as gaudily as us women. Gentlemen's dress today is so dull."

Tristan's lips quirked at the implied insult. "You'd prefer me in powder and patch, milady?"

No, she wouldn't. Those dark colors suited him perfectly: strict and severe, like the man. "I can't quite imagine you in pink silk and feathers."

How about in nothing at all?

Heat rushed to her cheeks at the unbidden thought—one of far too many she'd had in the past week.

She hastened to cover her confusion. "The most decorative male always seems to win the female. Imagine if other things were decided that way; instead of battles, wars could be won by whichever side had the best uniforms. Duels would go to the gentleman with the most attractive waistcoat. It would prevent a great deal of senseless bloodshed."

She was talking nonsense, but Tristan seemed to be entertained. "I'll be sure to mention it to Bonaparte, when next we meet."

The reminder that he might be called back to battle was a sobering thought. A world without Tristan in it, being superior and annoying, would be . . . dissatisfying.

Chapter 15

Tristan hid a smile at Carys's irreverent commentary. He'd always enjoyed her slightly off-kilter sense of humor. The way she looked at the world was so different from the way *he* looked at it that talking to her was like putting on a pair of someone else's glasses: He saw things in an entirely new way.

Of course, it also often left him dizzy.

He'd expected to find her dressed in her usual finery, like the reigning queen of fashion that she was, but this simple day dress was even more alluring. *This* was the Carys few were ever permitted to see, the real one he recalled from his childhood, unfettered and carefree.

The Carys she'd been before Howe had forced her to put up her guard.

The coppery red of her hair glowed like a vein of rose gold in the early morning sun, and the pale cotton of her dress outlined the glorious curves of her figure without the distraction of bows and frills.

"Why are you looking at me like that?" she demanded.

Her irritated tone made him smile. "I was just thinking how nice it is to see you let your hair down. Both literally and metaphorically."

A charming blush warmed her cheeks. "Yes, well, don't get used to it. As soon as I'm done here I'm going back to the house to get changed. I'm not exactly suited to the virginal white of a debutante, now am I?"

Her light tone was meant to be cynical and self-mocking, but his chest tightened at the thread of pain he sensed behind the words. She was all bravado, this girl, like a pale-faced new recruit getting his first glimpse of battle: grim with the knowledge that he had to go through with it, sick to the stomach at the thought.

He knew just how to shake her out of her misery. He let out a dismissive snort.

"You're only one bad experience away from being a virgin. You barely qualify to wear pale pink, let alone scarlet. You, Carys Davies, are a fraud."

Her mouth dropped open, as he'd known it would at the perceived insult, and he choked back a laugh. Outraged Carys was much better than miserable Carys.

"Being a virgin is a finite thing," she bit out. "You either are or you aren't. There's no gray area."

"True." He kept his tone to just the right level of amused and condescending guaranteed to drive her mad. "But sexual experience is a sliding scale. A marathon, as opposed to a sprint. You've barely stumbled across the starting line."

Her cheeks flushed a delicious pink and her knuckles

tightened on the handle of her bucket. He wondered idly if she was about to hit him with it. He got ready to duck.

"What point are you making, exactly, Montgomery?" she growled.

"For someone who's ruined, you've done a terrible job of it. Most women who suffer the consequences of losing their maidenhood have at least received some degree of *pleasure* for their trouble. You haven't even had that."

She lifted her brows, clearly irritated by his flippancy. "Well, there's not much I can do about that, is there?"

"Of course there is." He scoffed, as if she were a complete simpleton. "You can get more experience. With someone who won't hurt you. Someone who can show you a good time."

She choked out a laugh. "Of course. How logical. And where, exactly, am I going to find this paragon? A man who'll neither expect marriage, nor threaten to expose me?" Her tone was pure scorn. "Perhaps I should engage the services of a professional? Some kind of male tart?"

Tristan shrugged. He had no idea where this conversation was going, only that goading Carys was as natural, as *essential*, as breathing.

"I won't deny your options are limited. Especially here in Wales. But you really shouldn't make sweeping statements like you'll be happy with a celibate marriage when you aren't in full possession of the facts." He shot her another condescending look. "I know *I* prefer to make my decisions by having all the relevant information to hand, not just one small piece of the picture."

Carys lowered the bucket to the ground and placed her hands on her hips. Her eyes narrowed, and his pulse kicked up as if he'd just faced a French cavalry charge. He couldn't wait to see how she'd react.

"All right, Montgomery. If you're such an expert, why don't *you* provide me with 'all the relevant information'?"

His breath caught as his brain tried to make sense of what she'd just said. "Wait. What?"

Her russet brows lifted in challenge and her green eyes shot sparks hot enough to melt iron. "You're the one making sweeping statements like 'you don't need to like someone to have a satisfactory sexual encounter.' You think you're better than Howe? Well, then. *Prove it.*"

Carys's heart felt as if it might batter its way out of her ribs.

Good God. Had she really just challenged Tristan Montgomery to *make love to her*?

Why, oh why had she allowed him to needle her into saying something so outrageous?

Except, now that the idea had materialized, it felt inexplicably . . . right. Tristan had—unexpectedly—provided her with the perfect opportunity to voice the fantasy that had been lurking at the back of her mind ever since they'd spoken in the carriage. A fantasy that had become ever more insistent since their opera kiss.

Her cheeks were flaming, but the only way to master this situation was to brazen it out. To pretend she knew exactly what she was doing. To be as cool and logical as Tristan himself.

"Can you deny you enjoyed our kiss at the opera?" she heard herself say. "Be honest."

He met her gaze and her heart gave a funny little flip. "No. I don't deny it."

A tiny relieved breath escaped her at his admission, but she managed to nod, as if this were just a normal conversation about which fabric to use for a dress, or which dessert to serve for dinner. As if her chest weren't as tight as a drum.

"I don't deny it either," she conceded. "Which just goes to show that there might actually be some truth behind your idea that enemies can be . . . passionate. Together."

He inclined his head, but said nothing, so she forged on.

"I've come to realize that I owe it to myself to see if my experience with Howe was an anomaly."

His expression sharpened in interest. "Go on."

She rushed on before she could lose her nerve. What did she have to lose? She was already more embarrassed than she'd ever been in her life. If he turned her down it could hardly get more acute.

"I would like to make an informed decision. I need to know if making love with another man is as unpleasant as it was with Howe. If it is, then I can marry Ellington without any qualms about what I'll be missing." She took a deep breath. "And if I *do* find it more enjoyable, then I'll know to find a lover who can please me. Whether I marry Ellington or not."

"That sounds very logical," Tristan said evenly, and she couldn't tell if he was mocking her.

Be bold. Be brave.

"I assume you don't have a mistress at present?" she pressed.

"I do not."

"I also assume, from our kiss at the opera, that even though you disapprove of me, you desire me. Physically."

Her heart raced as his eyes bored into hers. "I do."

Her stomach somersaulted, but she cleared her throat and tried to sound cool and businesslike, as if she negotiated such intimate contracts all the time. "In that case . . . I would like you to be my tutor."

He flicked a nonexistent bit of fluff from his shirt cuff. "Explain."

"I can see how I might need some . . . rehabilitation," she said, careful to inject a note of defiance, and not self-pity, into her tone. "Like Buttercup, my bear. He needed to be taught that not all men are the same. That some touches can bring pleasure, not pain."

"And you think *I'm* the man for the job?"

"Why not? You seem ridiculously confident in your own abilities." She feigned a cool she most assuredly didn't possess. "I gave myself to a man I thought I was in love with, and it was a disaster. Perhaps making love with someone I'm definitely *not* in love with will be better?" She managed a wry smile. "We might be enemies, but in an odd way, an enemy can be trusted more than a friend. A friend can turn on you, let you down. An enemy is predictable. You already know their position, so you can't be taken by surprise."

He nodded, as if she was making perfect sense.

"I know *your* position," she continued. "You aren't in love with me. You don't want to marry me. You won't make empty promises or shower me with compliments just to get me into bed."

The corner of his lips quirked in that way that made her belly flutter. "True enough."

"Well, then. Why can't we be enemies with . . . benefits?"

He opened his mouth, but she threw down one final card before he could answer. "It will only be for this week, while we're here in Wales. No one else will know. When the party ends we'll go our separate ways. What do you say?"

Chapter 16

Tristan tilted his head, studying her, and Carys held her breath, both dreading and desperate for his answer.

"Very well. I accept."

She almost fainted with shock.

His gaze dropped to her lips and then flashed back up, and her heart beat even faster. His mouth curved into a smile. "I will make you two promises, neither of which is empty. One: I promise to give you pleasure, to the very best of my ability. And two: If you're dissatisfied with my performance, at any time, you can tell me to stop and I will."

Carys swallowed. His voice made her knees weak. "You really think we'll be compatible?"

He let out a soft laugh. "I really do. But you're just going to have to trust me until I can prove it."

Trust him. It all boiled down to that, didn't it?

Did she trust him not to hurt her? Did she trust him not to tell anyone?

Yes.

Tristan was nothing if not honorable, and he had nothing to gain by revealing their affair. Indeed, his own reputation would be damaged if it was known he'd seduced a woman of his own social class. He'd risk being forced to marry her if their involvement ever became public, and he certainly wouldn't want that. Not if he was planning to propose to Lavinia Purser by the end of the season.

Did she doubt his ability to teach her pleasure? *Definitely not.* Just kissing him had been enough to make her dizzy, and that quiet confidence of his suggested he could more than back up his claims.

A wicked flutter of excitement curled in her belly at the thought of him touching her, kissing her again.

But doubts began to crowd in. Tristan had implied that they could make love and feel nothing more than a pleas- ant physical response, but was the body so easily separated from the mind? From the heart? She'd had feelings for him for years . . .

On the other hand, she wouldn't have to worry about pleasing him, or whether he was having a good time. She wouldn't be trying to impress him, or even make him like her. It could be incredibly liberating.

Carys shook her head, scarcely able to believe that she'd blustered her way into a situation very few women ever achieved—carte blanche, the opportunity to safely explore her physical desires without fear of exposure or censure. The chance to be her true self for once, without artifice or pretense.

This might be a mistake of epic proportions, but she couldn't pass up the chance to have a little bit more of Tristan, even if it was only for a week. She'd been so miserable for so long. Why not grasp this fleeting chance of happiness?

"All right." Her voice was rather breathless. "How should we proceed?"

She could barely look at him. Her cheeks were hot and her heart was fluttering in her throat. "Will you come to my bedchamber tonight? The house is full of guests. How will you—?"

He stepped forward and tilted her chin, lifting it so she was forced to meet his eyes.

"Let's just start with the basics, shall we? A kiss." His expression was cool, but there was the hint of amusement at the corner of his lips.

"What, now?" she gasped.

"No, not now."

Her spirits plummeted and his smile widened, as if he knew how keen she was to get started.

"When, then?"

"You know the ruined folly, by the river?"

She nodded. She and her brothers had played there countless times. The thrill of trespassing on Montgomery land had only added to the enjoyment.

"Meet me there at four o'clock."

"All right."

She held her breath, hoping he'd kiss her then and there to seal their devil's bargain, but he merely brushed her cheek with his thumb and dropped his hand. She told herself she wasn't disappointed.

"Until later, then." He stepped back, gave her a short, formal bow, and turned on his heel.

Carys watched his broad shoulders disappear behind the rhododendron and slumped back against the bars of the ravens' enclosure with a feeling of stunned disbelief.

The click of a gun being cocked sounded off to her left.

"Muninn!" she scolded absently.

The raven followed through with the perfect imitation of a pistol being fired, and Carys let out a choked laugh. Was that warning shot for the man who'd just left? Or a hint that she'd be better off shooting herself than going through with their scandalous agreement?

Dear God, what *had* she done?

Chapter 17

It took all of Carys's acting skills not to show her impatience during the rest of the morning. She took breakfast, then helped Maddie welcome assorted guests as they arrived, showing them to their rooms in the various wings of the sprawling architectural monstrosity that was Trellech Court.

The imposing outer ramparts were just one part of the overall structure; the rest was an astonishing cluster of styles that seemed cobbled together as if by some mad, drunken architect. A crumbling medieval tower butted up against an Elizabethan gable—a half-timbered redbrick section that didn't have a straight line on it anywhere. Another wing, sprouting from the other side, was pure Palladian, all elegant cornices, huge windows, and pillars.

The overall effect was a confusing blend, almost too ridiculous to be believed. Every generation of Davieses had tacked on their own section, just to leave their mark. No doubt it gave Tristan—the architectural purist—heart palpitations. The disorder probably hurt his soul.

Carys herself loved it; it was chaotic and comfortable, brazen in its refusal to conform to any single architectural style. Much like herself, no one could ever accuse it of being *dull*.

"Have you seen Tristan?"

Carys willed the guilty blush on her cheeks to cool and shook her head at Maddie's unexpected question. "Err, not recently, why?"

"He said he might ride over this morning, but he must have forgotten." Maddie shrugged. "He's been so busy working on finishing that new house of his."

Carys had heard all about *that* during the carriage ride from London. Tristan was building a house on the Montgomery side of the river valley. It was several miles away from his father's estate, not far from the folly where they'd agreed to meet later, and Maddie seemed to think the project was to showcase his skills as an architect to potential clients.

Carys, however, strongly suspected that Tristan had a secondary motive: to get it finished so he had somewhere to bring a new bride. Her heart gave a funny little twist. No doubt Lavinia would approve.

The thought of Tristan married to Lavinia—to anyone, really—made her cross, and she reminded herself that it wasn't Lavinia who was meeting him in the forest at four o'clock. She would forget about the future and enjoy the present. Seize the day.

Rhys and Morgan's arrival shortly after lunch provided some respite from her impatience. She played a leisurely game of shuttlecock with Rhys, while Morgan bellowed unhelpful advice as if he were still on the forecastle of his ship and simultaneously flirted with shy Cordelia Rutledge, one of the single guests.

At two o'clock Carys took a couple of the visitors on a tour of the menagerie and introduced them to Buttercup, the South American spectacled bear she'd rescued from a street performer over a decade ago.

By three o'clock the butterflies in her stomach had intensified to an almost unbearable level. Since all three of her brothers were used to her riding out into the countryside unaccompanied, none of them batted an eyelid when she oh-so-casually said she was going to take a ride.

"Can't say I blame you," Morgan said. "Been feeling a bit cooped up myself."

Carys caught her breath, afraid he was going to offer to join her, but then he glanced over at the doorway to where Harriet, Tristan and Maddie's London cousin, had just arrived.

Morgan's expression took on a diabolical cast. "On the other hand," he muttered, "staying here has definite appeal. Just remember to stay on Davies property."

"I will."

Back in her bedroom, she dithered over what to wear. She needed to look her best—she had a reputation to maintain, after all, even in deepest Wales—but it was imperative not to look as though she'd gone to much trouble. No need to bolster Tristan's already insufferably huge ego by letting him know she'd made a special effort on his behalf.

Her hands shook as she unbuttoned her day dress. Perhaps Tristan had deliberately made her wait until this afternoon, to prolong the torture? She wouldn't put it past him.

What did one wear for one's own seduction? And how far was Tristan planning to go today? He'd mentioned kissing, but what else? He couldn't possibly be planning to make love to her in broad daylight in the middle of the afternoon.

Could he?

She settled on a forest-green riding skirt with a matching jacket, worn over her short stays and a thin cotton chemisette collared to look like a man's shirt where it showed between the jacket's lapels. The green made her hair shine like garnet and, remembering Tristan's comment about letting her hair down, she instructed her maid to dress it in a half-up, half-down style, as a symbolic compromise.

There was no sign of anyone as Carys rode up to the ruined folly, so she tied her mare to a tree, removed her hat and gloves, and strolled around the clearing trying to look as casual as possible.

On her third turn she jumped at a noise behind her and turned to find Tristan leaning against a crumbling pillar, his long legs crossed at the ankles. His smoky blue-gray jacket blended perfectly with the dappled shadows thrown by the trees. Her heart stuttered.

"I haven't been here for years!" she called out breathlessly. "The boys and I used to play knights and castles here all the time when we were younger."

She surveyed the tumbledown structure with affection. A few walls and part of one crenellated tower were just visible beneath a wild tangle of ivy and moss. When she'd been a girl she'd spun fanciful daydreams here, entranced by the lush green of the forest and the sunlight slanting through the leaves. The hushed, magical quality of the place conjured thoughts of fairies and secrets, of a time before humans walked the earth.

She glanced over at Tristan. "I love places like this. Just think of all the ancient history we're treading on."

"I hate to break it to you, but this place isn't that old. My great-grandfather had it built. He was of the firm opinion that no country estate is complete without a dilapidated classical temple somewhere on the grounds. He even paid for a live-in hermit."

Carys pouted in mock disappointment. "Oh. Still, I love a picturesque ruin. There's something so romantic about it."

She almost laughed at Tristan's expression of disdain.

"Romantic? It's like the setting of some dreadful gothic novel."

"Haven't you read *The Mysteries of Udolpho*? Ruins are a *necessity*. The overwrought heroine needs to trip over a crumbling staircase, or fall from a wobbly parapet. There's no potential for disaster if she's chased around a well-maintained castle."

Tristan shook his head, but his lips twitched, as if he was amused despite himself, and her heart gave another little jolt. Making him smile felt like such an achievement.

"What good is a wall without a roof? A window without glass?" he asked. "They're not doing their jobs, which is to keep people warm and dry."

"You're missing the point. They're romantic because they remind us of the passage of time, of our own mortality." Carys skimmed her fingers over a moss-furred wall. It was soft, like velvet. "Everything perishes. In a million years even these stones will be nothing but sand and water."

"That's melancholy, not romantic."

She shrugged. "Romantic poetry's *strewn* with rubble. Shelley's 'Ozymandias' is all about a giant sculpture, half buried in the sand, all that's left of a once-great empire. It reminds us to seize the moment."

As she was doing now.

Tristan pushed off the column and started toward her. Suddenly skittish, she scurried away to inspect a marble statue half hidden by the undergrowth. "Oh, I'd forgotten about these!"

Four statues stood guard at various points around the folly.

Tristan's boots crunched behind her and everything in her body tightened.

"Each one represents one of the four elements. Water, fire, earth, and air."

She didn't dare look over her shoulder to see how close he was. The scent of his cologne reached her nose and a coiling sensation twisted in her belly. She almost yelped in surprise when he reached out and smoothed the lock of hair that curled over her shoulder.

"You're fire, Carys Davies."

His voice was low, full of gravel. It made her knees go weak.

She managed a brittle laugh. "Ha! Little Flame. That's what my brothers used to call me, you know—because of my red hair. After Fiammetta, the writer Boccaccio's muse."

If she was fire, then what was Tristan? Her opposite, water?

No, he did nothing to dampen her desires. If anything, he was the wind, fanning the flames. She'd read a quote like that recently, by a French writer. *Absence is to love what wind is to fire; it extinguishes the small, it inflames the great.*

Tristan had been away for years, first at war, then on his Grand Tour. Had his absence fanned the flames of her love for him?

Carys stilled. Did she love Tristan? Or simply desire him? She didn't dare trust her own heart to make the distinction: She'd confused the two before, and look what trouble that had caused.

"Turn around, Carys."

His low command shivered through her. She sucked in a fortifying breath and swiveled to face him, but one glance at him, so close, had her on the verge of panic. This wasn't something impetuous and unplanned, like their kiss at the opera. If she kissed him now there'd be no blaming it on the excitement of the evening, or emotional distress.

"Maybe we should . . . wait for night?" she muttered.

A cynical smile curved his lips. "So you can pretend I'm someone else? Maybe you'd like me to come to your room in secret and make love to you in the dark, like Cupid and Psyche?"

Ugh. He could read her so well. In the dark she could deny she was thinking of him. Here in the daylight there was no pretending she was kissing someone else.

He took a step closer. "Darkness won't work, you know. You'd still recognize the scent of me. Just as I know the scent of you with my eyes closed."

Her heart fluttered as she inhaled his smoky cedar and spice.

"You'll know my touch too. And my taste," he murmured.

God, he was good. He wasn't even touching her and her body was already aflame.

"I'll know every inch of your body. Every line, every curve." His eyes lingered on the swell of her breasts beneath her jacket; they rose and fell faster as her breathing quickened. "Darkness won't make a blind bit of difference."

She swallowed.

"Are you going to cry off?" His soft tone was a challenge.

"No."

"Good."

She tensed, expecting him to touch her, but instead he took a step back, then another, retreating until he stood in the center of the leaf-strewn clearing. He crooked his finger at her. "This was your idea."

Her legs felt like jelly, but she forced herself forward and stopped when her skirts brushed his boots. He nodded his approval.

"Good. Now, did Howe kiss you?"

"Yes." She screwed up her face at the memory. "He pushed his tongue in my mouth. I didn't like it."

"Idiot," Tristan murmured. His clinical blue gaze searched her face and she felt like a botanist's specimen, a puzzle to be solved. "Has no one else kissed you since then?"

An embarrassed flush heated her cheeks. "No one except you. At the opera."

He nodded again, thoughtfully. "That was an angry kiss. A frustrated kiss. This one will be different."

"How?"

"Slower. More deliberate."

Carys gazed up at him, both excited and terrified. He was bigger than Howe. Taller, more muscular. He filled her entire vision, blocked out the sun. And yet she felt no trepidation. His physical power was so much greater than hers, but she trusted him not to take advantage of that fact. He made her feel oddly safe.

She was still marveling at that paradox when he raised his brows in definite challenge—a look that said, *I'm waiting . . .*

She reached out and cupped his jaw, her fingers tingling as they skated across his cool cheek. Giving in to temptation, she let the pad of her thumb slide over his lips, following the movement with her gaze as if spellbound.

He huffed out an unsteady breath. And when she lifted her face he dipped his head and settled his mouth against hers.

Chapter 18

Carys had expected force, or at least urgency. What she hadn't anticipated was the featherlight brush of his lips, a kiss so slight it was almost a question. But even that insubstantial touch was enough to make the embers inside her flare to life.

Tristan's fingers tightened at her nape. She closed her eyes and stayed completely still, only vaguely aware of the birds twittering overhead and the sunlight rippling over them.

His lips were soft, yet firm. He was right; this was nothing like their kiss at the opera. When he started to pull back she was the one who leaned forward to prolong the contact and to her dismay a needy little whimper escaped her. She felt him smile against her lips.

She pulled back and glared at him indignantly. "You're laughing at me."

"No."

"You think this is a joke. You're teasing me! Ohhh, you—"

Humiliation burned in her cheeks. What had she been thinking? He was a Montgomery. She'd been a fool to trust him. He was probably going to laugh about this later when he was alone—

"No!"

His lips cut off any further protest. One kiss became a multitude, playful yet persuasive, and Carys's anger evaporated. His thumb slid to her lower lip, rolling it down, and she felt a corresponding tug in the tips of her breasts and between her legs.

What magic was this?

She opened her mouth, inviting him in, but he moved to the side of her cheek instead, prolonging the torture. The faint stubble on his jaw dragged across her skin with a thrilling, unexpected roughness.

His breath tickled her ear and she shuddered. And when he kissed a trail down the side of her neck, barely grazing the skin, she tilted her head to give him better access. Sunlight danced against the inside of her eyelids.

It seemed an eternity before he made his way back to her lips. His tongue stroked inside and the intimacy of it was shocking, even though he'd kissed her just like this the night of the opera. It was like slipping into a hot bath: sweet, sinful decadence, and Carys dissolved into the sensation with a sigh of delight.

Even though her eyes were closed, there was no forgetting it was Tristan who was kissing her. He did it with such slow deliberation—as if he had infinite time and infinite patience.

She wanted to strangle him for his lack of urgency. How

could he be so restrained? She wanted to push him up against the ivy-covered wall and ravish him. To undo his cravat, yank his shirt out of his breeches, and slide her hands along the heat of his bare skin.

She wanted to be the one who made him lose his vaunted self-control.

She threaded her fingers through his hair, delighted that she was finally messing it up, and when he angled his head, she followed. It became a teasing game of advance and retreat.

Who'd have thought he knew how to play such a wicked game?

Thankfully, he seemed to be coming a little more unraveled. His hands slid to the front of her riding jacket and she gave a little gasp as the first button popped open. It sounded unnaturally loud in the quiet clearing. He made quick work of the rest, then parted the jacket to reveal her sheer chemisette. The shirt had no buttons, just a drawstring at the waist; he tugged it loose, exposing her stays and her upper chest to the dappled light.

Carys knew she ought to be embarrassed, but in truth she was no more exposed like this than she'd been at the opera, in her low-cut dress. Her stays supported her breasts like a balcony, leaving the top half of them enticingly bare.

Would they appeal to Tristan? The current fashion was for slim, flat-chested girls, but there wasn't much she could do about having such an ample bosom. Still, when had she ever conformed to fashion? She wasn't ashamed of her curves.

Tristan's expression was almost stern as he traced the top edge of her stays with his finger, leaving a trail of hot confusion in his wake. Then all rational thought fled as he bent and pressed a reverent kiss to the valley between her breasts.

Her pulse fluttered like a bird in a cage. Before she could fully fathom the sensation, he pushed the top of her stays down and the sudden brush of cool air against her nipples made her gasp.

His blue eyes captured hers. "You're beautiful, Carys."

He sounded so sincere that she couldn't possibly doubt him, and a tiny part of her tension drained away. Still holding her gaze, almost in challenge, he slid his hand around her ribs and cupped her breast.

Her face flamed.

Dear God, Tristan Montgomery had his hand on her naked breast!

To her horror, she felt her nipple tighten against his palm. Her shaky inhale only pressed her more fully into his hand, and the sight of his tanned fingers on her pale skin sent a primitive thrill through her. As she watched, he caught her nipple between two fingers and gently squeezed.

"Tristan!"

He looked up at her with a faint, quizzical smile. "Has nobody ever done that to you before?"

"No!" she gasped. "Howe mauled me through my dress like he was kneading bread dough, but . . . no, nothing like that."

"I don't suppose he did this either, then?"

He bent his head and kissed her, an inch above the nipple. Her stomach contracted. "He did not," she managed weakly.

"Or this."

His tongue darted out to flick her nipple and Carys stiffened in shock.

"Tristan Montgomery!"

He chuckled and did it again, and her knees almost gave way. Hot and cold shivers raced over her skin. And then he *licked* her, his wicked tongue circling in the most tormenting manner possible, and she grabbed his head and tugged on his hair—whether to pull him away or hold him in place she didn't know. A terrible impatience coiled inside her as he continued his exquisite torment, and when he finally lifted his head she could barely speak.

"You like that?" His gaze was as cool as ever, but there was a slight flush across his cheekbones.

"Very much."

"Then we'll do it again, but not today. That's enough for now."

What?

Carys almost stamped her foot in disappointment. *He was stopping? Now?* Her entire body was on fire, heavy with anticipation.

She glanced at him, but he seemed to have reverted to the serene, self-contained Tristan she'd always known. A wave of self-doubt assailed her. Had she been the only one to enjoy the past few minutes?

She forced herself to stay perfectly still as he straightened her stays and readjusted her chemisette as efficiently as any lady's maid. He re-buttoned her jacket with steady fingers, the backs of his knuckles brushing her sensitive nipples as he did so, and she ground her teeth, unsure whether he was doing it deliberately or not.

She wouldn't put it past him, the wretch. Perhaps his plan was to make her expire of unfulfilled lust? If that was the case, her days were numbered.

Just when she'd convinced herself that he'd been impervious to the squirming excitement surging through her own veins, he took a step back and she glimpsed the bulge in the front of his breeches. Her spirits soared, even as her mouth dropped open in shock. He clearly *had* been enjoying himself.

But dear God, surely Howe hadn't been that big? Not that she'd actually seen it, of course—it had been too dark and too hurried—but simple logic determined that something of *those* proportions hadn't been pushed inside her.

Tristan noted the direction of her gaze. He glanced down at himself, then back up with an expression that was part rueful and part grimace. "I liked it too. Obviously."

She gestured vaguely at his crotch. "Don't you need to . . . do something with that?"

His lips twitched. "Not today. We're not going to rush our fences. It'll pass, in a minute or two."

"But—"

He shook his head, and she was pleased to notice that while his cravat was still impeccable, she'd managed to disrupt the perfection of his hair. A tiny tuft was sticking out in the wrong direction, just behind his ear. It seemed like a small but important victory.

"No," he said gruffly. "Your experience with Howe was like—" He paused, searching for a suitable metaphor. "—like attending a six-course dinner. Except you missed out on the first five courses—all of which are quite delicious in their own right—and rushed straight to the dessert."

He tilted his head and the corners of his eyes crinkled. "Now, there's nothing wrong with dessert, especially if it's à chocolate gâteau, or crème brûlée. But Howe served you something revolting, like pease pudding, instead. It's no wonder you've lost your appetite." His gaze held hers and her blood heated at the wicked promise she saw there. "I'm going to make sure you enjoy every single course."

Her pulse fluttered in anticipation. What could one say to that? *Thank you*?

Feed me now; I'm famished?

He reached into his coat and consulted his pocket watch with an air of brisk efficiency. "It's almost five. You should get back to the house."

Carys sighed. "I suppose so. I promised Gryff I'd chat with the guests before dinner. Will I see you there?"

He shook his head and she quashed a little dip of disappointment.

"Not tonight. I've a meeting with my father and a couple of investors. But I'll be at the picnic Maddie has planned for tomorrow. She's showing everyone her latest archaeological discoveries, out near the wishing well on the western border. It's close enough to the house I'm building that I can attend to both."

Since her heart seemed to have finally resumed a more natural rhythm and the tingling sensations had subsided a little, Carys forced herself to stride over to her horse. She tugged on her leather riding gloves and settled her hat back on her head. Tristan started forward to help her mount, but she waved him away and used a tumbled piece of stonework to gain the saddle.

"I'll see you tomorrow, then," she said awkwardly. Now that there was some physical distance between them, it was almost as if the last few minutes had never happened. They were back to being begrudgingly friendly acquaintances.

Tristan, busy with his own horse on the other side of the clearing, nodded dismissively. "Yes. Tomorrow."

Tristan waited until he heard Carys's retreat, then dropped his forehead to his horse's saddle and took a deep, calming breath of leather and polish.

Bloody hell.

Her outrageous proposition this morning had come out of the blue and he'd struggled to keep the astonishment off his face. And yet, despite his shock, he'd only debated the wisdom of saying yes for a split second. He'd had a sudden, blinding vision of the rest of his life stretching out before him in the dutiful rut he'd preordained—utterly dull and predictable—and a kind of madness had seized him.

Just this once, he'd put pleasure before duty.

One week with the only woman he'd ever truly wanted.

One week to consign her to memory, to be as daring, as reckless, as she.

He was still rock hard in his breeches. He reached down and readjusted himself, but it did little to relieve the discomfort.

How could he be this turned on just from *kissing*? He'd thought it would be simple enough to maintain his cool, especially in the face of her obvious lack of experience, but Carys had thrown herself headlong into the lesson. Her innocent, explorative kisses had quickly transformed into deep, languorous swirls that made him want to keep on kissing her until they both passed out from lack of air.

He should have been prepared for this; she'd always been all-or-nothing. *Of course* she'd commit to kissing as fully as she'd committed to scandalizing the *ton* or to protecting her foolish brothers.

He clenched his hand on the pommel. God, her breasts were spectacular. He could still feel the ghosts of their imprints in his hands. And the taste of her skin? Every wicked daydream he'd ever had. He wanted to devour her, to eat her all up like the wolf in the tale. To tease her until she cried for mercy.

His cock throbbed in agreement, but he'd promised himself—and her—that they would take things slowly. His coolness under fire was legendary; if he could keep his head while facing a brigade of French hussars, he could bloody well control himself with an almost virgin like Carys. He was the one with all the experience, was he not?

And yet none of the women he'd ever slept with could hold a candle to her. Oh, they'd been witty and beautiful. Passionate and bold. He'd admired some for their intelligence, some for their brazenness. But while he'd desired them all, none of them affected him as she did. She was like a sliver of shrapnel under his skin, a constant presence impossible to forget. A niggling irritation from which he could find no relief.

Perhaps when he finally *did* make love to her it would cure him of his affliction. Familiarity bred contempt, as Chaucer said. The mystique would be gone, his desires would be quenched, and he'd be free to live the rest of his life without constantly wondering what it would feel like to bury himself inside her and see the look on her face when she—

His cock throbbed again. He ground his teeth and stared at a moss-covered wall.

Damn it. He couldn't ride in this state. He took another

deep breath and mentally set about designing the gardens
for his new house. The one he would share with his eventual
bride.

His manhood started to soften immediately, and he felt
an odd pang of guilt. It didn't bode well that whenever he
thought of Lavinia—or any woman who wasn't Carys—his
desire evaporated like mist in the sun.

Still, that was a problem for another day. Duty wasn't always a pleasure.

Chapter 19

The majority of Gryff's houseguests had gathered in the drawing room by the time Carys descended the stairs that evening.

She'd called for a bath after returning from the woods, and had blushed with guilty pleasure at the new sensitivity of her breasts as she slid the soapy washcloth over them. Her skin felt alive, tingling with awareness, and her flush intensified when she noticed the slight redness on her décolletage and realized that it must have been caused by the faint stubble on Tristan's chin.

She could barely believe what they'd done. The whole interlude seemed like a wicked, magical daydream, a secret entrusted to the forest. In a strange way she felt part of some timeless fellowship of lovers. How many other couples had met in those same woods over the centuries for a little clandestine amour?

All heads turned toward her as she entered the drawing room, unsurprising since she'd chosen a striking teal silk profusely embroidered with peacock feathers. Rhys caught her eye from across the room and raised his glass in a silent toast at her glorious extravagance. At least she'd given the guests something to talk about if conversation flagged.

Morgan stepped forward and handed her a glass of champagne. "You look like Geoffrey."

Carys inclined her head, almost jabbing his eye out with the ostrich feathers she'd placed in her hair. "Are you going to put me in a pie if I scream?"

"Don't tempt me."

"I might take a walk out to the menagerie later and show him this." She snapped open her peacock-feather fan and waved it with a dramatic flourish. "As a warning of what might happen if he continues to misbehave."

Morgan snorted. "I think even a birdbrain like Geoffrey has realized you couldn't harm a fly. I just hope Gryff's warned the guests they'll be woken at some ungodly hour of the morning by a screech that sounds like someone's being murdered."

Carys chuckled.

They drifted into the ballroom where Maddie had engaged a local string quartet to play a series of country dances and Carys spent the next twenty minutes deflecting the enthusiastic attentions of a young man named Thomas Herriott. His boyish adoration, while flattering, made her feel altogether ancient.

She interrupted an embarrassing attempt to woo her with a limerick about Lancelot and Guinevere. "Tell me, Mister Herriott, do you dance?"

Poor Herriott looked flustered at her direct question, as if he hadn't expected a goddess to actually speak, but he recovered quickly. "Er, oh, well, yes. Yes, of course. Would you like to—"

"Perfect!" Carys trilled. "In that case, perhaps you can explain something to me?"

Thomas looked as though he might collapse at her feet in gratitude. Even the tips of his ears turned pink.

"Anything!"

She sent him a smile, the one that brought out a charming dimple in her left cheek, and indicated a figure seated in one of the chairs on the opposite side of the room. The occupant, a slim girl with pretty features and flaxen hair, was clearly uncomfortable; her head was bowed, her shoulders stooped, and she fiddled relentlessly with the beaded tassels of the reticule in her lap.

"Do you see that lovely creature over there?"

Thomas frowned. "Err. Yes?"

Carys leaned closer, as if to impart some confidential information. "Then let me tell you, Mister Herriott, that I am quite horribly jealous of her."

"You are? Why?" Herriott seemed so genuinely mystified that Carys almost took pity on him. Almost.

She feigned astonishment. "Why, that's Cordelia Rutledge. Her father's General Sir Anthony Rutledge, the war hero. Not only is she a considerable heiress, but just look at her complexion! Not a freckle to be seen."

Herriott opened his mouth to insist that he adored Carys's freckles, but she was too quick for him.

"And I have always admired her lovely blue eyes. Why on

earth hasn't some lucky gentleman snapped her up? Are you all so lacking in observational skills?"

"She has a stammer," Herriott said bluntly. "That's what Fox says, anyway."

Carys waved her hand. "Only when she's nervous. It disappears when she's at ease." She went in for the coup de grâce. "Of course, an *intelligent* man would see past such a trifling obstacle. He might even see it as a challenge; can *he* be the one to vanquish the stammer? It's a quest worthy of any modern Lancelot."

Herriott, to her relief, seemed to find this idea rather appealing. He studied Cordelia with renewed interest.

"You should ask her to dance," Carys whispered.

He turned back to her, clearly torn. "Are you sure *you* wouldn't like to—?"

"Oh, goodness no! Not in this dress. Ask Miss Rutledge about fossils. It's a particular passion of hers, I believe."

Herriott straightened his cravat and smoothed his hair with new determination. "Do you know, Lady Carys, I think I will. I'm rather interested in geology myself. If you'll excuse me?"

Carys nodded graciously, and hid her smile when he left with a swift bow.

Her amusement increased when she saw Morgan shoot Herriott an irritated glare for conversing with Cordelia, but she felt no remorse for promoting the match. Morgan wasn't remotely serious about the girl—he was merely entertaining himself. Her brother needed a partner who would challenge him, not agree with every word he said, and Cordelia was too sweetly compliant.

Carys bit her lip. Now that she thought on it, the only woman who'd ever seriously affected Morgan was Maddie's cousin, Harriet.

She turned her head and located Harriet on the opposite side of the room. The other girl was looking lovely in a forest-green gown, but she seemed to be trying to disappear into the shadows.

Harriet lived in London for most of the year with her father, but came to Newstead Park each summer. Gryff, Rhys, and Morgan had spent most of their school summer holidays traipsing about the hills and valleys, looking for Maddie and Harriet to torment.

While Gryff had always returned from these adventures full of tales of what he'd done to annoy Maddie, Morgan's bragging had always been about irritating Harriet. He'd seemed to take a gleeful delight in teasing her.

But then Morgan had gone away to sea, and the man who'd returned was far more cynical and battle-hardened than the fun-loving brother who'd left. He'd thrown himself into the pursuit of pleasure with careless abandon, but Carys was worried about him. As someone who knew all about putting on a façade and only *pretending* to enjoy herself, she recognized the same signs in her brother.

His imprisonment on the island of Martinique had left a deep mark on him. Carys didn't know the full details, but Morgan blamed an incorrect maritime map for his shipwreck. He'd vowed to track down the mapmaker and extract revenge.

Carys sighed. Perhaps Harriet's presence this week would jolt him out of his slump. The two of them were good at keeping the other on their toes.

As if he'd sensed her thoughts, Morgan glanced over and

spied Harriet. His lips curved in a smile of anticipation. He rose in one smooth movement and started heading her way and Carys saw the exact moment Harriet realized she was Morgan's target; her eyes widened in alarm and she pressed herself back against the wood paneling as if hoping it would swallow her up.

Morgan's expression turned wolfish.

Harriet glanced first left, then right, clearly searching for an escape route, but found none. She was hemmed in by a giant potted fern and an elegant console table. Realizing her predicament, she drew herself up, but even at her tallest she was no match for Morgan when he stepped in front of her.

He offered his hand.

She shook her head, clearly trying to deny the dance Morgan was requesting, but he simply caught her fingers and spun her smoothly out into the newly forming line of dancers. Carys suppressed a smile at Harriet's furious expression and Morgan's answering look of mock contrition. How she wished she could hear what the two of them were saying . . .

A glass of champagne materialized at her elbow and she looked up with a surprised jump. Her heart rate tripled as she recognized Tristan, devastatingly handsome in black evening clothes and a snowy white cravat. She accepted the glass without thinking and took a healthy gulp.

How *did* he sneak up on her like that? The man was a magician.

His dark brows rose in greeting. "Matchmaking?"

Carys sent him a surprised glance. "What, between Morgan and Harriet? Are you mad?"

"No, those two." He sent a subtle nod toward Cordelia and Herriott.

"Ohh." She managed a creditable shrug. "Herriott was starting to annoy me. But I do think he and Miss Rutledge are well-matched. He simply needed a nudge in the right direction."

"And you provided the nudge."

"Why not?" Cordelia and Herriott were deep in conversation now. As Carys watched, a blushing Cordelia allowed him to lead her onto the dance floor.

"You found Herriott tiresome?" Tristan asked. "Why is that?"

"He's too young."

"He's two years older than yourself."

Carys sent him a teasing sideways smile. "I prefer a man with a little more worldly experience. Someone who doesn't have the rosy glow of optimism clouding his judgment."

"You'd choose age and cynicism over youthful exuberance? No wonder the *ton*'s dubbed you 'an original.'"

She laughed, genuinely amused. "Ha! That's the nicest thing they say about me. They also say that I'm extravagant and indecorous. And sadly lacking in feminine virtues like sweetness and humility."

She tossed her head, and the ostrich plumes danced. "In my defense, my 'profligate spending' keeps scores of people in gainful employment. I like to think I'm redistributing the wealth: from myself to the dressmakers, jewelers, and glove makers of London."

"Only you could argue that buying a new outfit for every day of the year is actually a public service. The King should give you a knighthood."

Carys suppressed an amused snort at his mockery. His

lack of deference was so refreshing. Any other man would have rushed to assure her that she was perfect.

"You don't like this dress either?" she teased.

"You'd look better out of it."

Her heart missed a beat. His expression was so bland she could scarcely believe she'd heard him correctly. Oh, he was wicked.

"I thought you said you weren't coming this evening?" she managed.

"My business took less time than anticipated. I decided to ride over here and help you fend off your raft of admirers."

His tone was so dry Carys couldn't tell if he was joking or not. She gestured at the empty space around them. "Well, thank you," she mocked. "You can see how besieged I am."

They were standing near the entrance of the ballroom and a commotion in the hallway heralded the late arrival of another guest. She twisted her head to see who the new guests were, and froze in shock as she recognized Victoria Howe handing her traveling cloak to their elderly major-domo, Beddow.

Dear God, no!

Her worst fears were realized when Victoria's husband entered close behind her, doffing his hat, closely followed by the portly form of her father, Obediah Jennings.

Chapter 20

"Damn those roads!" Christopher Howe's peevish tones carried along the hall. "I tell you, the farther one gets from London, the worse they get. It's a miracle we arrived before midnight."

Obediah Jennings sent his son-in-law an impatient glare. "Nowt wrong with the roads," he muttered gruffly, his northern accent pronounced. "It were the company that was wearing." He shared a humorous glance with his daughter. "And you could've come down in yer own carriage if you hadn't lost it at cards last week, my lad."

The floor beneath Carys seemed to tilt. Tristan plucked the champagne flute from her nerveless fingers and grabbed her elbow, and the steady pressure succeeded in grounding her.

"Breathe," he commanded gruffly.

She sucked in an unsteady breath, then another, and her

momentary dizziness began to fade. "I had no idea Gryff had invited them," she whispered.

"It makes sense," Tristan said evenly, keeping his voice low. "Gryff and my father have been talking to various businessmen looking to invest in the next stage of our joint mining project. They're going to lay a tramway to transport the coal and gold. Gryff must have invited Jennings to see the setup for himself. I can only assume he extended the invitation to his daughter and Howe too."

He glanced down at her, his expression enigmatic. "After all, Gryff has no reason to think you're avoiding Howe, does he?"

Carys frowned, unsure if he was blaming her for not confiding in her brother or not.

"I suppose not," she said stiffly.

They watched in silence as Lucas, one of the underfootmen, ushered the new arrivals up the main staircase to their rooms while Beddow sidled into the ballroom to inform Gryff and Maddie that more guests had arrived.

Carys's spirits plummeted, even as a flare of anger warmed her. *Damn Howe.* This place was supposed to be her refuge. Now any hope of a respite from the stresses of her life in London had been well and truly shattered. She would have to spend the rest of the week trying to avoid him while not appearing to do so. It was going to be a nightmare.

"I think I'm going to retire," she said shakily. "It's been a very long day." She glanced down pointedly at her elbow, where Tristan was still holding her in a firm grip. He dropped his hand with a start, almost as if he'd forgotten he was touching her.

"Carys," he commanded, and she glanced up into his

face. He was so handsome it always took her a little by surprise. "It will be all right."

Her heart clenched in her chest. His expression was so
earnest, like some medieval knight pledging allegiance to
his lady, and everything about his steady certainty inspired
confidence. No wonder he'd been able to lead so many of his
men into battle; he seemed so invulnerable, it was impossible to believe that he would permit anything bad to happen.

*And yet some of those men had still died, despite his best
efforts.*

Carys sighed. She suddenly remembered that he hadn't
actually agreed not to punish Howe, and was glad that he
was staying over at Newstead Park, rather than under the
same roof, for the next week.

"Promise me you won't do anything to Howe," she said
quietly. "He's not worth it. And I will never forgive you if
you do something to ruin Maddie's first house party. She's
already nervous enough about hosting as it is. She wants
everything to be perfect. You are *not* to make a scene."

Tristan's expression softened and a wicked flash of humor
curved his lips. He bent his head so his lips almost brushed
her ear, and a flash of heat raced through her.

"You do realize the irony of you, Carys Davies, lectur-
ing *me* about *making a scene*," he whispered. "I think most
people would agree that, of the two of us, you're far more
likely to do something outrageous. I'm not the one who wore
little more than a transparent handkerchief to a ball."

His gentle teasing went a long way to settle her nerves.
"Then promise you won't do anything stupid, like challenge
him to a duel, or a fistfight," she pressed.

Tristan's regretful sigh huffed against her ear. "Very well.

As much as I long to tear the bastard limb from limb, I promise not to engage in any kind of physical altercation with him while he's here. I won't touch him, unless it's in self-defense. Does that make you happy?"

Carys nodded, trying to ignore the little thrill that coursed through her at hearing Tristan speak in such a barbaric fashion. He was always so perfectly turned out she'd never really imagined him in any other state, but the muscles that he clearly possessed and his time in the army suggested that he was no stranger to brutal physical fighting.

Her brain was suddenly flooded with all manner of disturbing images of him, shirtless, glistening with sweat, like the bruising prizefighters she'd seen at the country fairs. She wafted her peacock-feather fan vigorously.

She'd be lying if she said she'd never imagined someone like Tristan or one of her brothers beating the senses out of Howe, but such violence, however satisfying, wasn't the answer. There would be no way of keeping such a thing quiet, and it wasn't fair to punish poor Victoria by association. Carys didn't know the other woman well, but she strongly believed in female solidarity. Life was hard enough for women without them turning on one another. She couldn't imagine Victoria was particularly happy, being married to a cad like Howe, and there was no need to add to her burdens.

Tristan's hand on the curve of her back pulled her from her introspection, and she fought not to fidget under the contact. The heat of his big palm burned through the fabric of her dress.

Since he was standing behind her, his familiar gesture was hidden from the rest of the room, but she was sure the flush in her cheeks betrayed her.

If his aim was to distract her from her woes by making her dizzy with lust, then he was doing an admirable job. She sucked in a breath as his fingers slid a teasing path up the back of her dress, catching at perfectly regular intervals on the laces that kept it secured.

Up. Up. Up.

How could such a simple touch—not even on her skin, for heaven's sake—be so suggestive?

The heat in her cheeks intensified as she felt her nipples harden within her bodice. Tristan's fingers finally reached the top of the scoop back of the dress and the jolt of skin on skin was like faint lightning. It made her stomach flip and her toes curl in her dancing slippers.

His lips were still by her ear. "Go to bed, Carys, and don't give Howe a second thought. Just think of all the things I'm going to teach you when we have our next lesson." His fingers traced a tiny circle on her back. "I'll see you tomorrow. At the picnic."

Chapter 21

The following day dawned warm and sunny and Maddie was delighted that her planned excursion and picnic could go ahead as planned.

Carys managed to avoid an awkward meeting with Howe and Victoria by skulking around the menagerie all morning, then offered to ride to the designated picnic spot. She kept her distance as the guests arranged themselves in their various carriages and quashed a malicious twinge of amusement when she saw a cross-looking Christopher climb into his father-in-law's coach.

Had Tristan used the carriage he'd won from Howe to bring him here from London? And would Howe recognize it, with the Montgomery crest now replacing his own?

She certainly hoped so.

Tristan was already at the picnic spot when they all arrived, and Carys nodded to him as she dismounted. Maddie had chosen this particular place—a charming wooded clearing around an ancient wishing well the Welsh called Ffynnon Pen Rhys and the English called the Virtuous Well—because it was where she'd inadvertently fallen into the cave system that had yielded the seam of gold the Davieses and the Montgomerys now jointly mined.

As Maddie pointed out the entrance to the tunnels to a few of the guests, warning them to take care on the uneven ground, Carys watched Gryff direct a small army of servants to set up various folding tables, rugs, campaign chairs, and picnic baskets.

Gryff's years of command in the army had never been more evident as he coordinated their efforts, and Carys smiled, glad that he finally seemed to be settling into the role of Earl of Powys he'd inherited upon their father's death last year. She sometimes worried that all three of her brothers—and Tristan too—might be finding life less than exciting after their adventures fighting Bonaparte on the Continent. The readjustment to civilian life was not an easy one.

She glanced over at Tristan again and was pleased to see him making his way across the clearing toward her, but her view was blocked by the last person she'd wanted to see. Howe had managed to sidle away from his wife and father-in-law without her noticing. He stepped up to her, slightly too close for comfort, as ever, just as Tristan arrived at her side.

Howe sent Tristan a wide, jovial smile, blissfully unaware that the other man knew about his treachery.

"Afternoon, Montgomery. Didn't expect to see you here.

What happened to the infamous Davies-Montgomery feud, eh? Thought you'd all be at daggers drawn."

Tristan barely inclined his head in greeting, but Howe didn't seem to notice the slight.

"This is a temporary truce for my sister," Tristan said coolly. "The feud itself is still going strong. Although—" He slid a glance at Carys and she caught a flash of wickedness in his eyes. "I think it's fair to say that it's . . . evolving. Davieses and Montgomerys seem to be finding new ways to collaborate. Wouldn't you agree, Lady Carys?"

Carys was certain her cheeks were pink with embarrassment, but she managed to respond to his innuendo-laden banter with sunny enthusiasm.

"Oh, absolutely. Just look at the way Gryff and Maddie have managed to get both families involved in the new gold mine. Nobody ever imagined a joint operation between our two families was possible, but here we are. Collaborating."

She sent Tristan a laughing glance.

Christopher, thankfully, was too self-absorbed to notice their teasing byplay. He was busy sliding a lecherous gaze over her body, from her intricately curled hair to her embroidered hem, and she tried not to shudder at the proprietary gleam in his eyes.

"You're looking lovely today, Carys," he said smoothly. "I do hope we can find time this week to catch up."

She forced a smile, in case any of the other guests were watching, but it was Tristan who spoke.

"Surely you don't mean *alone*?" His feigned surprise was so perfect that Carys almost smiled. He sounded as stern and disapproving as the *ton*'s highest sticklers. "You can't have anything to say to her that you can't also say in front of me. Lady Carys has her reputation to think of, Howe."

Christopher sent her a sly look. "Of course she does. And rest assured, her reputation is perfectly safe with me."

As long as she continues to pay for my silence. Carys mentally finished the rest of his unspoken threat, perversely glad that Tristan was here to witness his double-edged words.

"I'm delighted to hear it," Tristan said stiffly. "I would be most displeased if anyone did anything to hurt her."

He sounded so polite, and Carys could only marvel at the way he managed to imbue such innocuous-sounding words with an air of such menace.

Howe, however, gave a jocular laugh, oblivious to the threat. "That's an odd thing for a Montgomery to say about a Davies."

Tristan slid her another secret smile. "Hardly. Friends are easy to come by, but a good enemy's almost impossible to find. I like to think of Carys as my own particular Davies to torment."

Her stomach gave a wicked little somersault. She'd always thought of Tristan in exactly the same way. As her own personal adversary.

Howe looked confused, and she felt her lips curve up in a smile. How could Tristan manage to make her feel like *laughing* during a conversation with Howe? She'd never have thought it possible, but it was such a joy to be part of a team, beating Christopher at his own game of subtext and innuendo for once.

This is what it's like to have someone on your side. Someone of equal wit and talent.

Tristan glanced pointedly over Howe's shoulder: an easy task since he was several inches taller than the other man. Carys had never seen them standing so close together, but now that only a few feet separated them it was clear that Christopher was by far the less impressive specimen. How had she ever imagined that he could be a substitute for Tristan?

"I think your wife requires your attention," Tristan said coolly. He nodded to where Victoria stood laughing with Lord Prowse, and Maddie bit back another laugh. Victoria seemed to be perfectly content without her husband's presence. "Lady Carys, can I interest you in a tour of the house I'm building? It's not too far from here, and I seem to have lost my appetite."

"Thank you," she said. "That would be delightful. Good day, Howe."

She dismissed Howe with a regal nod, took Tristan's proffered elbow, and he steered her away.

"Thank you for rescuing me," she murmured when they were far enough not to be overheard. "He really is obnoxious. I can't believe I was ever taken in." She glanced up at Tristan, handsome as ever in a dark-blue jacket and tan breeches. "Were you serious about going to see your house? Or was that just an excuse to get away?"

He shrugged. "We can go there if you like."

"Won't it cause speculation, if we disappear off into the woods together?"

"Not the kind you mean. They'll think one of us is luring the other into the forest for a spot of murder. Lots of places to hide a body around here."

Carys rolled her eyes. "You wouldn't kill me, Montgomery.

Think how dull your life would be without me to disapprove of. You'd be bored in less than a week."

"I doubt I'd survive the loss," he mocked gently. "And neither would the British economy. It would collapse without your spending. London's dressmakers would be destitute, milliners begging in the streets."

She whacked him playfully on the arm. "Beast."

They stopped near the tethered horses and Carys glanced over at the rest of the picnickers who were now tucking into a feast of cold game pies and fresh fruit, courtesy of the Trellech kitchens. "I'd better tell Gryff we're planning to leave, or he'll send out a search party."

"Let Maddie tell him," Tristan suggested. He caught his sister's eye and beckoned her over.

Maddie's smile doubled in size when she heard their plans, and she gave Carys an impulsive hug.

"Oh, that's a lovely idea. It's so nice to see you two getting along for once." She sent her brother a playful warning glare. "You take good care of her, Tristan. That place of yours still has trenches to fall into and things to trip over. Gryff will flay you alive if anything happens to her."

"I'm not entirely lacking in coordination," Carys protested, laughing. "I'm sure I'll be fine."

It amused her that Maddie's only concern was for her physical safety, and not for her virtue. That Tristan might be taking her off for nefarious reasons was clearly so ridiculous it was not to be considered.

For some reason the thought was a little depressing. Was the idea of them as a couple really so outlandish?

She shook her head and mounted her horse as Tristan did

the same, and the two of them rode out of the clearing along the narrow leafy track.

The chance to see Tristan's new home aroused conflicting emotions in her chest. On one hand, she was genuinely interested to see the fruits of his architectural brilliance, but she was plagued by a niggling guilt too. Tristan should be showing it to Lavinia Purser, seeking *her* reaction to the place, not herself.

Chapter 22

It was worse than Carys could ever have imagined. It was love at first sight.

A valley opened up before them as they reached the edge of the woods, with a river curving playfully through the lush, rolling hills. And there, on a slight rise, was the most beautiful house she'd ever seen. Neat rows of windows reflected the afternoon sun, gleaming from a creamy white stone façade that was both elegant and yet surprisingly modern.

A poignant ache tightened her chest, the most visceral reaction she'd ever had to a building, and in a flash she recognized it for what it was: *yearning*. That gorgeous house on the hill represented everything she'd never realized she wanted until that very moment.

This was where Tristan was preparing to settle down, a place in which to raise a family of his own. After all his years of travels, he was finally putting down roots.

How ironic, when she'd always wished for the opposite—
for freedom, for wings with which to fly. Why did she suddenly pine for *this*? For permanence? It was so contradictory.

She knew why. As much as she loved Trellech Court, she
couldn't stay there forever. It was Maddie and Gryff's home
now. Rhys and Morgan would eventually marry and move
out, and she was expected to do the same. But how on earth
was she going to manage that, in her situation? How would
she ever achieve the stability and contentment this house em-
bodied?

She cleared her throat, acutely aware that Tristan had
reined in his mount next to hers and was watching her to
gauge her reaction.

"So, first impressions?" he asked gruffly, and the hint of
uncertainty in his tone was both endearing and unexpected.
It almost sounded as though impervious Tristan was nervous about her opinion.

How wonderful.

"It's beautiful," she said honestly, not bothering to hide the
reverence in her voice. "But why build another house when
you'll inherit Newstead Park from your father someday?"

"I wanted to design something for myself, to incorporate
the new classical styles I saw over in Italy. I'm a great ad-
mirer of Palladio, the Italian architect inspired by the de-
signs of ancient Rome."

"Hence your choice of costume at the ball."

He nodded and Carys hid a smile. She'd been studying up
on architectural styles ever since Maddie had let slip about
his love for an architect "called Paladin, or something," last
year.

Still, no reason to let him know just how far she'd gone

to learn about the things he liked. He was arrogant enough already, without that extra ammunition.

He tilted his chin toward the house. "It's been in construction for almost two years; I had a team of builders overseeing it while I was away. It looks finished from here, but there's still work to be done. You'll see when we get closer."

The house sounded very much like herself: an illusion. A vision that looked perfect from afar, but on closer inspection was still a work in progress.

"I intend it to be an example of what I can do," Tristan said easily. He nudged his horse forward and Carys followed suit.

"I'm hoping it will lead to more commissions." He studied the building's orderly façade. "Palladio felt that architecture should be governed by order and symmetry, and I agree. This design pays homage to antiquity with its harmonic proportions."

Carys suppressed a snort. The house wasn't the only thing with *harmonic proportions*; Tristan was as beautiful to look at as the villas he loved.

"I like the honesty of architecture," he continued, unaware of her ogling. "It's there, in plain sight, for everyone to see. There's no hiding a mistake."

"That's true. A doctor can bury his mistakes, but all an architect can do is plant vines to cover his up."

She was delighted to see his lips curve upward at her irreverence.

"Architecture isn't just about providing something as basic as shelter. There's more to it than that. It's about making something beautiful, about creating a space that makes people feel good. It's about pleasure and power. And sometimes illusion."

Her heart contracted sharply in her chest. If she'd ever

imagined Tristan to be cold and unfeeling, the quiet passion in his words disproved it. He practically vibrated intensity.

What would it be like to have him so passionate about *her*?

His blue eyes caught hers. "It's like we discussed at the folly. I wanted to build something that will outlive me. A legacy that will remain long after I'm gone."

Carys swallowed the sudden lump of emotion in her throat. "That's an admirable goal. You know, Goethe once described architecture as 'frozen music.' I thought that was rather nice."

He glanced at her sharply, as if surprised yet again by her knowledge. "Yes. Yes, it is."

They rode across the valley, and Carys could see teams of various workmen milling around the house. The place was a hive of activity.

Two men in paint-spattered clothes nodded at Tristan as they dismounted in front of the impressive front door. He returned their friendly greeting, then swept his arm in a theatrical gesture for her to precede him into the house.

She sucked in a breath as she entered a double-height hallway decorated almost entirely in pale marble. An elegant staircase swept up to a railed gallery ringing the upper level, but what caught her attention was the enormous glass chandelier being hoisted into place by another trio of men. The glittering tiered concoction swayed precariously on its temporary pulley, but after a few tense moments it was fixed in place without mishap.

Tristan heaved an audible sigh of relief and clapped the sweating foreman on the back. "Excellent work, Harding."

"Thank ye, my lord. That was the last one, I'm glad to say. The rest went in without trouble."

Tristan nodded and ushered her through one of the two doors on their left. "This way."

Carys lost count of the number of rooms they inspected, but she adored the way the place managed to feel both grand and yet comfortable at the same time. No one room was so enormous as to be daunting, even when devoid of furniture, and the proportions of each were close to perfect.

As Tristan had said, most of the interiors were nearing completion, and her spirits veered from awed admiration at his impeccable sense of style—the decoration was almost exactly to her taste—to outright jealousy of the woman who would eventually call such a jewel box of a house her home. When she found herself mentally imagining the furniture she would place in each room, she gave herself a stern mental shake.

"I purchased quite a few things on my Grand Tour," Tristan said as they exited a gorgeous salon lined in red velvet and peered into a room filled with enticing-looking wooden packing crates. "Paintings and sculptures and the like. Some are already here. The rest should be arriving soon."

Carys longed to grab a crowbar and start breaking open the boxes, but she forced herself to simply nod. They mounted the stairs, and he showed her the upper rooms, including several guest bedrooms. He swung open a door. "This is for the mistress of the house."

Her boots clicked on the newly polished parquet floor, an intricate pattern of diamonds in different-colored woods. The room was empty, awaiting furniture, but the walls had been papered in the palest of celadon green.

Her heart gave a strange stutter. There was no way he could know this was her favorite color, the same shade she'd chosen for her own bedroom back at Trellech. It was just a strange coincidence, but she was perversely irritated that another woman should enjoy that particular shade here. Why couldn't he have chosen a color she hated, like buttercup yellow, or pale pink?

She stepped blindly through a door to her right and found a sitting room, then ventured on, through another door she assumed led to a dressing room. She was wrong.

"And this is the master bedroom," he murmured.

Chapter 23

Carys stopped dead just inside the doorway. The walls of this room were darker, a more masculine, forest-green version of the suite next door. But whereas the other bedrooms had been devoid of furniture, *this* room was dominated by a beautiful four-poster bed that had been placed right in the center of the floor.

It wasn't one of the dark, heavily carved oak ones usually found in English homes, nor one of the overdecorated gilt monstrosities, encrusted with carved putti and scalloped shells. Four slim wooden pillars rose to support a square canopy designed to look like a classical Roman pediment. The painted style was neither overtly masculine nor feminine, just elegant and austere.

So perfectly Tristan.

There were no curtains, just a swathe of cream silk gathered in pleats on the underside of the canopy. A mattress, clearly new from the pristine white of the ticking, had been placed on the frame.

"Ah, it's here," Tristan said, pleasure in his voice. "I ordered this directly from a workshop in Siena."

His big body was close behind her in the doorway. His woodsy scent teased her nose, and something hot and wicked twisted her belly.

This would be Tristan's bedroom. He would sleep there, in that bed.

He'd probably be naked.

He probably wouldn't be alone.

A shaft of something that was almost pain pierced her chest. Green: the color of envy.

"I need some air."

She dashed for the door on her right, which thankfully opened back onto the corridor. Tristan's boot heels clicked a rapid tattoo behind her as she hurried down the stairs.

"Carys, wait!"

An open door led to the back of the house. She stepped through it and took the few precious moments before Tristan arrived to gather her wits. By the time he joined her at the edge of the terrace she'd regained her composure.

"Are you all right?"

She sent him a breezy smile and ignored the reckless, angry ferment simmering inside her. "Oh, yes. I was just feeling a little wheezy, that's all. It must have been the sawdust." She feigned a delicate cough. "I'm fine now."

She'd rather be burned at the stake than admit that the unexpected sight of his bedroom had almost undone her. She really could have done without that knowledge. It was bad enough fantasizing about him in bed at night using only her imagination. Now she'd be able to picture the exact setting.

With somebody else in his arms.

Ugh.

Tristan, thankfully, seemed to take her assurance at face value. He turned back to the house and gazed up at it.

"So, what do you think, now you've seen the inside?"

I think you should repaper your master suite and never tell me the color.

No, she couldn't say that. Still, the thought of him making love to another woman in that bed made her want to punish him, just a little.

"Honestly? It's beautiful, but a little . . . cold." His brows lowered, but she forged on. "It needs life. Personality."

"I'll admit it's a bit empty right now," he said stiffly, "but it won't be when it's full of furniture. You're just unused to a building that doesn't incorporate seventeen different building styles in one wing."

His scathing description of Trellech Court almost made her laugh, but she wasn't ready to forgive him just yet.

He turned and gestured at the half-finished gardens before them. Hundreds of shrubs and box trees, still in their pots, had been placed on the grass in an intricate pattern of scrolls and lines in the style of a formal French parterre.

"I'm still planning the gardens. Those will be formal beds, and beyond that there will be a maze, and an avenue of oak trees. I have hundreds of acorns—the Italians used them to pack around the paintings and sculptures for transportation. Might as well use them." He gestured to his left, where mounds of fresh earth lay piled on either side of several deep trenches. "And those are the foundations for the orangery."

Carys suppressed another pang of envy; she'd always wanted an orangery. And oaks were some of the slowest-growing of all trees; they would take years to come to maturity. Tristan was designing his future here, investing in the long term. What would it be like to look out over this same view in ten or twenty years, to see his children playing beneath the shade of those oak trees?

She'd never know.

She shook her head to dispel the depressing thought. "It's too ordered. Where's the spontaneity?"

He planted his fists on his hips and there was no mistaking the frown that darkened his features. She bit back a smile, delighted that she was needling him. He'd discomposed her by showing her his bedroom. It was only fair that she return the favor.

"I suppose you'd have it all gothic ruins and wild disorder," he said. "You'd prefer a tangle of brambles and wildflowers to a swathe of beautiful parkland."

"There's nothing wrong with parkland, I just think you need a bit of disorder to counter all these classical straight lines. It's too perfect. Too symmetrical."

"No, I don't."

"Yes, you do. Otherwise it'll be dull and formulaic."

"Dull?!"

She'd definitely hit a nerve. He glared at her. "It is restrained. Elegant. The very antithesis of all that rococo lunacy with its curlicues and trills and arabesques."

She sent him a serene smile, just to raise his blood pressure.

"I quite like the frivolity of rococo design. It has flair. Drama. It's like the peacock of the architectural world."

He snorted, but she was determined to make him concede. "Nature never uses such strict patterns. The countryside is full of beautiful wild places, and none of them conform to any particular order."

He scowled, and she pressed her point.

"You need a balance between the formal and the informal. There's beauty in both, but what makes it work is the contrast. The ordered parts set off the wild parts. They bring out the best in each other. They need each other to shine."

Carys paused, struck by the fact that she could be talking about the two of *them*, rather than about the gardens. She turned and gazed out over the hillside.

Tristan gazed at Carys's profile and wished, for perhaps the hundredth time, that he could read her thoughts.

It was only as they'd toured the house that he'd realized how impatient he was to hear her opinion of everything, how desperate he was for her to approve. His heart had been in his throat as she'd gazed around each of the rooms, and he'd found himself analyzing her every expression, searching for a frown of distaste or a glimmer of delight.

As he'd watched her take in the green walls of the mistress's suite an idea so shocking came to him that he felt as though he'd been punched in the chest.

He'd never envisaged Lavinia Purser here with him.

But he'd imagined Carys a thousand times, in every single room.

Each time he'd made a decision, some distant part of his brain had wondered: Would Carys like this? He'd chosen

green for those walls because the color was the most bea.
tiful against her red hair. Because he'd once teased her so
much when they were younger, taunting her that her bedroom was probably "a disgusting, girly shade of pink," that
she'd been goaded into telling him the real color.

And ever since he'd been old enough to fantasize about
making love to her, he'd had the clearest image of all that
glorious, fiery hair of hers spread out around her head
against a blanket of that celadon green. Every time she wore
a dress that color it drove him mad. She'd worn one to his
sister's wedding, and he'd spent the entire service thinking
about dragging her into the vestry and kissing her senseless.

A hot flush warmed his body as he forced himself to
face an uncomfortable possibility. Had he secretly—almost
unconsciously—built this house for her? For *them*?

Ridiculous.

Chapter 24

Carys turned back to Tristan and found him gazing out over the gardens with a strange, almost angry look on his face.

"We should get back to the picnic."

"Yes. Of course."

He ushered her back through the house and she sent a wistful glance over her shoulder as they mounted up and rode away. Tristan seemed disinclined to talk, so she rode quietly beside him, not commenting when he took a different route back. They joined up with the main road leading to Trellech village, and were soon greeted by the rhythmic sound of hammering coming from up ahead. A little farther on they discovered a field full of tents and wagons.

"What's going on here?"

A dozen workers were scurrying about, driving iron stakes into the ground and forking hay from wagons. A small crowd of local children had gathered by the low wall to gawp.

Carys squinted at the name painted on the side of one of the wagons. "Isn't that the menagerie we saw at Hampstead Fair a few weeks ago?"

As if to confirm her suspicion, a familiar roar echoed from one of the cages, causing a girl in the small crowd to scream in fright.

"It is! That's the angry bear!"

Tristan reined in beside her and she tried to look unaffected as his knee brushed hers. Even that innocuous touch made her skin tingle.

"The owner did say he would be touring the country."

She pursed her lips, locating the bear in the same barred wagon he had been in before. "Look at him, the poor thing. Still chained in that tiny cage. Don't they ever let him out? I'm going to talk to the owner."

She started to nudge her horse forward, but Tristan reached over and caught her sleeve. "Wait. Look."

She followed the direction of his gaze. The circus owner she recognized from the fair was sitting on an upturned barrel not far from the bear's cage, talking to another man in a shapeless brown overcoat. At first she thought Tristan's disdainful expression was for the jacket's lack of style, but then she caught a glimpse of Christopher Howe's face beneath the wide-brimmed hat.

Her mouth dropped open. What was Howe doing here? He, too, must have slipped away from the picnic.

From the circus man's angry expression and Howe's agitated movements it looked as though the two of them were arguing.

Back at the fair she'd suspected the two men knew each other, but it seemed that whatever relationship they'd once had, had soured. The circus man was glaring at Christopher as if he'd like to feed him to the bear and Carys bit back a cynical smile. She certainly knew *that* feeling.

As they watched, Howe turned his back on the man and strode angrily away, tugging his hat down low over his forehead as if he didn't want to be recognized.

A bubble of elation rose in her chest. "He's up to something," she breathed. "Something underhand."

"Men like Howe are always up to something underhand!" Tristan growled. "As you well know."

Carys was almost breathless with excitement. "Yes, but don't you see? If I can find out what it is, then perhaps I can get him to stop blackmailing me. If he has a secret he doesn't want made public, then I'll be in the perfect position to counter his demands. It will be stalemate—mutually assured destruction if either of us talks."

Tristan rolled his eyes. "I expect you think you can just waltz up to that bear owner, distract him with that pretty face and those magnificent breasts of yours, and he'll be so besotted he'll tell you everything?"

"I don't see why not." She sent him a sideways smile. "You think my breasts are magnificent?"

Tristan scowled, and her heart skipped a beat.

"What I *think*," he growled, clearly uncomfortable at being caught out in giving her a compliment, "is that Howe is going to come this way. We need to hide." He turned his horse and urged it back into the cover of the trees.

Carys glanced over at Howe and came to the same conclusion; she followed Tristan into the woods. She expected him to stop as soon as they were out of sight of the road, but he pushed on, only halting when the sound of hammering had completely disappeared.

They were in a small clearing, a natural impression that made her think of Titania's bower in *A Midsummer Night's Dream*. Moss made a springy green carpet underfoot, muffling the sound of the horses' hooves, and waist-high ferns sprouted between the twisted, ancient trees. The scent of damp earth and fresh greenery filled her lungs.

Tristan dismounted.

"What are you doing?"

"We need to wait awhile, or we'll come up behind Howe in the road."

"Good point."

She slid from her own saddle and tied the reins to a tree branch, then turned to find Tristan watching her, caught in a shaft of sunlight that slanted from above. Her stomach did a little flip as she realized quite how secluded they were. Back at his house they'd been surrounded by workmen, liable to interruption at any time. Here they were unquestionably alone.

A flash of daring seized her. "How long do you think we should stay, to be safe?"

"Half an hour?"

Her pulse rate increased at the amused, speculative look in his eyes. Was he thinking the same thing she was? She lifted her brows. "What should we do to pass the time?"

He crossed the clearing and she backed up, into the shade, only stopping when her bottom bumped against a huge, mossy boulder. Her heart leapt into her throat as he moved closer, placing his palms either side of her head, bracketing her with his body, just as he'd done back at the opera.

"I have a few ideas. Shall I tell you what they are?"

She felt almost sick with excitement as his eyes met hers. The amusement faded from his face, replaced with a look she could only describe as *predatory*.

Her blood began to sing as she inhaled the blood-warmed, masculine scent of him overlaid with the clean, earthy smell of the woods.

"I'd much rather you showed me," she whispered.

He leaned in until his chest pressed against hers. She reveled in his size, his masculine dominance—safe in the knowledge that the slightest word from her would have him retreat.

She didn't want him to retreat.

"I hope you're realizing by now that the man pushing his cock into the woman is only one small part of making love."

Her breath caught at the unexpected delight of hearing him use such coarse language. She wanted to hear him say every other filthy word in that cool, calm voice of his.

"What else do people do?"

His lips twitched. "Oh. All manner of wicked things."

"Show me."

He nodded, and she braced herself for his kiss, but instead he placed his hands on her waist, and lowered himself to kneel in front of her. Surprised, she put her hands on his shoulders and the vision of him at her feet was so extraordinary, so unexpected, that she tried to burn it into her memory so she'd have it for all time.

She gasped as he moved his hands around to squeeze her bottom, then slid them lower, down the backs of her thighs. "You're going to ruin your breeches," she protested weakly.

"I don't give a damn about my breeches. Lean back."

The soft command almost made her knees buckle.

Tristan, not caring about his clothes? The world was coming to an end.

She pressed herself back against the sun-warmed rock. His fingers encircled her ankles and she suppressed a shiver at the faint suggestion of restraint; then he ran them back up her legs—beneath her skirts. She wasn't wearing drawers. The heat of his hands bled through her silk stockings and she bit back a nervous laugh as his palms tickled the sensitive spot behind her knees.

"What are you doing?"

"I'm going to kiss you between your legs."

"What? Why?"

"Because it feels nice. And because I want to taste you."

Her stomach clenched, and the place he'd just mentioned seemed to pulse and throb. "Oh," she managed weakly.

He withdrew his hands and she bit back a groan of disappointment, but he merely caught the hem of her skirts and pushed the fabric up, gathering it at her waist in soft, looping billows.

"Hold this."

She complied without question. Then his hands were sliding up the front of her thighs and she pressed her legs together in embarrassment. This was so much more intimate than kissing, but everything inside her felt tangled and tight, like a ball of twine.

"No. Widen your stance, Carys."

She was sure her cheeks were burning, but she did as he commanded, then shivered as the cool air teased the bare skin above her silk stockings.

Surely this was a terrible sin, to be doing something so wicked in the full light of day? But if it was, then she was wicked too, because she was almost shaking with anticipation.

She clutched the gathered fabric against her thighs. She'd seen herself naked in the mirror enough times to know what he'd see if she moved it upward: acres of pale skin and a fiery red triangle of curls that matched the hair on her head.

Would he hate the way she looked? He'd probably been with many more beautiful—

His hands slipped beneath the silk and she jerked as his thumbs traced the ticklish crease at the top of her thighs. He leaned forward, and his breath warmed her skin a second before he pressed a kiss to the inside of her thigh.

A yearning ache settled in her belly.

His lips teased a path upward, and she grabbed his head with her free hand, tightening her fingers in his hair.

Oh!

His kisses got closer and closer to the hot, aching center of her, and then his fingers were there; parting the flesh, sliding easily in the slick dampness.

"Tristan!" She bucked against him in mortification.

A pair of birds flew, startled and cawing, into the air above them, but all she could think about was the way his clever fingers rubbed against her, back and forth, circling the tiny nub of sensitive nerves.

Her vision blurred. *Where had he learned such things? She'd lived inside this same body her whole life and never known it could produce such incredible sensations.*

A part of her rebelled against ceding her will; it was dangerous, imprudent, to surrender so much control. She tried to press her knees together, but he was there, between her legs, broad-shouldered and utterly focused on his task. His mouth joined his fingers, and all the strength left her limbs. He kissed her, softly at first, then with greater urgency, and she almost dissolved as his tongue flicked out and stroked her.

Dear God! Heat and heavy pleasure swamped her, such delicious torment she didn't know whether to die of shame or delight. She wanted to twist away and drag him closer at the same time.

A groan shuddered out of him, vibrating against her skin, and his hand tightened on her hip. "Carys, God. You taste . . . so good."

She couldn't answer. All she could do was pant as he renewed his attentions, his tongue and fingers working in some kind of magical harmony that must have been learned from the devil himself.

Just when she thought she could take no more of the exquisite torture his finger dipped *inside* her, pressing into the same place Howe had been that night. She tensed in sudden memory, anticipating pain, but there was nothing but glorious friction and sweet, sliding bliss.

Her head dropped back and she stared sightlessly at the leafy canopy above. Tristan's fingers moved, in and out, round and round, in wicked counterpoint to his tongue, and the coiling, tangled sensation in her belly began to build. Everything inside her grew hot and tight.

"Don't stop!" she begged, beyond shame, beyond anything but reaching the top of this astonishing ladder of pleasure.

His fingers increased their pace, gorgeous deep stabs that made her body clench around him. She fisted his hair, silently begging him to end the torment—and then pleasure flooded her; great rhythmic waves of delight that made everything flutter and throb. She sagged back, utterly bone-less against the rock.

"Oh, my God," she panted. "Tristan!"

Her entire being was suffused with a soul-deep, delicious satisfaction. Her limbs felt heavy and weak, as if she'd swum too long in the river.

Tristan withdrew his hand, and a little of her lethargy left her. She was still clutching his hair in a white-knuckled grip. She forced her fingers to release him, and unclenched her skirts at the same time; they fell back decorously around her ankles.

Tristan sat back on his heels and used his pristine shirt cuff to wipe his glistening mouth. His hair was a mess, his eyes almost completely black as he gazed up at her.

He hadn't even kissed her on the mouth. They hadn't even taken off any clothes.

His lips curved in a satisfied smile as he registered her dazed expression, and when he stood she caught the musky scent of her own arousal mixed with his cologne. Her belly fluttered again.

Her throat seemed inordinately dry; it took three attempts to get a word out.

"Well, that *certainly* never happened with Howe," she managed.

"It's called a climax. The French call it *la petite mort*—the little death. You're welcome."

Her heart was still thundering in her ears. "Is it . . . the same for a man?"

"Not being female, I couldn't possibly answer that question definitively," he said drily. "But if you mean 'Does a man experience a blinding surge of pleasure that makes him think he's hit his head on the ceiling of heaven?' then yes, I expect it's quite similar."

She bit back a shattered laugh. His face held that confident, *now admit I'm right* look she'd seen a hundred times before.

Oh, God. He was going to be insufferable now.

A belated pang of guilt seized her. "Oh, but *you* didn't . . . have any pleasure." She dropped her chin and stared at her feet. "I'm sorry."

His fingers tilted her chin back up and he gazed so deeply into her eyes she felt as if she were drowning. "That's not true. Doing that, with you, gave me a great deal of pleasure."

She flicked a glance back down at the irrefutable evidence in his breeches. "But you're still—"

He shook his head. "Remember what I said about dinner courses? It's good to come to the table hungry. Sometimes the anticipation is almost as good as the food itself."

"But . . . I want to please you. It's only fair."

He flicked her cheek with his finger. "You *will* return the favor, I promise. I'll show you how. But not today. We have to get back. Just give me a minute."

Tristan forced himself to retreat across the clearing, but the wanton image of Carys—eyes wide, cheeks flushed a delicious pink—was burned into his brain. He clenched his fists and strove for mastery over his own body.

Christ. He was on a knife edge, so close to losing his fabled control. Desire beat a pounding, insistent rhythm in his blood, a fierce mixture of lust and near violence, almost the same feeling he'd had after a battle. The heady scent of her was lodged in his throat: perfumed skin and slick desire. He could still taste her, sweet and tart, a delicious feminine tang on his tongue.

Breathe.

It would be so easy to turn back around, to lift her skirts and free himself from his falls. To take her, right there, standing up, hard and fast against the rocks, like wild animals. Or to lie her down on the mossy green carpet and strip her naked in the sunlight.

He could see it so clearly: all that glorious pale skin and flaming hair. He'd slide into her soft, sweet body and show her exactly what it felt like to come with a man inside her. He'd thrust and thrust until climax claimed them both. God, he craved her, like an addict in an opium den craved his next pipe.

He hadn't been lying when he'd told her it had been pleasurable for him too. He'd been almost delirious with gratitude that she'd entrusted him with her reeducation. He'd knelt between her legs like a supplicant. Worshiped her, with lips and hands and tongue, determined to show her the extraordinary world of pleasure that was open to her. Pleasure she'd been denied by that selfish bastard Howe. Pleasure she'd be denying herself if she married Ellington.

Tristan ground his teeth. The thought of Carys with either man still made his blood seethe. Carys deserved someone who would love her body *and* cherish her soul, and neither Ellington nor Howe was capable of that.

A wave of primal, savage satisfaction welled up in his chest. He might not have been the first man in her life, but he was the first to give her pleasure. That in itself felt like a crowning achievement.

Chapter 25

Carys declined to accompany the rest of the guests to the circus at Trellech the next morning, under the pretext that she'd already seen it at Hampstead.

While she was desperate to find out the owner's connection to Howe and repeat her offer to buy the poor abused bear from the man, it was unlikely she'd get a chance to speak with him privately, and she didn't want to arouse Christopher's suspicions. She would sneak away some other time to do some digging.

A steady stream of guests had been arriving from London all morning, invited for the final event of the house party tomorrow evening: Maddie's grand costume ball. Neither Frances nor James had been able to attend—James had been called to an ailing relative's estate in Cornwall and Frances was attending a christening with her family—but Carys had been delighted to see Lord Ellington among the

new arrivals. She was, however, glad to escape to the menagerie again. The unconditional affection of the animals
was always a welcome balm, especially when her body and
mind were in such turmoil. Flashes of what she'd done with
Tristan yesterday had given her a restless night.

She released Huginn and Muninn from their enclosure
and watched as they flapped off into the sky, cawing mer-
rily. No doubt they would have a wonderful time stealing
from the guests; they were as bad as magpies, delighting in
filching small, shiny objects. They regularly appeared with
such gifts for her: shoe buckles and hatpins and coins. She
cherished every one.

Buttercup's enclosure was one of the farthest from the
house. Since the bear spent most of his time up in the trees,
she put down the basket of scraps she'd collected from the
kitchens and picked up the battered tin music box kept by
the entrance to his cage. A jolly, tinkling sound floated from
the cheap instrument when she cranked the handle, and she
started to sing the words that accompanied the lilting melody.

"Bobby Shafto's gone to sea,
Silver buckles at his knee;
He'll come back and marry me,
Bonny Bobby Shafto!
Bobby Shafto's bright and fair,
Combing down his yellow hair;
He's my love for evermore,
Bonny Bobby Shafto!"

She trailed off into silence. She'd been as naively optimistic
as the girl in the song, once. She'd thought Christopher would

marry *her*, but now she could only be grateful he hadn't. Her life would have been ruined in an entirely different way.

I will make you two promises, neither of which is empty. One: I promise to give you pleasure, to the very best of my ability. And two: If you're dissatisfied with my performance, at any time, you can tell me to stop and I will.

Tristan's low words came back to her in memory and she tried to shake off the strange melancholy they provoked. She'd agreed to their scandalous bargain with her eyes wide open, and Tristan had done exactly what he'd promised, so why was she fighting a niggling disappointment, besieged by a gloomy sense that everything was coming to an end, just as she'd discovered a whole new world of possibilities?

Tristan had done her an enormous service. He'd shown her passion, true physical pleasure. She might have gone her whole life without ever experiencing something so sublime. How tragic would that have been?

And yet perhaps she'd have been better off *not* knowing what she was missing. What could she do with this incredible newfound knowledge except yearn for more?

Even if she discarded the possibility of marriage to Ellington and vowed to remain a spinster forever, it would be too risky for her to take a lover when she got back to London. She was bound to be caught, however careful she tried to be. The *ton* had a thousand eyes and an unerring nose for scandal. She'd be ruined in truth, and she would drag her family down with her.

She could stay here in Wales, she supposed. Take some strapping local lad as a lover and hide herself away, far from the gossips. She'd become an eccentric recluse, a cautionary tale for the debutantes.

There were several problems with that plan, of course, not least of which was the depressing fact that she didn't actually *want* any of the strapping local lads. The only man who made her burn that way was Tristan.

Second, she loved London. The fashion, the variety, the entertainment. To be banished from there forever would be unbearable. The city and the country fed two different parts of her soul; she liked the peace and the wildness of Wales just as much as she needed the sophisticated bustle of town. She needed a balance of the two—just like Tristan's blasted gardens.

As if the thought had summoned him, her skin prickled with awareness, and she turned to find him striding toward her along the shady avenue of trees.

Her breath caught in her throat and she watched him greedily, relishing the width of his shoulders, the muscular flex of his thighs above his leather riding boots. He was strong and lean and so handsome it was almost irritating. Why did he always have to look so perfect? It wasn't fair.

"I hoped I'd find you here."

The simple greeting was enough to make her pulse beat heavy in her throat, even though there was nothing remotely suggestive in his expression. Her body seemed impervious to pleasantries, however. It knew what wonderful things he could do, and it wanted them again.

A liquid heat, a thrum of anticipation, clenched her innards. Carys frowned. The damned man had bewitched her. Ensnared her. Made her a prisoner of her own desire.

In a flash, she truly understood the phrase *be careful what you wish for.* She'd wished to see the heat that Tristan hid beneath his cool exterior, and he'd given her a glimpse.

But if she was this addicted to him after the limited exposure she'd already had, what would she be like if they went
even further? If she actually took him inside her body?

She'd be lost.

The wisest course of action would be to stop now. To
thank him for his efforts and release him from their bargain.
He'd kept his word; he'd shown her pleasure, and surely the
climax she'd already experienced was the pinnacle of feeling? It couldn't be all that different with another part of his
anatomy, could it?

It was no good. She had to know. To find out what it was
to burn. Even if she was consumed.

She sent Tristan a wide, welcoming smile. "You've found
me."

Buttercup chose that moment to amble out of the undergrowth and provided a welcome distraction. He lumbered up
to the gate and she thrust her hand through the bars to give
him a welcome scratch behind the ears. The bear grunted in
appreciation.

"So this is the famous Buttercup?" Tristan's spicy cologne
teased her nose as he came to stand beside her.

"Yes."

He gave the music box in her hand a questioning glance.

"Oh, this is the music box his original owner used to play
to make him perform. I took it when I rescued him."

"You still make him dance?"

"Of course not. I wanted him to go back to being as wild
an animal as possible, not think he had to dance every time
he heard music playing." Carys ruffled the bear's furry muz-
zle as he pushed it into her hand, eager for attention.

"I realized I could change his bad memory into a good

one. At first I'm sure the music was an unwelcome reminder of how cruelly he was treated, but I played it to him every day, and each time I rewarded him with honeycomb. Now he only needs to hear the music, or me singing the tune, to come to the gate. I think he finds it soothing."

She reached into her basket and unwrapped a small chunk of honeycomb. Buttercup reared up in excitement, his black nose twitching, and swiped at it through the bars. When down on all fours he was only three feet high at the shoulder, but up on his hind legs he was as tall as Carys. Tristan took a wary step back.

Carys, however, laughed at the bear's eagerness. "Greedy!" she admonished fondly. She handed him the treat, taking care not to be scratched by his sharp claws or eager teeth.

"What kind of bear is he?"

"Do you see the white patches of fur around his eyes that look like eyeglasses? They give this kind of bear its name; he's a spectacled bear. He's come all the way from South America, haven't you, Buttercup?"

Buttercup was too busy devouring the honeycomb to answer.

"Each bear's markings are different, so they're instantly distinguishable."

The honeycomb had disappeared and Buttercup was snuffling around for more, so Carys handed him an apple.

"Does he not eat meat?"

"Not much. I did some research into his diet when we first got him. Spectacled bears are foragers, and he mainly likes fruit and vegetables. He especially loves strawberries and carrots."

Carys emptied the remainder of her basket of produce into Buttercup's cage and the beast gave a delighted whuffle.

"How long will he live?"

"I'm not sure. Bears like him haven't been studied much. I've had him for ten years already, but he could live for another ten, or more. It's definitely a long-term commitment. Like those oak trees you're planting in your garden."

She waved a hand to indicate the animal's roomy enclosure. "This is what I want for that bear at the circus. No chains. Lots of space to move around." She gave a wry shrug. "And yes, before you say anything, I *am* aware of the argument against menageries like this one. Though these cages are larger and more luxurious than the ones at the circus, they're still cages. And as someone who values her own freedom a great deal, I admit to being torn. I recognize the hypocrisy of keeping any animal contained."

Tristan looked like he was about to say something, but she pressed on, keen to make him understand. "I trust Buttercup to get this close to him because I got him when he was still a cub. He, in turn, knows I won't hurt him, but it's taken years to build that trust—and even then I still can't forget that he's a wild animal. He'll follow some commands, but he's only minimally trained. He has a will of his own."

As if to prove her point, Buttercup flopped to the ground and rolled over onto his back, paws in the air, so she could scratch his belly. Carys obliged.

"I would love to be able to release him back into the wild," she continued, "but for animals like him, it's just not possible. He's so used to human contact that he couldn't possibly survive on his own. I've spoiled him."

She sighed. "So the question becomes, is it better to set him free but risk him dying sooner, or give him a long and hopefully happy life here?"

She glanced over at Tristan and found him watching her. Her cheeks warmed at his scrutiny. "I don't know the answer. Maybe I should find him a female to mate with. But then that would be yet another animal in captivity, would it not?"

"You haven't 'spoiled' him," Tristan said gruffly. "His captivity isn't your fault. The blame lies with the men who captured him, brought him here, and sold him. You're just trying to make the best of a bad situation."

She bit her lip. That was true of both Buttercup's situation and her own. And now that she thought of it, what Tristan was doing for her was very much like what she was trying to do for the bear; both of them had taken a negative experience and turned it into something positive.

Ugh. Why did he have to be so understanding? It made him far too easy to love.

She caught in a breath. *No, not love.* To *admire.* Yes, that was it.

Most men saw things in terms of black and white, right and wrong. Tristan was intelligent enough to see that life really consisted of varying shades of gray. There was no perfect answer or solution. All one could do was try to stay closer to goodness rather than wickedness.

She glanced sideways at him and her pulse gave a funny little thump. She wasn't entirely sure she was succeeding at being good. Tristan made wickedness look terribly appealing.

"You are kind, Carys. And brave."

A blush warmed her cheeks. How often had a man

praised her for anything other than her looks, or her wit? Uncomfortable with the compliment, she tried to wave it away. "Oh, pish."

"And not just with your animals. I heard you took a caning for Frances, when you were still at school."

"Where did you hear that?"

"Frances told James, and he told me."

"You shouldn't believe everything you hear."

"Is it true?

"Well, yes," she admitted reluctantly.

"Why did you do it?"

"Because I was tougher than Frances. I had three rough-and-tumble brothers, and I'd fallen out of trees and been shied off my horse hundreds of times."

"Who hit you?"

"The schoolmistress, Miss Wickerstone. She was a humorless old bat."

"Where did she hit you?"

"Three strokes on my palms. And three on my bottom."

Tristan's gaze swept down to the rounded curves in question and her stomach gave another little flip. "Frances was always so skinny," she said breathlessly. "You could see her hip bones and her ribs. My bottom was always more . . . padded."

His lips twitched in appreciation, but his eyes were serious. "I wish I could have been there to take them for you."

He reached down and caught her hand, uncurling her fingers one by one, then pressed a kiss to the center of her palm, where the cane had landed all those years ago. Her heart stuttered.

He gave her hand a slight tug and she stepped forward until they stood toe-to-toe.

"And if I couldn't have taken them on your behalf," he murmured, "then I wish I could have been there to soothe the sting." His left hand slid to her hip, then lower, to cup her bottom. A wicked flare of heat flashed in his eyes. "I would have kissed it better."

Her lips formed a perfect *O* of surprise.

"We need to meet for your next lesson."

"It can't be here," she croaked. "There are guests everywhere. We'd be caught. No matter how discreet you try to be, the staff always know who's sleeping with who, and they *will* gossip. The news of a Davies and a Montgomery together would be too delicious to keep quiet. It would be all over the village by morning, and in the scandal sheets in London by teatime."

"Then meet me at my new house. We won't be disturbed."

Carys's blood pounded in her ears. If she was going to tell him she'd changed her mind, now was the time. "Yes," she heard herself say. "What time?"

"Eleven tonight. Can you get away?"

She nodded, almost dizzy at the sensation of being held in his close embrace. She lifted her face to his, shamelessly angling for a kiss.

His arm tightened around her waist and he caught her lips in a swift, hard kiss. She melted into him eagerly, but he pulled back with a sharp exhale.

"No. We're not starting something we can't finish!" he growled, and the savage yearning in his voice was enough to make her knees go weak.

He stepped back. "I'll see you tonight."

Chapter 26

Carys had never taken such pains to dress for an occasion, and her outfit was possibly the most scandalous she'd ever worn. Even the unflappable Madame de Tourville had raised one thinly plucked eyebrow when she'd ordered it. The costume had been meant for tomorrow night's fancy dress ball, but it would be just as perfect for tonight.

For the second seduction of her life.

Actually, it would probably be more accurate to call it the *first* seduction of her life. Whatever Tristan was going to do, it would be a thousand times better than Christopher's pathetic attempt.

Carys glanced at her own reflection with an impish smile. Her legs were enclosed in tight masculine breeches, and the smooth, soft buckskin did little to hide the feminine curves of her hips and waist. The cut of the jacket accommodated her chest, like a riding jacket, and a pristine white shirt and frothy cravat peeked from between the lapels like those of the most fastidious dandy. Even her leather riding boots had been made to her precise measurements by Hoby, ordered under the fictitious name of Signor Palladio.

She wouldn't have dared to wear the ensemble in London, not even if she'd been masked, for fear of being accosted, but here in Wales, at a private house party, it would be just about acceptable. Especially for one as scandalously eccentric as herself.

She had no doubt that Gryff, Morgan, and Rhys would find it highly amusing. She'd often worn their castoffs to ride or muck out the animals when they were younger. Of course, she'd had smaller breasts and less shapely calves back then.

Her eyes twinkled with devilry as she twisted her hair up and tucked it beneath a black top hat. She looked like a beautifully turned-out—albeit short—gentleman of the *ton*.

Her undergarments, in contrast, were deliciously feminine. Madame de Tourville had hinted that such gorgeous underthings were only suitable for an opera singer, or an elopement, but Carys had fallen in love with the pale-peach silk and lace. The blush tone was only a few shades darker than her own skin and it dripped over her body like poured cream.

She'd chosen the outfit to be memorable, to stand out from the crowd. She wanted to be like one of Shakespeare's intrepid heroines, the ones who disguised themselves as men in order to speak and move more freely. Rosalind in *As You*

Like It, or Viola in *Twelfth Night*. She'd dress as she wished to be: as confident and as liberated as a man.

Now she was even more glad of her choice. She wanted to be different from every woman Tristan had ever made love to before. He might have divested his lovers of a hundred skirts and petticoats, a thousand ribbons and stays, but she'd bet he'd never disrobed a woman dressed like *this*.

It might not be the first time for either of them, but it could still be a night to remember.

The house was nowhere near quiet as she slipped out of her room, but she had intimate knowledge of Trellech's secrets. The numerous additions and improvements to the building had produced a bewildering warren of hidden passages, priest holes, and hiding places. She and her brothers had spent hours playing in them when they were younger. Now she stepped through a bookcase in one of the upstairs bedrooms and emerged beside the stable block.

She was just saddling Medusa, her favorite mare, when Nanny Maude shuffled from the shadows, her diminutive form swathed in her customary Welsh shawl to ward off the chill.

Carys bit back a silent curse. Her old nursemaid had the unerring ability to know when one of her charges was up to mischief. The talent hadn't dissipated, even after twenty years.

"And where do you think you're off to, Carys Davies?"

"I have an assignation."

Nanny Maude's brows rose as she took in the masculine clothes. "Dressed like that? I hope you're not planning to join a game of faro down at the Red Lion in Trellech. You'll be fleeced. Again."

"I'm not, I swear. But there's something I have to do. To . . . gather information."

That much was true. She could just as easily be going to talk to the circus owner to dig up some dirt on Howe. She sent Nanny Maude a pleading glance. "Please don't tell the boys."

Nanny Maude's wrinkled face creased into a grin. "Ach. Well, I'd be lying if I said you were the first Davies I've ever caught sneaking about the place. I've lost count of the number of times I've heard those brothers of yours, six sheets to the wind, trying to climb in through that library window, thinking they were being quiet and making a racket fit to wake the dead!"

She shook her head with a fond chuckle. "I think it would be rather hypocritical to stop you. You're dressed as a man, so I'll treat you as one. Just take care, my love."

Carys gave the old woman an impulsive kiss and a hug. "Thank you, Nanny Maude."

Her fond squeeze was returned. "Now I know Morgan taught you an impressive right hook, but have you got a knife? Just in case?"

Carys patted her boot. "Just as you taught me."

Nanny Maude had been most disapproving of Carys's formal education at Miss Wickerstone's academy. The old Welshwoman was of a far more practical and pragmatic disposition. She firmly believed that a woman needed to know how to look out for herself.

"Good girl. Make sure you're back before you're missed." Her black eyes twinkled with a knowing mischief that made Carys wonder if she didn't suspect her mission was of the more passionate kind. "And remember: If you can't be good, be *careful*."

Carys's heart was pounding with a mixture of terror and anticipation as she secured Medusa in the newly constructed stables behind Tristan's house. The feeling that she was trespassing, doing something naughty and forbidden, sent a frisson down her spine.

The house was dark, but the back door from the terrace was unlocked, so she slipped silently into the vast white hallway. The huge chandelier tinkled in the disturbance of air, sending a shower of refracted moonbeams onto the floor beneath her feet.

Her boots made a series of staccato clicks on the stairs; there were no rugs or carpets to soften her tread.

Was Tristan even here?

Drawn by some invisible force, she pushed open the door to the master suite with hands that were not quite steady. Faint moonlight shone through the curtainless windows, outlining the bed in a silvery halo, and she swallowed back a nervous laugh.

The fact that the bed was the only piece of furniture in the room was certainly symbolic, a stark reminder of the reason she was here. There were no other pieces to detract the focus, nothing to lend the room a personal touch.

Because this *wasn't* personal. It was just a physical transaction, one body showing another body pleasure. No deeper emotions were supposed to be involved.

And yet something that felt very much like guilt nibbled at her, the sense that she was somehow being unfaithful.

Or forcing Tristan to be. This was the bed where he would eventually make love to his wife; he shouldn't be making love to *her* in it. It seemed disrespectful.

But a petty, vindictive part of her wanted to give Tristan this memory of her, here, in his arms, whenever he closed his eyes.

She wanted to bloody well haunt him.

The creak of a floorboard behind her was her only warning of danger. She started to turn, but an arm snaked around her waist and another clamped over her mouth. Her hat went flying as she was lifted bodily off the floor and crushed against a huge, rock-hard body. She let out a muffled scream against her assailant's palm.

"What the fuck do you think you're—*Carys?*"

Tristan's murderous growl softened in a heartbeat when he realized his mistake. His arms loosened and his hand dropped from her mouth as he spun her round to face him.

"Bloody hell, I thought you were a trespasser!" he scolded. "Why in God's name are you dressed like that?"

Carys let out a wheezing exhale and willed her racing heart to calm. "It's a disguise, you dolt. In case anyone saw me on the way here. It's my outfit for tomorrow night's costume ball."

His features relaxed. "I assumed you'd be wearing your handkerchief dress again."

"Me? Wear the same dress twice? I'd never live it down."

Tristan's grip on her upper arms tightened as he raked another—slower—glance down her body and his dark brows lifted in obvious appreciation. "I didn't think any outfit could be as provoking as your handkerchief, but you've proved me wrong."

Her blood warmed at the compliment, but she sent him a severe look from under her lashes. "You said I looked like a Venetian courtesan."

"You looked a hundred times better than a Venetian courtesan, and you know it. You looked like a Renaissance work of art."

"Don't you dare say I looked like a Michelangelo," she warned. "I've seen pictures of his women, and they all look like muscly men with breasts added on as an afterthought."

"Your breasts are definitely not an afterthought," he said, solemnly. "They're perfect."

"I believe you called them spectacular."

"Magnificent," he corrected. "I called them magnificent. But *spectacular* will do just as well."

His gaze slid to where they were constrained beneath her jacket and her nipples beaded against her silk chemise.

"I'm amazed you can even see me, with so little light," she said breathlessly.

The corner of his mouth twitched, and she inhaled the delicious scent of night and cedar from his clothing.

"I don't need light to see you. I know what you are: a beautiful, infuriating force of nature."

She opened her mouth to argue, but he pressed his fingers over her lips. "And for the rest of the night, you're mine."

Chapter 27

Tristan's possessive growl made her stomach twist with delicious anticipation. She could hardly believe this was real, that *Tristan Montgomery* was going to make love to her.

The practical, cynical side of her was convinced it would be a disaster. What if she found it as unpleasant as she had with Howe? What if there was something wrong with her? Tristan was bigger than Howe in every possible way. If Christopher had hurt her with his invasion, surely it would be even worse with someone of Tristan's size? It was foolish to hope it would be different.

And yet the part of her she'd thought long dead—the girl who still believed in fairy tales, despite all the proof she'd gathered against the likelihood of happy endings—that girl still craved Tristan's touch.

She braced herself and stared him straight in the eye. "All right. I'm ready. Let's do it."

His soft chuckle fanned the hairs at her temple. "Always so impatient," he chided. His hands slid to her shoulders and his thumbs traced a soothing pattern over her collarbones. "You're *not* ready. But you will be."

Carys swallowed. She'd never thought herself a coward, but the reality of what they were about to do was starting to sink in. "Should we . . . light a candle? A lamp?"

"No. This house is supposed to be uninhabited, remember? We don't want anyone coming to investigate." His lips brushed the outer corner of her eye and she felt him smile against her skin. "We'll be just like Cupid and Psyche. You can pretend I'm your faceless lover, come to seduce you in the dark."

Her heart clenched. The comparison was apt, but not in the way he meant. He was as perfect as any god, so beautifully constructed she wished she had the skill to paint him, whereas she was the foolish mortal, rife with imperfections. But unlike Psyche, she knew exactly who was making love to her. That was half the problem; she had no idea what their relationship was now. Were they friends? Enemies? Lovers? Was it possible to be all three at once?

Moonlight caught the slash of his cheekbone and the sinful curve of his eyelashes. Almost in a daze, she lifted her hand and threaded her fingers through his hair, amazed that after imagining it for so long, she finally had the right to touch him like this.

He dipped to nuzzle the sensitive skin beneath her ear, then angled his head, rubbing against her hand like a lion, silently demanding attention, and her blood heated at the thrilling scrape of his stubble against the tender skin of her jaw.

He made a sound of masculine contentment, a deep growl that rumbled from his chest, and she had the sudden thought that he was marking her with his scent, *claiming* her as his mate in the most primal, animalistic way. Goose bumps pebbled her skin and a wicked skein of longing coiled in her belly.

Her hair had partly fallen down when she'd lost her hat, and she stayed completely still as he removed the remaining hairpins with devastating casualness. The heavy waves fell down and he combed them with his fingers, smoothing teasing paths from her shoulders to the tips of her breasts.

She shivered.

He pushed the jacket from her shoulders, then slid his hands down her sleeves and gave the cuffs a practiced tug. She shrugged, and the jacket dropped to the floor with a soft thump. Having him act as her valet was astonishingly sensual.

"Raise your chin."

His face was a study in concentration, and she quaked a little at his intensity. It was rather intimidating, to be the focus of so much attention. Intimidating, but strangely addictive.

She did as he directed, and the backs of his knuckles brushed the underside of her chin as he deftly untied her cravat, unwound the long strip of fabric, and let it fall.

Her heart was pounding so hard she was sure he would hear it in the silence.

Her shirt was next, and she struggled to keep her breathing even as he tackled the buttons with deliciously slow purpose. Her desire increased with each additional inch. The cool cotton slid down her arms and joined the jacket in a puddle of moonlight at her feet, and he sucked in a breath as he took in the scandalous silk and lace chemise underneath.

She hadn't bothered with stays or a corset, and the peaks of her nipples were clearly visible, poking at the delicate fabric.

Why didn't he say something?

Did he really not want to remind her who was undressing her? Did he honestly think *that* was the illusion she craved? Carys bit back a despairing little laugh. Nothing could be further from the truth. Tristan Montgomery was the only man in the world she wanted. Had ever wanted, really.

She caught his wrist, her fingers barely meeting around its circumference, and he glanced up at her in question.

"I'm not . . . thin. Or willowy," she warned, suddenly desperate to temper his expectations. He was looking at her as if she, too, were a goddess, and while she might have pretended to be Diana for the ball, she knew she was far from perfect.

"No," he agreed huskily. "You're not thin. Or willowy. You're delicious. And I'm a starving man who wants to feast."

Oh, she was in so much trouble.

"Sit on the bed. We need to take off your boots."

Carys did as she was told, and watched in mute amazement as he knelt at her feet and pulled off her boots with one strong hand on her calf and another at her heel. She steadied herself with a hand on his shoulder, feeling the muscles shift beneath her palm, remembering in a fierce blush what he'd been doing the last time he'd been kneeling at her feet.

A throbbing ache pulsed in the tips of her breasts and at the juncture of her thighs, and she squeezed her knees together. Would she find the same pleasure tonight, in his arms?

He tossed her second boot aside and stood. From her seated position she'd never been more aware of his size, his strength. He was a powerful shadow in the still room, sleek and dangerous and beautiful, like the leopard at the Tower. Grace and menace, all for her.

He reached down and her stomach contracted as he unfastened the buttons of her falls.

"Lie back."

She did so, keeping her feet on the floor, staring up at him as he caught the waist of her breeches and eased them down. She lifted her hips to aid him, shivering as he drew them off, then divested her of her silk stockings too.

She was left in just the scandalous silk chemise; it skimmed her hips and finished just above her knees, shifting on her body like liquid pearl.

Tristan gazed down at her and she resisted the urge to sit up, to cover herself. His expression was shuttered, almost impossible to read, but she took heart from the way his gaze roved over her, flitting from place to place like an indecisive butterfly looking for a place to land.

As she'd done so many times before, she feigned a confidence she didn't feel and lifted her brows in challenge.

"Well, this isn't fair. I'm nearly naked, and you still have on all your clothes."

Her teasing comment seemed to snap him out of his trance.

"I can remedy that."

He toed off his boots and stripped off his jacket with the ease of long practice. His cravat dropped to the floor beside hers. He stepped to the edge of the bed, his knees brushing hers, and tugged the tails of his shirt from his breeches. His hungry gaze never left hers, and her heart beat loudly in her ears as she read the challenge, the promise, in his look.

He wasn't going to call a halt tonight.

She swallowed down a combination of excitement and terror. She felt naked, stripped bare already.

He extended his arms toward her, wrists upward, in a silent demand for her to unbutton his cuffs, and if she hadn't been so nervous she would have smiled at the imperiousness of the gesture, the unthinking expectation of compliance.

She was only too happy to assist. She'd imagined undressing him a thousand times.

The silk chemise slid with a wicked promise against her skin as she sat up, caught his wrist, and flicked open the small pearl studs. His skin was warm, and the intimacy of the service made her catch her breath. The sight of his exposed wrists did something strange to her insides. The blue veins and shifting ridges of sinew seemed both vital and yet oddly vulnerable, and she couldn't resist stroking the pad of her thumb over the pulse that beat, strong and steady, beneath the tawny skin.

He hissed out a breath, and she let her hand drop, flustered by the sudden urge to cradle his hand in her own and draw it to her lips for a kiss.

In a swift move he stepped back and removed his shirt in that way particular to men, the way her brothers did it; he reached up and caught the back of it, behind his neck, and drew it up and over his head.

Oh, goodness.

The white fabric slid down his arms and pooled at his wrists, and her mouth went dry as he tossed it aside. Moonlight traced the curves of his biceps and the bony ridges of his shoulders, and she wished for a lamp, a thousand lamps, to see the full glory of him.

Her hungry gaze moved down, to the hard planes of his chest and the triangle of his ribs that tapered into a trim waist and a flat stomach dusted with an intriguing line of hair.

God, he was beautiful. Tall and straight and insolent, like a sublime piece of architecture, perfectly designed and constructed.

Carys bit back a wild giggle. She wanted to scale him like a building, to find all his handholds, the jut of his hips, the ridges of his shoulders. Anywhere she could gain purchase to drag herself closer.

She wanted to touch him everywhere.

She lifted her eyes and met his gaze, then blushed at having been caught ogling.

She waited with bated breath for him to unfasten his breeches, but instead he bent and placed his fists on either side of her hips, caging her within his arms. The mattress dipped, rocking her off-balance, and she leaned back, suddenly nervous again.

He pressed forward, his warm exhale fanning over her cheek as his knee depressed the bed next to hers and he prowled up her body like some sleek jungle cat. She sank back to the mattress with a little gasp.

The scent of him—warm spice and male skin—engulfed her as he lowered himself until his chest was only inches from her own.

"I've imagined this," he whispered. "A thousand times."

Her eyes widened at his unexpected admission. The heat of his chest burned through the layer of silk and kindled an answering fire in her blood. Unable to bear the exquisite tension for a minute longer, she lifted her head and kissed him.

For a split second he tensed, as if surprised by her forwardness, and then his mouth opened on hers in a kiss that could only be described as *carnal*. He cupped the back of her head and pulled her to him, his tongue stroking hers with a fierce, almost desperate urgency.

He angled his head, pressing her more forcefully back onto the bed, and she closed her eyes, lost in wicked sensation.

Yes!

His lips were as exquisite as she remembered, teasing, coaxing, demanding a response.

She shouldn't want this. It was lunacy.

She wanted it with every beat of her heart.

He pulled back with a groan, breaking her grip on his hair.

"Don't stop!" she gasped.

He pushed back, and she sat up, panicked, thinking he was leaving her, but her protest died on her lips as he flicked open the buttons of his falls and stepped out of his breeches.

Carys forgot to breathe.

He stood, unashamed of his nakedness, giving her the chance to look her fill. Even partly hidden by shadow, she could see that his male part was like the rest of him: thick and strong. It jutted proudly from the dark nest of hair between his legs.

She huffed out a slow breath. She'd never seen a fully

aroused man before. He was magnificent; curves and muscles aligned in perfect symmetry.

"Show me how to give you pleasure," she breathed. "You said you would, back in the woods."

"Giving you pleasure gives me pleasure."

She shook her head. "That's not what I mean. I want to be an equal partner in this. An *active* partner. I don't want to just lie here while you do things to me—that's what I did with Howe. I want—I don't know what to do." Embarrassment warmed her cheeks at her confession, but she kept her steady gaze on his. "Show me, Tristan. Please."

Chapter 28

Show me, Tristan. Please.

Tristan bit back a groan and tried to ignore the pounding of his heart and the insistent throbbing of his cock. His name on her lips was torture. He wanted to hear it again.

Her shy demand had taken him by surprise. Up until now he'd managed—barely—to maintain some emotional distance by telling himself that he was doing her a favor. He was the one with the knowledge, the greater experience. She needed his help. It was a logical solution.

But she'd just cut straight to the heart of the matter; the reason he'd been comfortable going along with their agreement was because he'd been the one to set the pace, to parse out the information, to give or withhold the pleasure. If he showed her how to please *him*, they would be equals in truth.

Was he ready for that? The hold she had on him was strong enough already. She could twist him into knots with just a look, a word, a touch. Once she realized the full extent of her potential she would be unstoppable.

And he would be lost.

Tristan bit back a wry laugh. *God help him*, he was already lost. He'd always suspected this outrageous girl would be his downfall. He'd tried to avoid it—avoid her—for as long as he could, but now it seemed like fate had finally caught up with him.

Did she even realize the magnitude of what she was asking? He'd stupidly thought he could hold himself apart when he made love to her. That he'd be able to pretend she was just another willing body in his arms.

That she would touch his skin, but never his heart.

She'd seen right through him. And, God, he loved the way she challenged him. She was demanding equality. The least he could do was give it to her.

"All right," he heard himself say. "I'll show you. Come here."

He forced himself to remain motionless as she slid to the edge of the bed, that wicked silk negligee riding up the creamy perfection of her thighs. She stood and gazed at him uncertainly, her eyes huge and shadowed in the half-light.

"Closer," he rasped.

She stopped when they were toe-to-toe and a shudder of awareness ran through him.

"Touch me. Wherever you like."

She lifted her hand and flattened her palm directly over his pounding heart. He bit back a hiss of need. God, he'd miscalculated so badly. He was going to go up in flames.

He tried not to flinch as she explored him, petting him

as if he were one of her wild creatures. Over his shoulders, across his chest. His stomach muscles tensed in relay as she slid her palms down his ribs, then lower, stroking his waist and hips with an innocent fascination that increased his desire tenfold.

When he could stand it no longer he caught her wrist and drew her hand to his cock.

"Here." His voice was gravel in his throat. "Put your hand around me. Like this."

He folded his hand around hers, showing her how to hold him, and when she curled her fingers around his shaft he sucked in a low groan of pleasure.

"God, that feels so good."

Carys could barely see what she was doing, but oh, she could feel. The rough, springy hair, the velvety hardness of him.

It was a revelation. She'd never seen Howe's member, let alone touched it; it had all been a confused blur as he'd shoved up her skirts and pushed between her legs, rough and uncaring.

This, with Tristan, was different. It was give-and-take, a slow discovery, and her heart contracted for the care he was taking with her.

He lifted his hand from hers and cupped the back of her head, his long fingers stroking the fine hairs at her nape, and she continued exploring on her own, fascinated by the way his breathing deepened and hitched.

She brushed the smooth top of him with her thumb and discovered a slick bead of liquid. He threw back his head and muttered a curse up at the ceiling. A tremor went through his body and a thrill of delight warmed her. *Yes!* He'd made *her* wet, with his wicked ministrations. She was finally doing the same for him.

He bent and pressed a kiss to her neck, his lips warm on her skin, and she tightened her fist, eliciting another groan.

"God, Carys. What you do to me—"

His hand covered hers again as he caught her lips in a ravenous kiss. Stars sparkled behind her eyes, darkness and swooning pleasure. His tongue slid in and out of her mouth and he rocked his hips in tandem, sliding his length within their joined hands. He showed her the rhythm, how to stroke him, up and down, and Carys marveled at the unexpected combination of violence and tenderness.

He pulled her even closer, resting his forehead on her shoulder, and she reveled in the strength of him, his ragged breaths against her neck.

His movements became more rapid, his hand tightening around hers until it was almost painful, and then with one final stroke he let out a long, low groan of bliss. His body convulsed with a series of shuddering spasms and his length pulsed in her hand. A flood of warm wetness coated her fingers, her belly; she felt it through the thin silk of her chemise, and her lips broke into a triumphant smile.

She'd given him the male version of the pleasure she'd experienced back in the clearing!

It took him a few seconds to come to his senses, which Carys fully understood. *Her* brain had been like porridge afterward too.

When he finally released his grip on the back of her head she pulled back, smiling up at him as he opened his fist and freed her hand. Her hold on him had been so tight it was hard to uncurl her fingers; they seemed fused to his skin, but he finally stepped back and bent to retrieve his cravat from the floor. He used it to wipe the dampness from her, then tossed it aside.

He cleared his throat. "Well, that was . . . unexpected. I hadn't planned on that."

Carys suppressed another smile. She *loved* the fact that she'd derailed his plans and made him forget himself. It made this evening less a meticulously planned seduction and more of a joint voyage of discovery.

She sneaked a glance downward to get a better look at him in the moonlight, and was shocked to find his member still standing proud. Her elation vanished. Had she done something wrong? Had he *not* received pleasure, after all?

She swallowed. "Have I . . . ruined it?"

His brows drew together. "What are you talking about?"

She gestured between his legs. "Shouldn't it have gone down?"

His expression cleared, and his lips split into a smile of comprehension. "Oh, sweetheart. No. You haven't done anything wrong."

"Then why isn't it going back to normal?"

He stepped up close, and her stomach fluttered as he brushed her cheek. "The fact that it *hasn't* just proves how much I want you." His eyes crinkled and he gave a self-deprecating shrug. "And what we just did doesn't mean we're done for the night. Not by a long shot."

Carys tilted her head, still not entirely convinced he wasn't just trying to make her feel better. "Do you need time to recuperate?"

He sent a cheeky glance south and his arrogant smile made her catch her breath. "Apparently not."

He bent as if to kiss her again, but she pressed her hand to his solar plexus and summoned her courage to the fore. There was still one topic they had yet to discuss.

"Wait. I might not know much about this whole lovemaking business, but I *do* know the woman can get pregnant from doing it."

Embarrassment burned her cheeks, but she forged on. This topic was simply too important to ignore. She'd seen enough animal couplings to understand that not every act of procreation resulted in offspring, but it had surely been pure luck that she hadn't been made pregnant by Howe.

The horror of that possibility still made her shudder. She would *not* take that risk again.

"My brothers have clearly enjoyed the physical company of a number of women," she said briskly, "and since none of them have produced any unwanted offspring, I can only assume there's some way of avoiding that outcome."

"There are. Several ways, actually."

"What are they?"

She couldn't quite believe she was having such a mortifying discussion, but Tristan seemed reassuringly unaffected, as if this was a completely natural conversation.

Perhaps it was. Did a man discuss such things with his mistress before starting an affair? Had he had this same conversation with those Venetian courtesans he'd mentioned?

A wave of irrational jealousy swept through her.

"There are times in a woman's monthly cycle that make it less likely for her to conceive," he said quietly, and she experienced a rush of relief that he was answering her, instead of mocking her ignorance.

"But it's not the most reliable method. Another way is for the man to wear a sheath over his cock, to catch his seed. They're made from linen, or animal intestine."

Carys's grimace wasn't feigned. "*Intestine?* Truly? That's horrible. Isn't there a way that *doesn't* involve animal innards?"

"Yes. The man can withdraw from the woman before he spills inside her." He touched the damp patch on the front of her chemise with his thumb. "This liquid contains my seed. It could grow into a baby if it's inside you."

His words produced a strange flutter in her belly. Carys frowned. "So the woman has to trust the man to get out?"

"Yes." His eyes bored into hers. "It requires a great deal of trust, but I swear to you, Carys, I won't risk it."

Carys stared up into his handsome face. Tristan Montgomery was many things, but there was no doubting that he was a man of his word. She put her palm to his jaw, thrilling at the slight roughness of his evening beard against her palm. "I trust you. Now show me what I've been missing."

Chapter 29

Her words released the last of his restraint. Tristan caught her face between his palms and claimed her lips, and she went up on tiptoe to meet him with a joyous little laugh.

In a flurry of movement he caught the hem of her chemise and tugged it over her head, and the feel of her bare breasts against his naked chest made her suck in a wondrous breath. His hands were everywhere, skimming her body with a touch that brought goose bumps to her skin and a knot of desire to her belly.

He lowered her to the bed in a blur of motion and Carys braced herself for him to fall on top of her, but instead he rolled them both to their sides and wrenched his lips from hers.

"Slow!" he growled, almost to himself. "We are going to take this *slowly*."

It sounded as if the words were pushed through clenched teeth, and she bit back a smile of delight.

He propped himself up on his elbow and used his free hand to trace the top curves of her body, down her arm. It was so dark she could barely see his outline, just the swell of his shoulder and the ripple of biceps.

"Your body is beautiful, Carys," he whispered. "Like a church, a temple."

She stifled a shaky laugh. "Trust you to compare me to something architectural. I warn you, if you start talking about my flying buttresses, I'm leaving."

He chuckled. "I meant, it's a place I want to worship."

"Oh. Well, that's fine."

He traced his forefinger across her collarbone and back in a lazy movement. "I hope you're not suggesting that architecture is boring, Lady Carys?"

His mock severity made her blood sing with anticipation. She loved this teasing side of him.

"Allow me to teach you some architectural terms." His fingers plucked a lock of hair that had fallen over her shoulder. He flattened the curl against her skin, then released it to bounce back into shape. "This looping spiral, for example, we call a curlicue, or an arabesque."

"Hmm," Carys managed. Her body was liquid, melting heat.

"Lie back."

She complied, rolling to her back as he remained propped on his side like a Roman statesman at a feast.

She glanced down at her own body. Pale moonlight highlighted the highest parts, but much of it remained in shadow.

That helped her feel less exposed, despite her nakedness. She could imagine herself a wicked siren in the darkness. A woman who'd had countless lovers, instead of one single, painful disappointment.

Tristan's finger traced lower, drawing a delicate M shape over the top curves of her breasts, taking a teasing dip into the central valley.

"And here we have arches—very useful for bridges. Excellent shape for support."

Carys snorted a laugh. "Those need a *lot* of support."

"Your breasts?" He cupped one gently and her blood heated even more. "The architectural term for these is *domes*. I'm a great champion of domes. They're one of my favorite features." He bent and kissed one, and she sucked in a breath.

God, the man was a natural tease. He was talking about architecture, for heaven's sake! But with his wicked smile and his burning eyes, he could probably even make geometry arousing.

His fingers were still exploring. He moved them with mind-stealing slowness in ever-decreasing circles until he reached her nipple. It was already a taut peak—thanks to the combination of a cool room and hot desire—and she gasped as he caught it between thumb and forefinger and gave it a gentle tug. She felt a corresponding tug low in her belly.

"Now what do we call this? A cupola? That's a small, useless tower on the top of a building, in case you were wondering." He shook his head, apparently dissatisfied with the analogy. "No, this is more of a *finial*. A decorative embellishment."

Carys arched up with a moan of blind need as he took it into his mouth. He suckled her, hot and wet, swirling his tongue, drawing a deep pull of desire from her core. She fisted her hands on the mattress.

He kissed his way down her body and she tensed her stomach as he pressed a light kiss on her navel, then continued his leisurely investigation. She squirmed in delight, desperate for him to touch between her legs again.

"Stop wriggling," he chided with a laugh. "I need to take a full inventory."

He ran his hands with almost reverent care down her sides, shaping the dip of her waist and the slope of her hip. "You have an excellent assortment of curves, Lady Carys. And curves are some of the most desirable forms in all of architecture. Beautiful and strong."

He stroked her again, and she practically purred in pleasure.

"What we have here is an S shape, or ogee. A concave curve in the lower half, a convex curve in the upper."

Carys reached the end of her patience. "My turn."

She wrapped her fingers around his length. It leapt in her hand, fully stiff again, and she bit her lip in delight. "What's this in architectural terms? A pinnacle? A spire?"

"A column," he groaned. "A tower."

She chuckled, even as he rolled over her and pressed himself full-length to her body.

They both stilled. The contact was incredible, all that naked skin on top of her, the press of muscle and bone. He wasn't even giving her his full weight—his upper body was supported on his elbows—but she felt deliciously crushed. Not in the helpless, smothered way that Howe had made her feel, but in a sheltered, protected way. As if she was precious. Desired. As if his strength was hers.

"Enough playing," he growled, and she thrilled at the gravel in his voice. This wasn't the coolly controlled Tristan of the ballroom. This was Tristan stripped down to his bare essentials, a lusty man in his prime. A man pushed to the edge of his endurance.

She *loved* this Tristan. She'd been trying to meet him for years.

He kissed his way down her quivering belly and then held her hips still as he sank between her legs. Carys opened for him with a willing sigh. He teased her with his hands and his mouth, just as he'd done in the forest, but this time the beast took his time, drawing out the torture, building a slow, luxurious heat . . .

He pulled back.

Carys gaped down at him, ready to hit him in frustration.

"Not this time," he said on a laughing exhale. "It's finally time for dessert." His eyes caught hers and the laughter faded from his face. "Last chance, Carys. Do you want me inside you? Say yes. Or I'll stop."

Her throat was tight, but she managed to nod. "Yes. Yes, I want that."

Want you, she almost said, but bit her tongue.

Inside me. All around me.

He'd joked about Cupid and Psyche, but she would never pretend he was another man. It was Tristan she wanted. Only him.

He crawled up her body and planted his hands on either side of her, arms straight to relieve her of his full weight. She could feel him, hot and hard against the inside of her thigh, and she tensed instinctively at the almost-forgotten sensation. He moved his hips, nudging at the opening of her body, and she tried to relax, to welcome him.

He reached down, guiding the slick head of him against her. "Relax, Carys. Breathe."

He'd said that to her before, somewhere, but the memory fluttered away. She was too busy concentrating on the pressure between her legs: a deep, burning stretch as he pressed forward.

It wasn't the sensation she remembered. There was no pain, only a slow, delicious friction.

Tristan stilled, hovering above her, giving her time to adjust. She could feel the tremors in his arms as he battled not to move and her heart ached in gratitude for his restraint. In every other area of her life she might mock his control, but in this one instance it made him the perfect lover. He wasn't like Howe, to lose himself in a selfish frenzy.

Gradually her body yielded. He slid in even deeper, and they both sucked in a breath.

What an incredible sensation.

Carys lifted her arms and cupped his face, forcing him to look at her. "Tristan. It's good. I'm good." How ironic, that she was the one reassuring him.

"I'm inside you." He sounded fierce and almost incredulous. "God, you feel good."

"So do you." She sent him a tremulous smile.

He let out a groan of relief and rocked his hips, sliding out of her a fraction, then back in, and the corresponding ripple of pleasure had her arching her back in delight.

Now he could lose a little of that control. There was a time and a place for restraint, and it was over. She wanted him to shout her name and forget his own.

Almost as if he heard her thoughts, he increased his rhythm, pulling her closer as if he could fuse them together. She caught his hair, burrowing her fingers into it, pulling him down for a kiss, and lifted her hips, pressing and flexing against him as the promise of ecstasy shimmered through her blood. Her hands roamed the warm expanse of his back, his lean flanks. She stroked the mounds of his buttocks and when he groaned in encouragement she tightened her grip and drew him even deeper. The world narrowed to the two of them, male and female, in fierce, elemental simplicity.

The tension built inside her and she grasped for it, pulling it closer with every wicked slide of his body inside hers.

And then, with a gasp, she was flying; pleasure so sweet it was almost misery, joy so strong her heart ached. Spasms of pure pleasure beat against her like the rhythmic flap of wings.

Tristan was planted inside her, anchoring her to the bed, to the earth, and yet she was soaring in the heavens, breathless and weightless.

Roots and wings.

Such a beautiful paradox.

Even as she drifted back to earth, she was aware of Tristan still moving within her. Her body was convulsing, little aftershocks of pleasure, and he hissed out an impassioned curse as her climax pushed him even closer to his own.

With one last thrust he withdrew and pressed himself against her. His hands gripped her hips as he shuddered against her belly and she held him close as he buried his cry of completion against her neck.

A fierce joy bubbled up inside her. *This is what it felt like to be a properly pleasured woman.* Not some empty vessel, used and discarded for a man's pleasure.

Would she have bruises on her skin tomorrow? She almost hoped she did. They would be proof of the heaven they'd just shared.

Tristan's heart was thundering against her chest, a pounding gallop that matched her own, and she cherished the rapidly cooling sheen of sweat on his skin, the hot rasp of his breath against her shoulder.

She would never accuse him of being cold and passionless again.

He loosened his grip in slow increments. His body relaxed, and she bit back a smile at his uncharacteristic vulnerability. She could probably stab him in the back and he wouldn't notice.

Considering their long and acrimonious family history, some long-dead Davies femme fatale had doubtless done exactly that to a Montgomery male at some point.

Then again, if Tristan's kinsman had possessed half as much skill in bed as his descendant, maybe *her* ancestor would have been the one to meet her maker. Carys herself was so boneless, she wouldn't bother to struggle if Tristan chose to smother her with his body.

There were worse ways to go. She'd die in a state of bliss.

Tristan finally rolled off her, but he didn't move away. He gathered her in his arms and pulled her close, her back to his chest, and released a deep sigh.

"If that wasn't better than your first time," he rasped, a weary laugh in his voice, "then I'll give up sex forever."

"So modest," she snorted.

He squeezed her lightly in punishment.

"Seriously, though," she said, "it *was* better. A hundred times better. Thank you."

"You're very welcome." He chuckled sleepily. "If I ever decide to become a male tart, I'll use that quote on my trade cards. 'Tristan Montgomery: a hundred times better than your previous lover.'"

Carys shook her head at his levity. His gentle teasing didn't dismiss her trauma, but it *did* help to put it in perspective. One bad experience wasn't the end of the world, and she would be foolish to let it overshadow the rest of her life.

He'd done an excellent job of exorcising Christopher's ghost. Like a master composer, he'd erased Howe's tuneless first draft and replaced it with a symphony, a joyous new song she'd never get tired of hearing.

Carys fought a dangerous feeling of contentment. It felt surprisingly natural to be here in Tristan's arms. She wanted to close her eyes and sleep in his embrace, to wake in the morning and make love all over again.

Impossible. They couldn't stay here all night. She had to return to the house before she was missed.

Would she ever have the luxury of falling asleep in someone's arms? Of being able to reach out, at any time, and simply touch him without fearing the consequences?

Her heart squeezed in her chest. "Cupid and Psyche" was the wrong fairy tale for them. They were more like a Norwegian tale she'd heard once, called "East of the Sun and West of the Moon," in which a handsome prince was cursed to appear as a bear in the daytime and only took the form of a man to visit his wife in the dark.

Tristan was like that, someone different in the darkness.

Someone uninhibited and free. Would he turn back into a metaphorical bear in the light of day? Would he treat her as if nothing had happened between them? Would she be able to do the same?

Carys stared blindly into the darkness. There were only a few days of the house party left. Would he consider this the end of their bargain? She couldn't imagine there was any *more* to lovemaking than he'd shown her tonight. This, surely, had been the pinnacle.

Or the spire. Or the turret. Or whatever architectural term he might give to it.

She quelled a wry smile at her own foolishness.

There was no future for the two of them beyond this bargain, and yet the thought of never making love with him ever again was truly depressing. He was like those opium sellers she'd read about in the newspapers, who gave the first pipe for free, knowing their mark would become addicted. If she wasn't careful, she'd be desperate for him, begging for more.

It might already be too late.

Chapter 30

It seemed only minutes before Tristan loosened his grip and sat up. "We have to get you back home."

He slid to the edge of the bed and pulled on his shirt and breeches, then retrieved her clothes from the floor. She pulled them on, grateful for the darkness that hid her sudden blush.

Why on earth was she embarrassed now, after everything they'd done? It made no sense.

He slanted her a look as he shrugged into his jacket. "How do you feel? Sore?"

She did a quick inventory, then sent him a shy smile. "No. A few parts of me ache, but not in a bad way."

"It's all those muscles you aren't used to using on a daily basis." He grinned. "The only remedy is to keep using them. To avoid any stiffness."

She couldn't hide her smirk. "I thought *stiffness* was to be encouraged? Perhaps I misunderstood?"

"Perhaps you need another demonstration."

Her heart fluttered, but he shook his head. "No, not now, minx. You need to get back."

"So practical," she grumbled, even as her spirits soared. *Not now* left room for the possibility of *maybe another time*.

They finished dressing in companionable silence, and descended the staircase side by side.

"I'll ride with you to the edge of your gardens."

"You don't need to act the gallant with me," Carys said. "I rode here perfectly well on my own."

He vaulted up onto his horse. "Yes, but that circus is in town, which means there could be all sorts of unsavory characters lurking about the countryside. I should have insisted on meeting you at Trellech to ride here together."

Carys rolled her eyes. She'd be willing to wager that *he* was the only danger to her body in the vicinity. He seemed to be having quite a devastating effect on her heart too.

They set off, and she tried to enjoy the simple pleasure of riding beside him, but her brain refused to settle. As wonderful as their lovemaking had been, a sense of unease nibbled at her. What if it had only been that good because it had been with Tristan? What if he was the only one who could make her feel this way?

He'd said it was just bodies, that she might have an equally good experience with someone else who knew what he was doing, but she wasn't so sure. What she felt for him was more than just a physical attraction. More than just lust. Those things were all well and good—and perhaps for a man they *were* the only things required for a satisfactory experience—but for a woman she rather thought there might be other factors that came into play. Factors like trust. And respect.

And love.

Her heart missed a beat. She gazed at the tuft of hair between Medusa's twitching ears as the uncomfortable truth hit her in a blinding flash. This whole time she'd been telling herself it was "just Tristan." A handsome man whose opinion didn't matter. A worldly, sardonic acquaintance she could use for sexual experience and then forget.

What an idiot she'd been.

He'd never, ever been "just Tristan." What she felt for him was more than desire, more than infatuation.

She loved him, heart and soul.

Ugh.

Tristan stared at his horse's ears as a host of conflicting emotions swirled in his chest.

The bloody woman was tying him in knots.

On one hand, he was experiencing the purely masculine triumph of having *finally* made love to her; he wanted to crow like one of those ridiculous cockerels of hers. He felt elated, filled with a savage animal satisfaction.

The difference, though, was that animal rutting involved very little emotion. It was a mindless, pleasurable act of procreation, something basic and uncomplicated, whereas there was nothing uncomplicated about what he and Carys had just done.

His fingers tightened involuntarily on the reins.

He'd always suspected that the combination of the two of

them would be incendiary, but the past hour had surpassed his every expectation. It had been perfect. Or, rather, perfectly *im*perfect.

He'd planned a cool and choreographed instruction, but it hadn't been like that. It had been wild and honest, sweaty and desperate.

Unpredictable.

He hadn't even been in control. He might have started out that way, but by the end he'd lost all sense of who he was. He hadn't been Tristan Montgomery, architect, ex-soldier. He'd simply been *hers*. Lost to sensation, aching with need.

He couldn't remember the last time he'd teased and laughed so much in bed. Or wanted to linger after the glow of his climax faded and his heart rate returned to normal.

But he'd wanted to stay there with her. All night. Wrapped up in that glorious hair, feeling the sweet curve of her derrière nestled against his crotch, the warm silk of her skin beneath his palms.

It hadn't just been good sex. It had been *more*.

More fun. More intense. More confusing. He'd veered between wanting to laugh at her, comfort her, and fuck her, all in the space of five minutes.

Had it been the same earth-shattering revelation for her?

He bloody well hoped so.

He sneaked a glance over at her riding quietly beside him. He should be congratulating himself. He'd done what he'd set out to do, which was to show her how good sex could be, with the right partner. But he'd also given her a reason to leave him. She could take a lover now, armed with the knowledge that she should walk away if she didn't find it as satisfying as what they'd just shared.

Except . . . he didn't think she *would* find it. For all his experience, he'd never encountered such astonishing synchronicity, such a soul-deep connection.

A perverse part of him rather hoped she'd never find it with anyone else. That she'd come to appreciate just how rare and extraordinary their joining had been.

No, that was a ridiculous thing to wish for. There was no reason to think that she wouldn't find another man caring enough to ensure her pleasure. It was himself who'd spend the rest of his life trying to recapture the bliss he'd just found in her arms. He already had a horrible feeling he'd compare every woman in his future to her—and find them wanting.

Because he'd never feel for any other woman what he felt for her.

He let out a silent, frustrated exhale. God, he should never have agreed to this ridiculous arrangement. Ignorance would have been bliss. He could have gone his whole life without knowing the heaven of her taste, her touch.

And now it was too late.

He wanted more. Which was precisely why he should end this . . . whatever *this* was. Experiment? Education? Exorcism of her past? He should end it now, before he lost even more of himself. He should escort her home, gently inform her their liaison was over, and that would be that.

He stole another glance at her profile.

And yet.

There were still so many variations of pleasure he could show her. How to take him in her mouth, for example. In a flash he saw her kneeling between his legs, that glorious hair of hers fanning over his thighs like molten copper, those green eyes looking up at him with teasing intent. He imagined himself, twisting her hair into a long rope, looping it over his fist to tug her upward for a kiss—

His wicked thoughts had him repositioning himself in his saddle, but Carys, thankfully, seemed so lost in her own thoughts she didn't even glance his way.

Tristan scowled into the darkness. Where should they go from here? The party was almost over; the grand ball was tomorrow evening, and the chances of more private moments together were slim.

Frustration and longing churned in his belly. Should he suggest extending their agreement after this week? A week wouldn't be long enough for him to show her everything he dreamed of doing to her. Even a month would be too short.

He was beginning to think a *lifetime* might not be enough.

He shook his head, annoyed with himself. Impossible. Maddie's marriage to Gryff might have broken the unwritten rule precluding a union between a Davies and Montgomery, but there was no chance of anything similarly permanent between himself and Carys. She couldn't continue to be his lover once they got back to London. It would be impossible to keep it a secret, and the last thing he wanted was to ruin her reputation when she'd gone to such lengths to protect it and—by extension—her family. Besides, he was returning to London to choose a bride, not find a mistress.

Tristan let out a sigh. This madness with Carys would end as planned, at the end of this house party.

But the memories would last him forever.

Chapter 31

Maddie had stolen the idea of a costume ball from Lady Banbury, and Carys found the general bustle and excitement as the house prepared for the evening ahead a welcome distraction.

It forced her not to think too much about what had happened between herself and Tristan the night before. He'd ridden with her to the edge of Trellech's boundary, but when she'd waited anxiously for a goodbye kiss, for some indication of what came next in their unusual arrangement, he'd simply given her a gruff, "Well, good night, then," and galloped away.

She'd fought a sense of disappointment and pique ever since. It wasn't as if she'd expected him to declare his undying love, but surely she deserved a little more than, "Well, good night, then," after what they'd done?

Had he lost interest already, now that they'd lain together? Had the thrill of the chase gone?

She tried not to think about it.

The entire Montgomery family would be in attendance tonight. Tristan's father, Tristan, plus his two spinster aunts, Prudence and Constance, who inhabited one wing of Newstead Park with a random assortment of cats.

Carys had met the Aunts on a number of occasions, and she'd always found them great fun. Despite their fifty-year age difference, she had the feeling that the three of them could be great friends. They shared her irreverent, mischievous sense of the absurd. How such playful, gossiping old dears were related to cool, reserved Tristan was a mystery.

It was still too early to get dressed in her costume, so she headed down to see the animals, and since she was feeling antisocial, she avoided the main garden and took a shortcut through the yew maze. It had been planted by some Elizabethan Davies over two hundred years ago and unwary visitors often got lost in its shady corridors for hours, but Carys knew every twist and turn.

She was almost at the center, near the courtyard that held the sundial, when she rounded a corner and froze in surprise. Victoria Howe and Lord Prowse were locked in a passionate embrace.

Carys clapped her hand over her mouth to stifle her instinctive gasp and ducked behind the hedge, praying that neither of them had seen her.

Victoria and Prowse? They'd seemed comfortable in each other's company at the opera, and at the picnic, but she'd never have imagined they were conducting an affair.

A swell of something almost like pride warmed her chest. *Good for you, Victoria!* Howe certainly didn't deserve any allegiance.

Carys tiptoed away, checking around each successive corner in case any other couples had decided to take advantage of the maze's secrecy, but she reached the animal enclosures without further mishap.

When it was finally time to get dressed, she tried not to blush as she donned the same masculine outfit she'd worn the night before. It was impossible not to remember the way Tristan had divested her of each item with heart-pounding deliberation. Was she eager to see him tonight or not? She couldn't decide.

She'd just plucked up the courage to descend the stairs when a knock sounded at her bedroom door and she opened it to find Victoria Howe standing there, looking nervous, as if unsure of her welcome.

"Victoria! Can I help you? Is something the matter?"

The other woman glanced furtively over her shoulder. "I wanted a word with you in private, if you don't mind. May I come in?"

Carys opened the door wider and stepped back, not sure whether to be intrigued or alarmed. "Of course."

Victoria was dressed as Good Queen Bess. The golden embroidery of her skirts shimmered in the light from the lamp, and the pleated ruff around her neck bobbed as she stepped forward. When Carys indicated the pair of gilt chairs that flanked her dressing table, Victoria perched on one and folded her hands in her lap.

"I think you might have seen me in the maze this afternoon," she said without preamble.

For a moment Carys debated whether to feign ignorance, but then she simply nodded. She was sick of secrets.

"I did. With Lord Prowse. I'm so sorry, I didn't mean to intrude. But you needn't worry. I won't tell anyone."

"I love him," Victoria said simply. She placed her hand over her stomach. "And in point of fact, I'm carrying his child."

Carys blinked, stunned by this new revelation. She wasn't sure why Victoria was telling her this, but perhaps the other woman felt the need to unburden herself. Carys could certainly sympathize with that. She'd carried the weight of Howe's blackmail alone for almost two years, and it had been almost unbearable. Until she'd confessed to Tristan, that night in the carriage.

How long ago that seemed.

Victoria fiddled with her pleated skirts. "The world will think Christopher's the father, of course, but I'll know the truth. And so will *he*," she said, with a glimmer of satisfaction. "I haven't shared his bed for months, but he'll be too proud to say anything. He won't want anyone to know he's been cuckolded."

She sighed. "I wish I could be with Prowse in public, but a divorce is out of the question. And at least my son will inherit Howe's title. It's the only thing of his I want."

She glanced up, and her eyes searched Carys's face. "I'm telling you this because I don't think *you* hold any love for Christopher either. I believe I know what happened between the two of you before he married me," she said quietly. "He's said things, from time to time, to make me suspect. I'm sorry for any distress he's caused you."

Carys's heart began to pound at having her secret revealed so unexpectedly, but Victoria's gray eyes were kind, not gloating or angry. She swallowed a lump of emotion at the other woman's compassion.

"It's not your fault," she managed. "He's the one who behaved badly."

"You needn't worry *I'll* tell anyone," Victoria reassured her earnestly. "I swear I won't. We women have to stick together." She gave a faint smile and shook her head. "I never should have married him, you know. The title my father wanted doesn't begin to make up for being tied to such a pathetic excuse for a human."

Carys reached over and gave her hand a friendly squeeze. "I'm sorry."

Victoria shrugged. "I'm tired of paying for his mistakes. His gambling and his intrigues." She let out a dismissive snort. "Actually, I don't care about his affairs. I certainly don't want him in *my* bed. But he's got himself tangled up with all sorts of unsavory characters—I even heard him talking to a bear handler the other day about repaying some debt. I live in daily dread that he'll do something foolish."

Carys grimaced. "Not that I don't appreciate you taking me into your confidence, but . . . why are you telling me this?"

Victoria's eyes met hers. "Because I don't want you to make the same mistake *I* did, and marry for something other than love. I know I shouldn't meddle in something that's none of my affair, but I heard you might be considering Lord Ellington and I have to say, I think you'd be making a grave mistake if you accept him. The way you look at him is nothing like the way you look at Tristan Montgomery."

Carys's stomach swooped. *Dear God, were her feelings for Tristan so obvious?*

Victoria sent her a gentle smile of understanding. "I've always admired the way you face down society, Carys. You're so much braver than I am. Just . . . don't be afraid to do what makes you happy."

Carys nodded, still a little dazed. "Thank you, Victoria."

The other woman stood, and Carys followed suit.

"I'll go down to the ballroom now," Victoria said. "I'll see you there."

Carys nodded again, her mind swirling with everything the other woman had revealed.

How sad for Victoria not to be free to marry the man she loved. And how would *she* feel in the same situation? Could she really marry Ellington if she was in love with someone else? It would surely be a recipe for heartache.

As soon as she entered the ballroom, Carys was accosted by Tristan's aunts, who'd settled themselves near the door at the side of the dance floor to have the best possible view of the proceedings.

Constance, the older sister, sent her a delighted smile. "Why, Lady Carys, you look marvelous! How original, to come dressed as a gentleman. I doubt even Beau Brummell himself could find fault with your appearance. Is that who you're supposed to be?"

"Excellent choice," Prudence interjected, without waiting for confirmation. "You're almost his female equivalent. Every lady copies your style."

"Don't let it go to your head, though," Constance cautioned. "Poor George has been spending beyond his means for years. I hear he's close to being hounded out of London by his creditors."

Prudence nodded sagely. "It all went wrong a couple of seasons ago when he called Prinny fat, to his face. He's running out of people to lend him money."

Like Christopher, Carys thought darkly.

"I'm not Beau Brummell, actually," she said.

"Then who are you?"

She sent the two women an enigmatic smile. "I'll leave you to guess. But to give you a hint: It's someone you know very well indeed."

Prudence opened her mouth to ask more, but at that moment Lord Ellington stepped up to join them.

"Good evening, ladies."

Carys suppressed a chuckle as both her companions sat up a little straighter. It seemed neither of them was immune to Ellington's timeless charm.

He bowed at them, then offered his arm to Carys. "If I may steal Lady Carys for the next dance?"

Constance sent him a wide smile. "Of course, my lord. Take her away. I do love to see you young things swirling around the dance floor." She lifted her lorgnette to her eye and pretended to study Carys's outfit again. "Although there won't be much swirling with *both* of you in breeches." She chuckled. "I hope you can decide which of you should lead."

Ellington laughed, enjoying the byplay, and pulled Carys away.

Carys sent the Aunts a farewell smile, and just before she was out of earshot she heard Prudence whisper, "I wonder what Tristan will make of *that*?"

Her heart missed a beat. Were they referring to her scandalous outfit, or the fact that she was dancing with Ellington? That Tristan might actually be jealous of her dancing with another man was something she'd never dared to hope.

The first thing Tristan saw when he entered the ballroom was Carys, dressed in those damned alluring breeches, laughing up at Ellington as they joined a country dance. Something hot and possessive clawed at his innards. He purposefully glanced away and saw his aunts seated strategically near the door to catch unsuspecting new arrivals and pump them for gossip. Prudence waved him over with her fan, so he dutifully made his way toward them.

"Whenever I see the two of you smiling at me like that I just know you're up to no good," he said by way of greeting. "What scheme are you concocting now?"

Constance tried to look offended, but her grin ruined the effect. "How rude, Nephew dear! Why, the two of us are just sitting here, minding our own business."

"And poking your nose into everyone *else's*," he said drily.

Neither of them bothered to deny it.

Prudence looked up at him. "I thought Lavinia Purser would be here. Was she not invited?"

Her tone was so carefully nonchalant it was clear she was fishing for information, and Tristan suppressed an inward groan. An unaccustomed flush rose on his cheekbones. In truth, Maddie *had* asked him if she should add Lavinia to the guest list—and he'd said no.

He'd used the excuse that the new house wasn't finished, that he didn't want to invite her down to see it until it was ready, but that wasn't entirely true. He hadn't *wanted* Lavinia here. He'd only wanted Carys.

It was extremely vexing.

"I heard you were paying her particular attention, my boy."

Tristan started guiltily, before he realized his aunt was referring to Lavinia, and not to Carys.

"What? Oh, yes. I admire Lavinia very much."

Pru wrinkled her nose in a childish gesture more suited

to an infant than a seventy-year-old woman. "Admire her!" she snorted. "One *admires* a horse, or an elegant table, not a flesh-and-blood woman."

Constance bobbed her head in agreement. "I'm sorry to say it, Tristan, but I've always found Lavinia Purser rather a cold fish."

"Just like her mother," Pru chimed in. "Letty Purser's a *stickler*. We went to school with her, you know. She was always the first to go tattling to the teachers whenever one of the other girls got into mischief."

Constance elbowed her in the ribs. "You're still cross she caught you kissing the stable boy."

Pru sniffed. "She didn't have to tell Miss Manners, did she?"

Tristan bit back a bark of laughter, but the two of them weren't finished.

"Lavinia's cut from the same cloth. There's no fire in her."

"Unlike that Davies girl," Constance said slyly. "She's a firecracker."

As if on cue, they both swiveled their heads to watch Carys, twirling around the dance floor in Ellington's arms.

The attempt at matchmaking was so unsubtle that Tristan almost rolled his eyes. Now that he thought back on it, it wasn't the first time they'd tried to nudge him toward Carys. They'd approved of her—despite her dastardly Davies heritage—ever since he'd been a boy.

He had to admit that Carys and Ellington made a striking couple. They were both wonderful dancers, moving perfectly in time with the music. Ellington was wearing the outfit of a sixteenth-century musketeer, with fold-over boots and a dress sword swinging from the sash across his torso.

Because of Carys's outfit, they gave the appearance of two men dancing, and Tristan bit back a bitter laugh. Ellington probably fancied her even more, dressed like that. Maybe he was regretting her constant refusals to marry him.

Constance gave a soulful sigh. "She's so beautiful. That red hair, and that figure! Rubens could have painted her. It's such a shame the current fashion is for reed-thin chits with breasts scarcely bigger than a bee sting. Men like a nice handful. Wouldn't you agree, Tristan?"

Before he could formulate a reply to that outrageous pronouncement—which sadly wasn't unusual for his relatives, who seemed to think that their advanced age gave them carte blanche to say whatever they liked to whomever they liked—Prudence gave an approving chuckle.

"Bit of a hoyden, though." She shot him a mischievous glance. "When she was twelve or so, Connie and I came across her in the woods. She was flat on her back, gasping for breath because she'd tried to take a fence that was much too high and tumbled from her horse."

Pru nodded. "The poor child was dreadfully winded. She had leaves in her hair, mud all over her skirts. She looked like a wild little wood sprite. I suspect she'd cracked a rib or two, but she was such a brave thing. She didn't cry. Instead, she forced a laugh and admitted it was her own fault for trying to be too ambitious. She was more concerned for her horse than for herself."

"That sounds like Carys," Tristan said.

"We gave her a lift home in our gig."

"Always admired her spirit." Pru nodded.

"Me too," Tristan murmured.

The aunts shared a knowing look.

"We helped her again, just recently, you know," Pru said, a little too casually.

Tristan raised his brows. He'd heard that particular studied casualness from her before. It almost always boded trouble.

"Oh, God, you interfering old harpies. What did you do?"

"It was a few weeks ago, back in London. At Lady Banbury's costume ball. You went as a Roman senator or something like that. And Lady Carys went as Diana, in the most marvelous see-through dress. Do you remember it?"

Tristan clenched his teeth. "Yes. I remember it." *He'd probably still think of it on his deathbed.* "What did you do to help her?"

"I overheard Lord Caseby boasting that he'd be the one to 'bring Carys Davies to heel.'" Prudence's tone dripped with disapproval. "As if she was a disobedient spaniel!"

Connie shook her head. "I was going to trip him with my cane, but then Pru had an even better idea."

Tristan didn't even try to stifle his groan. "What did you do?"

"I poisoned him," Pru said placidly.

Chapter 32

"You did what?" Tristan demanded, aghast.

"Poisoned him," Prudence repeated. "But only a little." She patted the beaded reticule on her lap. "I never go anywhere without my little vial of blackthorn syrup. One never knows when it might come in handy. I slipped a few drops into Caseby's port, to spare poor Lady Carys his company."

Tristan raked a hand through his hair. "Good God. What does it do?"

Prudence's smirk was triumphant. "It's a purgative, helps empty the bowels. It worked like a charm. Not fifteen minutes later, Caseby was taken ill with a bad case of stomach cramps and had to go home."

"Serves him right, the old lecher." Constance chuckled.

Tristan shook his head, torn between fond awe and utter disapproval. If Pru had administered the same medicine to Christopher Howe that evening, Howe would have gone home prematurely and Tristan would never have discovered Carys's secret.

He'd never have made his impetuous suggestion.

Never have made love to her.

That would have been a tragedy. For all his misgivings, he wouldn't change what they'd done for the world.

He sent his two aunts a chiding glare. "You're like the witches in *Macbeth*. One of these days you're going to get into a lot of trouble."

Constance waved her hand. "Oh, pshaw. Whoever would suspect two sweet little old ladies like us? Do you know, Pru, I rather think we could get away with actual murder, if we put our minds to it."

"Do not *ever* put your minds to it!" Tristan growled. "However tempted you may be. And let me tell you now, Carys is not the person to ask for any eye of newt, or ear of bat, or whatever it is you need for your witchy concoctions. She loves all animals."

Both aunts chuckled; then Constance became serious once more. "You know, if we're the witches from *Macbeth*, then Lady Carys is Katherine, from *The Taming of the Shrew*."

Prudence nodded. "Men like Caseby think they need to 'tame her,' to crush her spirit, but they're wrong. Her spirit is what makes her so attractive. But most men are too insecure to want a woman who can outwit them."

His aunt was right. Tristan loved Carys's intelligence, her irrepressible energy. He loved the fact that she challenged him constantly.

Lavinia had never voiced an opinion that didn't exactly correlate with his own. Now that he thought about it, it was surprisingly annoying. If he wanted a companion who simply repeated everything he said, he might as well borrow one of Carys's parrots.

Constance took a sip of ratafia. "Yes, well, most men are fools, Prudence." She sent Tristan a sideways glance. "Present company excepted, of course."

"Thank you," Tristan muttered. "And you're right, only a fool would want to change her. She's perfect as she is."

Both aunts raised their brows and looked at him with identical, knowing expressions. He'd seen that look a hundred times in his childhood: when he'd said or done something stupid and they were waiting for him to realize what it was.

Prudence sent him one of her wicked, stirring-the-pot grins. "You should ask Lady Carys to dance, Tristan."

Tristan clenched his jaw and sent them both another *stop meddling* glare. "Do you know, I think I will."

He strode off to the opposite end of the ballroom, grateful to escape.

Prudence took another sip of her wine and watched Tristan's hasty retreat.

"Do you think the poor boy knows he's in love with her?"

Constance snorted. "I doubt it. Our dear Tristan is as stupid as the next man when it comes to matters of the heart. He thinks the reason he can't stop thinking about her is because she's the most vexing creature on the planet."

Pru chuckled. "Should we tell him, do you think?"

"Oh, heavens no. We've done quite enough interfering. Let's just hope he manages to arrive at the right conclusion before he does something truly stupid, like propose to that dreadful Purser girl."

Pru patted her reticule again. "I might put some black-thorn syrup in *his* brandy, if he does."

Chapter 33

Tristan was waiting at the edge of the dance floor when Carys and Ellington whirled to a breathless stop.

Ellington sent her an intrigued glance. "Lady Carys, are you sure you want to risk dancing with such a ruffian?" He gave Tristan's costume an appreciative look.

Tristan, against all expectation, was dressed as some kind of pirate, in an open-necked white shirt and black leather breeches, with a red handkerchief tied around his throat in lieu of a cravat.

"I do believe I'll cede the field." Ellington chuckled good-naturedly. "Forgive me, my dear, but he's armed to the teeth."

It was true. Tristan had a brace of pistols thrust into his waistband. He really did look like a disreputable buccaneer, and she found this less-than-perfectly-attired version of him shockingly enticing.

She swallowed down her delight. "How good to see you finally embracing the wilder side of your nature, Montgomery."

Tristan's hot look made her toes curl. "It delights me to please you, Lady Carys."

Carys felt her cheeks flush at his deliberately wicked double entendre and prayed Ellington wouldn't notice their byplay. Flustered, she took Tristan's arm and allowed him to lead her onto the dance floor.

A glance to her left showed Gryff and Maddie already in each other's arms, looking besotted and paying no attention to anyone else. Rhys and Morgan, however, had both noticed her accept Tristan's invitation. Both of them were staring at her with the same combination of incredulity and suspicion.

Ugh, brothers.

The musicians played the opening bars of a waltz. Tristan put his hand at her waist, and anticipation surged through her.

"Pretend to look reluctant," she hissed through her teeth. "As if we're only doing this to keep Gryff and Maddie happy. Rhys and Morgan are watching and I want them to think we're making a heroic attempt to heal the rift between our families."

Tristan's lips twitched, but he quickly schooled his expression back into its usual stern disdain. "How's this?"

"Perfect," she teased. "You look like you'd rather be anywhere else."

"I *would* rather be anywhere else!" he growled.

Carys tried not to laugh. Sharing a joke with him was just as much fun as teasing him. She forced her own face to look as though dancing with a Montgomery were worse than being stretched on the rack.

"I heard a Davies woman once stabbed a Montgomery man

at a party just like this," she said. "Back in the sixteen hundreds. She slipped a knife between his ribs during a gavotte."

Tristan's hand tightened on her waist. "I can believe it. You Davieses always aim for the heart."

"I didn't think Montgomerys *had* hearts," she said lightly. "She must have nicked his liver."

Tristan swirled her around in punishment for that little jibe, and she tried to contain her instinctive whoop of delight. It was an effort to keep a cool distance between them, to keep her elbows locked and her chest away from his, when all she wanted was to melt into him like warm candle wax. It was even more of a challenge to pretend she was hating this, when it was heaven to be in his arms.

She'd waited her whole life for this.

A lady's skirts usually created a barrier that prevented her partner from getting too close, but her breeches meant that their legs were often entwined. Tristan's thigh insinuated itself between her own as they circled and turned, and her blood heated to a low simmer. She was sure he was doing it deliberately, the scoundrel. The gossips would be having a field day.

It was a strange paradox, but dancing with him in public felt almost more scandalous than making love to him in private.

She glanced up at him, smiling with her eyes, if not with her mouth. "Do you know, I've been trying to get you to dance with me for years. Were you afraid I'd ruin your reputation?"

She kept her tone light, but there was a kernel of hurt behind the words. His constant rebuttals had stung.

"No. I was afraid you'd ruin *me*."

Her heart stuttered. What did *that* mean?

"And have I?" she breathed.

"Completely."

She missed a step, but he steered them effortlessly into another twirl, and when she glanced back up at him the intensity had gone from his eyes. She quashed a feeling of disappointment. He wasn't being serious.

Determined to appear unaffected, she gave him a head-to-toe inspection, as Ellington had done.

"If anyone's doing any ruining tonight, it'll be you. You look as if you'd ravish a dozen virgins before breakfast and steal the silver on your way out."

His lips quirked. "I believe I already told you I've never had a virgin, and I don't intend to start. But if you've changed your mind about having someone avenge your honor, I'd be more than happy to put a bullet in Howe for you. He wouldn't be the first person I've ever shot, but he'd certainly be the most satisfying."

Carys caught a breath, secretly thrilled at this new, slightly bloodthirsty side of Tristan, but she shook her head. "I appreciate the offer, but no violence, remember?"

She cast her gaze around the room, looking for Christopher, but while she saw Victoria and her father talking to Doctor Williams, there was no sign of him.

Thankfully, Tristan seemed to take her refusal in good part. "I still haven't figured out who you're supposed to be, you know."

"Your aunts think I'm George Brummell. But they're wrong."

"Who are you then?"

She couldn't resist a grin. "Someone I've long admired."

"A swordfighter? A lion tamer? A highwayman?"

"I'm *you*."

Carys held her breath, afraid she'd revealed too much, but his reaction was not what she expected at all.

"You *admire* me?" He let out a bark of laughter that made several nearby couples glance over at them in shock. "I wish my aunts could hear you now."

"Why?"

"Because they think *admire* is a dreadful word. Too weak."

Carys tilted her head. "They're probably right. Davieses and Montgomerys should use stronger terms to describe one another. Like *hate*, and *loathe*, and *despise*."

His eyes glittered with mischief. "Or *lust. Desire. Need.*"

The simmer in her blood became a boil. She tossed her head and summoned her most flirtatious smile. "In that case, let me rephrase. I don't admire you. I adore you. I pine for you. I'll die if you don't make love to me again."

He laughed at her exaggerated dramatics, but her heart quailed a little at how close the words skirted to the truth. She tried to temper her expression, tried not to stare up at him like a besotted idiot, but surely the stars in her eyes would give her away. The attraction sparking between them must be obvious to every observer.

The waltz ended on a triumphant note and they swirled to a breathless stop.

"You look hot, Lady Carys," Tristan said, loud enough for those nearby to hear. "Allow me to escort you to the terrace."

He turned them away from a glowering Rhys and Morgan and steered her deftly through the open French windows that led out into the gardens. Carys went without demur.

A few other couples were already outside, enjoying the balmy evening air, but Tristan drew her down the shallow steps and away from the house. Lanterns had been placed on hooked poles at intervals around the flower beds, and the sound of the music floated after them as they strolled along the avenue of trees leading toward the menagerie.

Carys's stomach was a writhing mass of nerves, and when Tristan finally stopped and turned to her she decided to grab the bull by the horns.

"We need to discuss our arrangement," she said breathlessly. "We agreed it would last until the end of the party, and you've more than fulfilled your side of the bargain, so if you want to consider it over, then—"

"We're not finished," he growled. "The party doesn't end until the fireworks at midnight. Or maybe not even until tomorrow, when the last guest leaves."

Her stomach flipped in relief. "Well, if you want to be *technical* about it—"

He took a step closer and her heart began to pound. "I do."

"We still have a few hours left, then."

He nodded. "And until then, it's my duty to show you pleasure."

"Duty!" She scowled. "You make it sound like a chore!"

"Oh, it is." He drew her into his arms, and she went with only token resistance. "A terrible chore. See how bravely I'm overcoming my natural revulsion for a wicked Davies."

She stifled a giggle. "You're doing a sterling job." She pressed against him and wriggled provocatively. "I can feel how *hard* it is for you."

"That's my pistol," he said, straight-faced.

She wiggled again.

"My other pistol."

She flattened herself full-length against him, from breasts

to thighs, and with them both wearing breeches there was no mistaking his desire. A thrill of feminine triumph coursed through her.

"And this?" she teased.

"That's all for you."

She laughed in delight.

"I can't imagine what else you still have to show me," she murmured, quite truthfully. "I thought we covered it all last night?"

His slow smile made her weak at the knees. "Which just proves your education in debauchery is still sadly incomplete, because *I* can think of a thousand wicked things to do out here in the dark."

He slid his hand around her nape and tilted her head upward, and her stomach clenched in delightful confusion.

"It sounds as though you admire me, Montgomery."

He shook his head. "You're dreadful. You drive me bloody mad."

She lifted up on tiptoe so her lips brushed against his. "Good. Because you do the same to me."

Tristan kissed her, hard, and Carys shivered in delight. She'd never dreamed she'd have this effect on him. His tongue stroked into her mouth and his hands molded her body as lovingly as a sculptor smoothing clay.

A fierce joy filled her. She wanted him naked, beneath her, their layers of clothing gone. Would he forget himself so much that he'd make love to her here, in the gardens? The irony of that almost made her laugh against his mouth; for the second time in her life she was in danger of being made love to in a garden, but unlike the first time, she desired *this* ravishing with all her heart.

Was it still "bedding" if they did it in a *flower* bed?

She'd just grabbed his lapels and started to peel off his jacket when Tristan froze. She stifled a frustrated moan of denial, but then she heard it too: the heavy thump of rapidly approaching male footfalls.

She straightened with a curse. "Oh, damn it! I bet that's one of my stupid, interfering brothers."

But the sound was coming from the direction of the menagerie, not the house, and she gasped as Christopher Howe suddenly stumbled out from behind a bank of rhododendrons.

Chapter 34

Carys's spirits plummeted.

Dear God, had he been spying on them? If so, he'd have even more fodder for his hateful blackmail.

Howe caught sight of her and skidded to a halt, panting. "Ah! Carys. Thank God I've found you."

She frowned at his panicked tone. "What are you doing out here?"

Tristan stepped forward, out of the shadows, and Howe gave a visible start. He obviously hadn't expected to see him there with her. *How odd. Maybe he hadn't been spying, after all?*

"Yes, Howe. What do you want?" Tristan's voice was hard. "I hope you weren't following Lady Carys to accost her."

Howe somehow managed to look offended, as if he'd never dream of accosting a woman in a garden, which considering his far-from-spotless behavior was deeply ironic.

He rested his hands on his hips as he tried to catch his breath. "I came to find her," he said, still gasping, "because I didn't want to cause a panic. Her bear has escaped. I saw him running off into the woods."

Carys shook her head. "Buttercup? Don't be ridiculous. He's safely in his cage. It's probably just a guest, dressed up. Why, Squire Digby's come as Hercules. He's got a lion-skin rug over his—"

"I'm certain," Howe insisted. "I saw him myself! I heard him growl. He ran off into the woods, that way." He pointed behind him.

"Buttercup couldn't possibly have opened his own cage. Someone must have let him out." She narrowed her eyes in sudden suspicion. "Was it *you*?"

Howe drew himself up. "Of course it wasn't. Why on earth would I do that?"

"I don't know. Just to make mischief, probably."

"What were you doing in the gardens?" Tristan demanded.

Howe shot him a smirking, knowing, look. "Same thing you are, I imagine, Montgomery," he drawled. "Taking the night air."

Tristan looked like he might say more, but Carys caught his sleeve. "I'd better go and take a look. If Buttercup *has* managed to get out, I can coax him back into his cage. He's probably already frightened, with the extra noise and the music."

Howe let out an audible sigh of relief. "Excellent. I knew it would be better to tell you than those hotheaded brothers of yours."

"Shall I get some food from the house?" Tristan offered.

"I'll go," Howe said quickly. "You should stay with Carys. She shouldn't be out there facing that monster alone."

"He's not a 'monster,'" Carys scolded. "And he's no danger to me. But I can't guarantee how he'll react if he meets anyone else. The poor thing must be terrified." She glared at Howe. "Go and ask Cook for some fruit."

"What if *I* come across him?" Howe asked. "What shall I do?"

"Let him sniff the fruit. He's not very fast. He'll lumber after you. Draw him toward his cage, throw the fruit inside, and when he follows it in, close the door. If that fails, sing 'Bobby Shafto.'"

Howe's look of confusion would have been funny if the situation weren't so dire.

"What, the *sea shanty*?"

"Yes."

"But—"

"Just sing it to him," Carys said impatiently. "It calms him down. Now go!"

Thankfully, Howe turned and loped off toward the house. Carys turned to Tristan, who was checking his pocket watch. "How much time do we have before the fireworks?"

"A few hours yet."

"That should be enough." She started purposefully toward the animal cages. "He can't have gone very far."

The lanterns didn't extend to the edge of the grounds, but there was enough moonlight by which to see, and her heart sank when they found the iron door to Buttercup's enclosure swinging open. She'd been hoping Howe had been playing a cruel trick on her, worrying her for no reason, but that clearly wasn't the case.

Had he been the one to release the bear? She wouldn't put it past him; he was certainly vindictive enough, the swine.

She squinted into the recesses of the enclosure, but it was so large and full of greenery there was no hope of seeing if the bear had returned of his own free will.

"Buttercup!" she crooned softly. "Are you in there, sweeting?"

Not a rustle came from the darkness, so she picked up the little music box from its place near the door. "I suppose we'd better start looking."

A dark shape swooped overhead and she let out a startled yelp. "Huginn!" she scolded. "Shoo! Go to bed."

The raven cawed loudly, delighted to have surprised her, and Muninn's answering call came from deeper in the woods. Carys let out a defeated sigh. "Oh, fine, if you want to come, come. But no silliness, you hear me? We need to find Buttercup."

Huginn blew her a noisy kiss.

"Should we go and get horses?" Tristan asked.

"No. They might get spooked."

He pulled one of the pistols from his belt.

"What are you doing? You are *not* shooting my bear."

He sent her an exasperated look. "Of course I won't shoot him. But if he threatens a guest, we might need something a little more drastic than *singing*. I assume he dislikes loud noises and bright lights?"

"Yes. Firing that would scare him witless."

"Well, then. I'd rather be prepared. Just in case." He unhooked the brass powder flask from his belt and tipped a small measure into the barrel of the pistol.

"I can't believe you came fully armed to a costume party," Carys marveled. "I thought those were just for show."

He sent her a cynical smile. "A Montgomery on Davies land *always* comes ready for a fight."

She rolled her eyes. "This is the nineteenth century, for heaven's sake. Not the eleven hundreds. Haven't we moved on from that now?"

"You'd think so," Tristan said, "but you Davieses have an uncanny ability to attract trouble. I've come to realize I always need a little extra firepower when you're around."

He produced a metal tin from his pocket, extracted a tiny square of fabric wadding and a round lead shot, and pushed them both down the barrel with the slim metal ramrod secured on the underside of the pistol. Carys watched his brisk efficiency with a dazed kind of awe. His final task was to pour some powder into the pan on the side and flip closed the little cover that shielded it from the wind.

"All right. Let's find that bear of yours."

Chapter 35

Carys had been sure they'd find Buttercup feasting on the vegetables in the kitchen garden or stealing apples from the orchard, but there was no sign of him in either location, so she and Tristan ventured into the woodland that surrounded the formal gardens.

She was glad she wasn't wearing skirts. Brambles scratched at her hands and clawed at her breeches, while the uneven ground threatened to twist her ankle at every step.

"Buttercup!" she cooed. "Where are you? Come to Mummy."

Behind her, Tristan snorted in amusement, so she pushed back a tree branch and let it go, stifling her own laugh as it slapped him in the face.

"Bloody hell!"

A plop and a sucking sound indicated that his pristine boot had landed in a muddy puddle, and she grinned. The possibility of a fully disheveled, mud-spattered Tristan was delightful.

"My God," he muttered. "I feel like I'm in one of those Shakespeare plays where everyone gets lost in the woods and blunders about like idiots."

"Like *A Midsummer Night's Dream*? I love that one."

"Of course you do," he groused. "You thrive on chaos. I bet you like the ones where the girls all dress up as boys too."

"They're fun. I bet *you* like the stuffy, serious ones where everyone dies. Like *Macbeth*, or *Hamlet*." She wrinkled her nose, even though she knew he couldn't see her in the darkness. "So gloomy."

"This feels very much like the one that has 'exit, pursued by a bear.'"

"That's *A Winter's Tale*. Poor Antigonus gets eaten. But don't worry, Buttercup only likes sweet things. You're too bitter to interest him."

Carys listened for his reply, but heard only the sound of sliding pebbles followed by a splash and another curse.

"Damn it all! These are my favorite boots!"

"Watch out for the little stream!" she called back cheerfully.

He gave an enraged growl.

Carys scanned the trees. They'd been walking for at least half an hour, by her reckoning. This particular patch of woodland was almost untouched. A few animal runs crisscrossed the ferny floor and in the shifting shadows every rock, bush, and stump looked like a bear.

Tristan cupped his hands around his mouth. "Buttercup, you hairy little miscreant!" he bellowed, in a voice he'd probably last used to direct troops on the battlefields of France. "Where the bloody hell are yooooou?"

Carys glared at him over her shoulder. "Don't shout at him like that. He won't come if you sound angry."

Even in the semidarkness she could see him roll his eyes. "We've gone so far we're almost on Montgomery land now. My new house is just over that rise. We should go back."

Carys bit her lip. He was probably right. They'd looped around the eastern edge of the estate, and even though it was hard to tell in the darkness, they couldn't be too far from the road to Trellech. Where on earth was Buttercup?

She was about to turn around and face defeat when she heard a faint puffing sound, and a flare of glowing blue light shimmered to life just ahead of them.

She gasped in delight. "Oh, look! Fairy fire!"

Tristan stepped up next to her and squinted. "What? Oh."

"I've only ever seen it once before," Carys whispered reverently. "When I was a little girl. Welsh folklore says it's a light held by the fairy folk, the pookas—naughty goblins who lead travelers astray. The humans follow the light, thinking it will lead them to safety, but when it goes out they're left lost in the bog."

Tristan snorted. "In English we call it a 'will-o'-the-wisp' or a 'jack-o'-lantern,' which I suppose is the same thing. A little sprite called Will or Jack holding a light."

"It isn't always dangerous. In some stories, if the travelers are kind, it guides them out of the woods, and leads them to gold and treasure!"

"There's no need to whisper," he scoffed. "There's nothing magical about it. It's a perfectly natural phenomenon caused by swamp gasses escaping from the marshy ground."

Carys glared at him. "You're so blasted *logical*, Montgomery. Don't you believe in magic?"

He shook his head and tilted his chin at the flickering light. "Another name for that is 'ignis fatuus,' which is Latin for 'foolish fire' or 'giddy flame.' Because only a fool would fall for its tricks."

She put her hands on her hips. "Not everything can be explained in a logical, scientific way."

"This can."

"Yes, maybe. But not *everything*."

He lifted his brows in that condescending manner that made her want to kick him in the shins. "Name something."

"All right, clever clogs. What about love? That's not logical or scientific. But it definitely exists. It makes people do all sorts of extraordinary things. If that's not magic, I don't know what is."

Tristan couldn't decide whether he wanted to strangle Carys or kiss her for her stubborn, irrepressible optimism.

Here, in the moonlight, dressed in those damned alluring breeches, she looked like a naughty little wood sprite herself. And just like the pookas, she had an uncanny ability to lead him astray. Here they were, tramping around some godforsaken bog when they could be warm and clean inside. Kissing. Or, better yet, in bed.

His boots were never going to be the same.

He wasn't entirely sure about his mind either.

Or his heart.

He huffed out a breath, half-amused, half-exasperated. Forget the fairy fire, *she* was the giddy flame. La Fiammetta, with her red hair and her endless intrigues and adventures.

Following in her wake would lead to disaster of the worst kind. And yet he was powerless to resist her special brand of magic.

Ignis fatuus. Tristan suppressed a snort. How apt. He hadn't mentioned it to Carys, but the Latin word *fatuus* gave rise to the English word *infatuate.* That was clearly his current problem; he was infatuated with her, like half the other men in the *ton.* But unlike the other men, his obsession with her seemed to be permanent.

There was no time to dwell on the subject, because Carys thrust her pert nose in the air and sent him a withering glance.

"You, Montgomery, have the emotional range of a . . . a rock." She pointed toward the fading blue glow. "I'm going that way."

"Toward mortal peril or untold riches," he said drily. "My money's on the peril."

"Follow me or not, it's your choice."

A twig snapped off to their right and Tristan stilled. He tilted his head, his senses honed from years of listening out for enemy patrols and ambushes. The hairs on his forearms prickled.

"Wait!" He reached out and caught her arm. "Listen!"

Carys, thankfully, did as she was told.

"Do you hear that?" he whispered. "It's coming from over there."

They both squinted into the darkness. Sure enough, a rustling that wasn't the wind in the trees could be heard. Something large was pushing through the undergrowth.

"It could be poachers," she murmured. "Or a stag."

He leveled his pistol toward the sound.

The ferns rustled, and he caught a glimpse of dark fur.

Carys let out a sigh of relief.

"Buttercup! There you are! Who let you out, hmm?" She thrust the metal music box into his hands. "Quick, turn the handle."

Since there was nothing else for it, Tristan lowered the pistol and cranked the little handle on the side of the box. A tinkling, slightly off-key tune sprang forth, and Carys took a breath and began to sing.

"Bobby Shafto's gone to sea,
Silver buckles at his knee;
He'll come back and—"

A deep growl interrupted her serenade.

Carys stopped with a surprised little gasp and Tristan ceased turning the handle. In the sudden silence the growl came again, and Tristan's stomach plummeted in dread. The low vibration indicated an animal far larger and far angrier than Buttercup.

"I. Don't. Think. That's. Buttercup," Carys whispered.

Chapter 36

Even as Carys said the words, an enormous creature lumbered out of the woods about thirty feet from where they stood, and for one endless moment time seemed to stop.

Tristan blinked. It was the bear from the circus. Out of his cage.

How in God's name—? Was every bear in Britain suddenly loose in these bloody woods?

He held his breath, praying that, by some miracle, the beast would ignore them and move on.

The monster stopped and sniffed the air, then shook his shaggy head in obvious agitation. A splatter of saliva whipped from his jaws. With a jerky movement he reared up on his back legs and let out a blood-curdling roar. Even at this distance, he was taller than Tristan, and probably weighed five times as much.

As quietly as he could, Tristan cocked his pistol and rapidly weighed their options. Shooting the thing would likely do nothing but enrage him. If he chose to attack, they were in very serious trouble indeed.

"You know about bears," he hissed. "What should we do?"

Carys had been staring at the creature as if transfixed. She didn't even turn her head to reply. "Back away. Slowly."

He started to move, keeping the pistol trained on the bear, backing toward the protection of the trees. Carys followed. Every snap of a twig made him wince.

The bear crashed back down on his front paws with a grunt. His huge head swung in their direction and this time there was no doubt that he had spotted them. His beady black eyes glinted in the moonlight as he emitted another low growl that curdled the marrow of Tristan's bones.

"Keep going," Carys whispered urgently. "But don't run, or he will give chase. Don't turn your back either."

Tristan could feel the pulse pounding in his throat, a rush of terror burning through his blood. He'd felt like this before every cavalry charge—this doom-laden sense that his life hung in the balance, that every heartbeat could be his last.

Damn it all. He'd never expected to find such danger so close to home.

They kept backing up, trying not to trip over the branches and brambles that carpeted the ground, and for a short distance it seemed as though the bear would let them leave. Then, to Tristan's horror, the animal started lumbering toward them.

"Oh dear," Carys muttered. "That's not good."

The bear didn't seem to be in much of a hurry, but to

Tristan's eyes his slow, measured pace felt very much like a deliberate stalk. They were being hunted.

"Shit," he breathed, incredulous.

From the corner of his eye he saw Carys lift her hand to her throat and swiftly untie her cravat. She let it fall to the ground in a flutter of pale cloth.

"That might slow him down."

Sure enough, the bear stopped to investigate. He lowered his long snout and Tristan could hear him snuffling and scratching at the fabric with his claws. They gained another vital few yards.

Tristan bent and placed down the music box on the ground, then risked a glance behind him. The woodland had thinned, and his heart gave a leap as he recognized the looming hulk of his new house through the trees.

"My house is just over there!"

Carys nodded. "Run, while he's distracted."

Tristan didn't need telling twice. He grabbed her hand and began to sprint through the undergrowth, heedless of the noise, lifting his knees high to clear the fallen branches and brambles. Carys, thank God, kept up with him; he tugged at her arm, urging her onward, wrenching her upright when she stumbled, dragging her along with him by sheer force.

Behind them, the bear gave a bellow of irritation.

Tristan didn't dare look back; he could hear the bear give chase, crashing through the undergrowth with terrifying speed.

They burst from the cover of the trees and emerged on one side of the pot-filled gardens. In the moonlight the neat rows of shrubs formed a nightmare labyrinth between them and the safety of the house.

Tristan's lungs were burning with exertion, his thighs on fire from the sudden sprint.

No time to reach the house. Too far. The bear would be on them before he could kick open the door. The stables? No, they'd be cornered—

A series of rhythmic grunts sounded behind them. Tristan whirled Carys out to the side, out of the line of fire, and leveled his pistol at the huge shape barreling toward them.

He shot blindly into the darkness. The powder flashed, briefly illuminating the beast, but the single shot went wide. It splintered a sapling, and the bear barely checked his pace.

"Bollocks." Tristan tossed the spent pistol aside and whirled around again, searching for an escape. "This way!" He tugged Carys's hand and stumbled toward the mounds of earth that marked the future site of his orangery. They'd only just dug the foundations.

"Run!" he urged breathlessly. "And when I say jump, jump as far as you can."

"Yes."

He glanced at her. Her face was pale in the moonlight, her eyes wide with fear, but her chin was set in a determined line. Together they sprinted forward, with Tristan desperately trying to gauge the distance and the perfect time to leap.

The black pit of a newly dug foundation yawned in front of them, five feet wide and fifteen feet deep.

"Jump!" he bellowed.

He pushed off and threw himself forward with all his might and felt Carys do the same. For one soundless moment they hung suspended in the air above the drop, and then they both landed on the mound of earth piled on the opposite side.

He fell to his knees at the impact, felt a tug as the seam of his jacket ripped beneath his arm. Since he was still clutching Carys's hand, she tumbled down with him, and they both scrabbled madly for purchase in the shifting soil. He turned to see the enormous bear almost upon them, his jaws wide in a snarl. And then, in a blur of dark fur and flashing claws, he half tumbled, half slid into the pit.

The bear's bellow of fury mingled with Tristan's shout of triumph as he realized his plan had worked. Still clutching Carys's hand, he edged forward and peered over the side of the trench. His calculations had been correct—the sides were vertical, crumbling soil. Despite his size, the bear wasn't big enough to climb out, nor could he gain purchase on the muddy walls. He was trapped.

"Dear God!" Carys panted, her voice quavering with emotion. "Is he stuck in there?"

"I bloody well hope so."

Her brow furrowed. "He isn't hurt, is he?"

Tristan bit back an incredulous laugh. "*Isn't hurt?* That thing was about to eat us!"

"Well, you can't blame him for that. He's only acting on instinct. The poor thing's never been treated well by humans. It's no wonder he feels the need to attack."

Tristan shook his head and pulled her back from the edge, then staggered to his feet and steered her a safe distance away, only stopping when they neared the terrace. His heart was still pounding in his chest and now that the immediate danger was over he felt both weak-limbed and utterly invincible. He'd been sure they were about to be mauled to death.

"I think that just knocked ten years off my life," he panted.

Carys tugged her hand from his and bent double, trying to catch her own breath. "That's the bear from the circus," she gasped. "We need to let them know where he is."

"Not yet." Tristan shook his head. Elation, pure primitive emotion, was coursing through his veins. His hands were shaking.

Both of them were covered in mud. Carys's hair was a wild tangle around her face, and her skin was milky pale in the moonlight. He'd never seen anything more beautiful.

She could have been seriously hurt. She could have been killed.

His stomach clenched. God, he couldn't imagine a world without her in it. He would have fought that beast with his bare hands to protect her. He would have died for her.

It was that simple. And that complicated.

She straightened and glanced up at him, those bottom-less green eyes of hers searching his face, and he didn't even question his desire. He simply reached out, caught her face between his muddy palms, and pulled her in for a kiss.

She came to him with a tiny whimper of relief, as if she was as desperate for this touch as he was. She grasped his lapels as his lips found hers and he groaned into her mouth. Urgency seized him, to touch, to taste—every one of his senses needed reassurance that she was safe. Alive.

He needed to be inside her. Now.

She made a low moan of protest as he dragged his lips from hers.

"Need you," he managed, barely able to form the words. His brain was a mess. He could hardly think. Hardly speak. She'd ruined him.

She tightened her fingers. "Yes."

That was all the permission he needed. He recaptured her lips and in the same moment tugged her shirt roughly from her breeches. *Why the hell wasn't she wearing skirts?*

She caught his urgency. Her small hands pulled his own shirt free. His remaining pistol fell to the ground with a thump.

They sank to the grass in a tangle of limbs. He rolled over her, half covering her as he unbuttoned the falls of her breeches and did the same to his own in a desperate blur of motion. His fingers were jerky and uncoordinated with need.

Too many clothes. Breeches. Boots.

God damn it.

His cock sprang free, hard as iron, as he shoved her breeches down over her slim hips. She tried to help and their hands tangled, adding to the desperation. She wasn't wearing drawers. He kissed her again, harder, deeper. Sweet, decadent darkness and bright, singing life.

He slid his fingers between her legs. She was slick, wet, and he entered her with his finger, then another. The floral, addictive scent of her mingled with the damp grass and the mud; every beat of his heart sent it coursing through his blood. He pumped his fingers, loving the way she clutched at him, the gorgeous hot slide toward oblivion.

Her nails dug into his shoulders. "God, Tristan. Yes."

He wanted to push himself inside her now, this very minute, but her riding boots had stopped her breeches midthigh, trapping her legs together.

In a swift move he withdrew his hand and rolled her over, urging her up onto her hands and knees. He pressed himself behind her, his chest to her back, and nudged her legs apart.

His cock slid into the furrow between them, sliding in her wetness, and he couldn't contain his groan of bliss.

She gasped as she comprehended this new, wicked possibility. "Like this? Oh!"

She wriggled her backside, urging him on, and he almost blacked out, the pleasure was so great. He changed the angle of his hips and then—sweet miracle—he was inside her, pushing deep.

He couldn't contain his groan. She arched her back and he pressed his head to her shoulder with a throaty curse.

He had no finesse. This was filthy and elemental and he'd never felt so desperate for anyone, anything, in his life. He drew back, grinding his teeth against the almost unbearable pleasure, then pushed inside her again. Her inner muscles tightened around him as if she wanted to keep him there forever. He thrust again, harder, then stilled in panic, afraid he'd been too rough, but she simply reached back and caught the back of his head, pulling his face down into the lee of her shoulder with a little laugh.

"Yes. Show me. Everything."

The last of his control vanished. She wasn't a prim society girl he needed to coddle. She was Carys, fierce and demanding, and she could take everything he wanted to give.

Thank fucking God.

His lungs were burning, his heart bursting in his chest, and he let himself go. He thrust into her, again and again, gasping her name as he felt her flutter around him. He clutched her hips, and she rocked back on him, catching the rhythm as if they'd done this a thousand times. The world spun away. They were just two bodies, vital and free, sending a glorious two-fingered gesture of defiance to the universe.

She moaned his name as her climax hit. Her body clamped around his and the rhythmic pulses triggered his own release. He tightened his arms, buried deep inside her, and convulsed with shudders of bliss.

Awareness slowly crept back to his sluggish brain. The sounds of the night intruded: the angry grunts of the bear as he tried to escape the pit, the calls of the birds in the trees. He rolled them both to the side, sliding from her body as he did so, and hugged her tight against his chest.

Carys let out a delighted, breathless laugh. "Now I see why you said I needed more lessons. I had no idea you could do it *that* way!"

Tristan's heart was still pounding, but the cool night air was rapidly restoring his wits. A doom-laden weight settled on his chest.

He'd finished inside her.

Disbelief and self-recrimination fought for supremacy. How could he have forgotten himself so completely? *Damn it all.* This was everything he'd sworn to avoid—an entanglement of epic proportions. What if she fell pregnant? He'd be honor bound to offer for her, and she'd be so devoid of options that she'd have no choice but to accept, or face scandal and ruination. They'd both be trapped.

He gazed blankly over her shoulder and tried to think logically, but it was impossible to think with her nestled so trustingly in his arms. God, he'd become as impetuous as she was. And the worst thing was, he didn't entirely dislike it.

A strange, self-destructive part of him wasn't even outraged by what they'd done. It was almost as if he *wanted* his fate to be sealed.

He frowned into the darkness. *Did* he want to be married to her? Two weeks ago he would have answered with a resounding *no* . . . and yet the idea wasn't truly unappealing. Being bound to this brilliant, irresistible creature for the rest of his life wasn't the worst thing he could imagine. In fact, being married to anyone else—to someone as cool and passionless as Lavinia, for example—seemed far worse.

Carys might be infuriating and unpredictable, but she was the one person in the world who made him truly come alive. For years she'd spurred him to outrage and frustration, and now she pushed him to the heights of passionate sensation. She kindled a fire inside him, and he wasn't sure it would ever burn out.

Tristan shook his head. He would think about their personal predicament later. They had more pressing matters to deal with. Like a bear in a pit. And the fact that *her* pet was still missing.

God, what a night.

Chapter 37

"We have to move," Tristan said quietly.

Carys sighed in reluctant assent. Her body was still tingling, her mind fuzzy with delight at the deliciously rough way Tristan had just made love to her.

The fact that he'd given himself so completely gave her a rush of purely feminine satisfaction. Such frantic lovemaking was probably just a natural reaction to their near-death encounter with the bear, but even so, she cherished the way Tristan had been so desperate. It had been impetuous and unplanned—and oddly endearing.

Who would have thought people could make love on their knees, like animals? It made sense, of course, considering humans were animals too, but she'd never imagined it could be so enjoyable.

How many more ways were there that Tristan hadn't shown her yet? She wanted to try them all.

But only with him.

Her spirits sank. Oh, she was in so much trouble.

He sat up behind her and the rush of cool air against her backside brought her fully back to reality. There was dampness between her legs—both her own and that which Tristan had left. Her heart stilled.

He hadn't pulled out of her before he spilled his seed.

Dear God, they'd been so lost to sensation they hadn't even noticed, but would he think she'd done it on purpose, to try to entrap him into some kind of a relationship?

Her stomach tensed. Surely he knew her better than that? She'd never marry a man simply because he'd compromised her.

She took a deep, steadying breath. This was not the time to fall apart. There might not be any consequences from this moment of rashness. She hadn't conceived from her coupling with Howe, had she? Luck had been on her side then. She might be equally fortunate this time. Yes, she'd been stupid, but there was no point in worrying about it now. Time enough to panic if she missed her monthly courses.

With awkward, fumbling fingers she pushed down the tails of her shirt and tucked them into her breeches, then got to her feet. Her limbs still felt shaky.

She turned to Tristan. "We need to find the circus owner and tell him what's happened to his bear."

"Agreed. We can't leave him here all night. He might dig his way out." Tristan bent and retrieved his pistol from the grass. With one long, searching look at her face—which made her want to squirm under his scrutiny—he turned and headed off around the side of the building. "The road to Trellech's this way. Come on."

Carys threw a last glance at the pit containing the hapless bear, then tramped after him. She had no idea of the time. Had her absence—and Tristan's—been noted? Would her family be worried? Had Buttercup been found?

Tristan was striding along as if all the devils in hell were after him, and she had to quicken her pace to keep up. Within minutes they reached the end of the long drive and started down the tree-lined road. Her legs were aching at the unaccustomed exercise, and she was about to tell him to slow down when he stopped and held up his hand in a gesture for silence. She stilled a few paces behind him, and heard what he had: the clanking sound of a wagon and men's voices, just around the bend.

Her mood lifted. They were still some distance from the village, but the circus owner must already be aware that his bear was loose. He and his men were clearly out looking for the creature.

She started forward eagerly, but Tristan caught her arm.

"No," he whispered. "Wait."

He steered her to the side of the road and pushed her into the cover of the trees, and she bit back a growl of impatience. The man expected trouble at every turn. Perhaps it was a remnant of his years of being in the army, or maybe their run-in with the bear had made him overly protective, but while she appreciated him looking out for her safety, this, surely, was an overabundance of caution.

"Hoi!" A masculine shout hailed the vehicle from the opposite side of the road. The horses drew to a halt.

With his finger to his lips, Tristan ushered her forward, using the foliage as cover. The wheeled bear cage had stopped in the middle of the road. A burly man stood at the horses' heads, while two more figures were conversing to one side.

"Have you found it yet?" The urgent demand carried easily to them in the still night air.

"No, damn it. The devil's still out there," came the reply.

Tristan sucked in a breath. "That's *Howe*."

Carys squinted, trying to make out the faces beneath the hats. "Don't be silly. He's back at the house looking for Buttercup. Why would he be out here?"

"He'll be found, soon enough," the first man said. "We can't let it delay the delivery."

Carys gasped. That *was* Howe. She'd know those whining, dissatisfied tones anywhere.

"What are they up to?" Tristan murmured.

Howe tilted his chin at the empty wagon. "It's all there?"

"Aye. Just as 'Is Lordship ordered."

Carys wrinkled her nose. That second man was the circus owner; she recognized his battered top hat.

"You don't mind if I check?" Howe's tone was sarcastic, belligerent. "Not that I don't trust you, of course, but it's my neck in the noose if it's not right."

The circus owner swept his hand toward the empty cage. "Be my guest." He reached over and slid open the bolt that fastened the door on one side. The bars swung open, and Howe, to her amazement, climbed up into the cage.

"What's he doing?" she whispered.

Tristan shrugged.

As they watched, Howe proceeded to kick around in the straw that lined the bottom of the cage. Huge clumps fell through the bars onto the road. When he'd cleared a patch, he reached down and caught at something in the middle of the floor. Carys assumed it was one of the iron rings used to secure the bear's chains, but to her surprise a section of the floor lifted up. It was a hidden trapdoor. Howe leaned over and reached inside, and whatever he found clearly satisfied him.

He nodded. "Good."

The circus owner spat on the floor, an eloquent indication of his disdain. "As I said. I'm getting my cut. I ain't greedy for more."

His tone suggested it was Christopher himself who was guilty of that sin.

Howe released the trapdoor with a heavy thud, jumped down, and brushed his hands on his coat. "Your contact will be waiting at the harbor. His name's Masson. Give him the money and leave, and you'll be paid when you get back to London. His Lordship will see to it."

The circus owner wiped his nose on his sleeve. He nodded at his bulky friend, who was still standing at the horses' heads. "All right. Let's go, Will."

He clambered up onto the wooden seat. Will joined him, rocking the carriage with his weight, and the circus man tipped his hat to Howe in mocking deference.

"Pleasure doin' business with you."

Howe stepped back, and Carys crouched low as the empty wagon continued along the road. She lowered her face and held her breath as it passed, but their dark, mud-covered clothing was the perfect camouflage.

Tristan's hand on her sleeve held her back until the sound of the horses' hooves faded away. She glanced at him in question, scarcely able to see his face in the shadows, and he leaned over so his lips were close to her ear. "Stay here. I'll get Howe."

She nodded. Howe had watched the cart roll out of sight, but now he turned up the collar of his coat and began to trudge toward them.

Tristan slid into the shadows, silent as a cat. As Howe drew level with her, Tristan materialized in the road behind him.

"Nice night for a stroll," he drawled.

Howe nearly jumped out of his skin. He turned with an undignified yelp as Tristan caught him by the collar. His hat tumbled to the ground, revealing a face rigid with panic.

"Montgomery!" he panted. "Good God, man, you almost scared me to death!" His face fell as he suddenly realized the ramifications of Tristan being there. He tried to brazen it out. "Hoi, did you find the bear?"

Tristan's jaw hardened. "Oh, we found a bear. But not the one you claimed was loose. We found an entirely different, far more dangerous animal. *Explain*."

Howe's mouth opened and closed like a fish out of water. "I don't know what you're talking about."

"Bollocks!" Tristan growled. "The bear that should have been in that cage"—he stabbed the air in the direction of the departed circus cart—"was loose in the woods, and I think you were perfectly aware of that fact. You deliberately sent us into harm's way."

Howe gulped and tried to pull his coat from Tristan's grip.

Carys stood, relishing Howe's look of dismay as she, too, stepped into the road. She placed her hands on her hips.

"Yes, Christopher. Explain. Where's Buttercup? And what are you up to with those men?"

Howe was still trying to extricate himself from Tristan's hold. Tristan lost his patience, grabbed his wrist, and twisted it up behind his back, effectively imprisoning him.

Howe let out a shriek of pain. "Aah! Stop! That hurts!"

"Answer her," Tristan demanded.

Howe bent over to relieve his discomfort. "Your precious bear's still in his cage," he panted. "I gave him a pitcher of cider. He drank the lot and went to sleep."

"But . . . why send us out into the woods?" Carys frowned.

"Because the circus bear escaped when they tried to move him into another cage. He ran off and I knew you'd be the best person to deal with it."

"So why didn't you tell us we were looking for that bear? You could have warned us. We could have been killed!"

Tristan gave the still-flailing Howe a shake that produced another howl. "He couldn't tell us," he said grimly. "Because that would reveal he had something to do with it."

"That's not true!"

"We just heard you discussing it with those men." Tristan's voice was hard. "What's hidden in the cage?"

Howe's face paled even more in the moonlight. "Nothing."

Tristan shook him, hard enough to rattle his teeth. His expression was fiercer than Carys had ever seen it.

"Stop lying to me." He swung Howe round so he was facing Carys. "*Look at her*," Tristan ordered. "She could have been killed, you bastard. It was a miracle we escaped. Don't tell me it was for 'nothing.'" He glanced over at Carys and his eyes met hers. "I know I promised not to hurt him unless it was self-defense, but surely—"

Carys nodded. "Oh, this is definitely an exception. Hit him. He deserves it."

Tristan raised his fist and Howe cringed in fear. "No! Wait! It's gold. Gold in the cage."

Tristan paused. "Gold? What for? Where's it going?"

"To France," Howe sagged in defeat. "It's for the Emperor."

"Bonaparte?" Carys gasped. "Where's it from? *You* don't have a penny to your name."

"I can't tell you!" Howe wailed. "He'll kill me. He said he'd hold me responsible for every guinea."

"Who?" Tristan growled. "Tell, me, Howe, or I'll finish you right here." He tugged the pistol from his waistband and pressed it to Howe's temple. Carys blinked. She'd forgotten Tristan had the second weapon. It wasn't ready to be fired, of course, but Howe didn't know that.

"Lord Holland!" Howe gasped.

Carys's mouth dropped open. "Lord Holland?"

"Why did he get *you* to help him?" Tristan demanded.

"I lost a fortune to him at cards. I can't pay, so he said I had to do this for him instead."

Carys gave a humorless laugh. "He blackmailed you? Oh, that's perfect. How do you like being on the receiving end? Not much fun, is it?"

"He said he'd turn me over to the moneylenders," Howe cried pitifully. "They'll break my legs. Or worse."

"I wouldn't blame them," Carys snapped. "Why is the money here, though? In Wales?"

"The ports near London are too closely watched by the coast guard. Here, the smugglers can still get through."

Carys shook her head in disbelief. "So you hid the gold

beneath the bear. It's the perfect hiding place—who'd be stupid enough to get near the creature to check for a trap-door?" She frowned in sudden recollection. "You were planning this back at the fair at Hampstead Heath. I saw you."

Howe shrugged, but didn't deny it.

"Does your wife know about this?" Tristan asked.

"God, no. She'd hurt me worse than the moneylenders."

Carys glanced at Tristan. "It's not hard to believe that Lord Holland's behind something like this. He's made no secret of his sympathy for the French."

"This is more than sympathy," Tristan's voice vibrated with quiet fury. "It's *treason*. Thousands of men are dead because of Bonaparte and his allies. My colleagues. My *friends*." He pressed the barrel of his gun to Howe's sweating temple. "And this bastard sends the man gold." He cocked the pistol with his thumb. Howe whimpered. "You'll be lucky if you don't hang for this, Howe," he growled. "I should do you a favor and put a bullet in you right now."

Carys's heart was pounding. Tristan looked so fierce, so coldly furious, she could quite believe he would go through with his threat. Her heart clenched for all the trauma he'd suffered during the war. His rage was entirely justified, and a wave of admiration caught her off guard. His control was impressive. She would probably have punched Christopher in the teeth before now.

"We need *proof*," she said softly. "Otherwise it's just our word against his." She glanced behind her, along the empty road. "We need to get that gold."

Tristan nodded. "Agreed."

Chapter 38

Carys glanced at Howe. "You can't shoot him, Tristan."

Tristan gave a growl of disappointment. "You're right." He uncocked his pistol with a click and replaced it in his waistband. "He's not worth hanging for."

Howe sagged to the ground. "Oh, thank God."

Tristan sent him a look full of loathing. "Shut up, or I'll throw you in the pit with the bear." He took a step toward Carys, but Howe seemed to recover some of his spirit. He surged to his feet, fists flailing.

"No! You won't stop that shipment!"

Tristan swung his arm and clipped him neatly on the jaw. Howe's eyes rolled back in his head as he crumpled to the ground in a boneless heap.

Tristan shoved him with his boot. "Don't worry, he's not dead," he grumbled. "Just unconscious."

"That's a very useful trick." Carys tried to look disapproving, but a surge of savage satisfaction bloomed inside her. She'd never been able to physically hurt Howe herself. Having Tristan deliver the blow she'd always longed to give was just as pleasing.

"Should we tie him up?"

"No. He'll be out for a while. We have to stop that coach. Come on."

Carys caught his sleeve. "How? Even if we catch up with it, those men are armed. We have one pistol between us. We can't hold them up like a couple of highwaymen." She glanced down at their outfits. "Even if we are dressed like them."

"Well, we can't just let them get away either." Tristan picked Howe's hat from the ground and settled it on his own head. "We'll think of something."

Carys sighed. "All right. The road loops around that next rise and doubles back on itself. If we cut across the fields we can get ahead of them."

"Lead on."

She shot him a teasing look from under her lashes. "You know, I've always admired you in evening dress, but you make a very passable ruffian."

His brows rose, and his eyes darkened. "Oh, I do, do I?"

He caught her waist and dragged her up against his chest. His hand slid down to cup her bottom and he gave her a playful squeeze. "Poor George Brummell would faint dead away if he saw me dressed like this, but I'd very much like to show you how much of a ruffian I can be. Unfortunately, now is not the time." He pressed a swift kiss to her lips. "We'll continue this discussion another time, my lady."

Carys bit back a groan of disappointment, but nodded. "This way."

With her in the lead, they pushed through the hedge and hastened across the adjoining fields, heading steeply downhill. Mud splashed their boots as they leapt over a stream and scrambled up the opposite bank.

Carys was panting when they finally slipped back into the thick strand of trees that lined the road. She hushed Tristan, listening for the telltale sound of the cart, and her pulse quickened as she heard it descending the lane. "Now what?"

A dark shape swooped low across the road, narrowly missing her head.

"Huginn!" she gasped, horrified at the bird's unfortunate timing. "Shoo! Go home, you pest."

The raven let out a soft caw of greeting.

The rumbling of the cart was getting closer. "I have a plan," Tristan whispered. "My French is pretty good, thanks to my time on the Continent. I'll pretend to be their contact."

"What if they recognize you?"

He sent her a lazy grin. "In this outfit? Tristan Montgomery wouldn't be seen *dead* wearing this." He touched Howe's hat and tugged the brim low over his eyes, then pressed the pistol into her hands. The wooden stock was warm from his body.

"There's no time to load it. Hide."

Unable to think of a better plan, Carys ducked down behind a fallen tree trunk. Huginn flew down, hopped onto her shoulder, and pecked at her hair. She stroked his wing in greeting. "It's nice to see you too, but you have to go!" she whispered.

Huginn merely fluttered up onto the mossy tree stump and perched on the end as if ready to be entertained, and

Carys cursed silently as the familiar silhouette of Muninn circled down and landed in a tree across the lane.

Tristan positioned himself in the center of the road and her heart pounded as the cart clattered around the bend. Tristan raised his arm in greeting and the driver drew the horses to a stop with a startled command.

"Hoi, you! Stand aside!" The barrel of a pistol glinted in the moonlight as the second man lifted it from the seat beside him. "Stand aside, I say."

Tristan held his hands higher, displaying his lack of weapons. "*Non, non,* monsieur," he said, in heavily accented French. "*Je suis* Masson. Masson." He patted his chest to underscore his words. "I collect. For Lord 'Olland. You 'ave for me?"

The man frowned, apparently not entirely convinced by Tristan's performance. He settled the pistol on his knee, still pointed at Tristan. The driver peered suspiciously into the hedgerow, clearly expecting some sort of attack.

"What you doin' out 'ere, man? We was to meet you at the 'arbor."

Tristan gave an excellent Gallic shrug. "Custom patrol. We move to ozzer beach."

The man sniffed. "What's the password?"

Carys heart sank. *Password?* Howe hadn't mentioned a password.

Tristan, however, seemed entirely unfazed. He gave another shrug. "Password? I forget password."

The man cocked his weapon. "You was supposed to give me a password," he said belligerently. "I ain't givin' you the blunt until you tell me what it is."

Tristan opened his mouth, but whatever he'd been about to say was interrupted by the sound of a rifle being cocked just to Carys's right. She snapped her head around and gaped at Huginn in horror. The wicked bird had produced a perfect imitation of the firearm.

The circus owner whipped around, trying to pinpoint the source of the sound, and her heart stopped in her throat as the barrel of his gun pointed straight at her. She didn't dare move a muscle.

"What was that?" he demanded.

Carys glanced at Tristan, and was amazed to see his teeth flash white in a wicked grin.

"Ah, my friend. Zat is the reason I don't need ze password." He chuckled. "My men surround you. Put your guns away."

Her heart swelled in admiration of his brilliant buff. He'd clearly remembered the ravens' ability to mimic. But would the smugglers believe it?

As quickly as she dared, she reached over and nudged Huginn with her hand, trying to make him repeat the sound, and to her delight he obliged.

You're getting extra strawberries for a whole year, she promised him silently.

The driver of the cart swore viciously. He cocked his own weapon, but with perfect timing the sound of another rifle came from the opposite side of the lane.

Carys almost laughed aloud.

Muninn, you glorious mischief-maker! You copy whatever Huginn does, don't you?

Tristan took full advantage. He gestured calmly at the two men. "Please, messieurs, get down. I take ze cart from 'ere."

The man in the top hat shook his head. "You ain't takin' this wagon. I need it for my bear."

"If we ever catch the bugger again," the other man grunted. He uncocked his weapon and lowered it slowly to the seat.

"I leave ze cart in ze village." Tristan said dismissively. "You come in ze morning."

The circus man looked like he might argue, but Tristan made an impatient gesture with his arms. "*Allez!* Make haste, or we miss ze tide."

With a growl of assent, the other man lowered his weapon, and both men clambered down from the cart.

Tristan kept his chin down, his hat shielding his eyes. "Merci, messieurs. *L'Empereur* is in your debt."

The circus owner spat onto the road. "That's what I fink of your *empereur*!" he growled. "I'm only doin' this fer the blunt."

Carys glimpsed Tristan's grin beneath his hat as he clambered up onto the box and took up the reins. "As are we all, monsieur," he said silkily. He snapped the reins and clucked his tongue to move the horses forward.

"Oy, wait a minute," the circus man growled belatedly. "You can't just leave us 'ere."

Tristan shrugged. "My men will be 'appy to keep you company." He gave a shrill whistle. "Armand! *Avec moi. Vous autres, restez avec ces anglais jusqu'à ce que nous soyons partis. S'ils font du bruit, tirez-leur dessus et cachez les corps. Retrouvez-nous à la plage.*"

Carys's eyes widened at Tristan's perfect French. The man continued to surprise.

"What's that you're sayin'?" the burly man demanded. "Bloody foreigners."

Since Tristan had glanced in her direction, Carys deduced

that she was Armand, and that he meant for her to join him on the box. She hastily stuffed the ends of her hair into the collar of her jacket and hunched her shoulders, then stepped out of the trees, keeping her face averted, but making sure the men saw the pistol she held.

They took a step back in surprise. If they hadn't entirely believed Tristan's tale about being surrounded, her appearance had them doubting again.

"It means," Tristan said, recapturing their attention as she scrambled up onto the cart next to him, "that my men are to watch you until we are gone. If you make a fuss, zey will shoot you. I suggest you go 'ome." He made a swirling gesture with his finger. "*Allez.*"

The two men apparently swallowed his tale. They both turned and started trudging back up the lane. "You'd better not damage my cart!" the circus owner called over his shoulder.

Tristan sent him an airy wave and spurred the horses.

Carys hardly dared to breathe as the cart picked up the pace. She kept expecting the men to realize they'd been duped, for the sound of a bullet to ring out, but as the distance increased and the two men disappeared behind them she allowed herself to slump onto the seat with a gasp of relief.

"I cannot believe we got away with that!"

Tristan glanced away from the horses to give her a triumphant grin. "Well, to tell you the truth, neither can I," he admitted with a chuckle. "But 'fortune favors the brave' and all that. The real triumph belongs to your birds. They were magnificent."

As if sensing his praise, Huginn and Muninn both burst from the trees, wheeling overhead and then swooping back around the cart with a series of noisy caws that definitely sounded as if they were celebrating. Carys laughed in delight.

"You made good use of their tricks," she said. "That was quick thinking. Especially for a Montgomery."

"Why, thank you." Tristan smiled. "I do believe that's the most complimentary thing a Davies has ever said to a Montgomery."

She nudged his shoulder with her own, as she often did with her brothers. "I thought we made an excellent team."

His answering silence made her look up at him in question, and her heart missed a beat at the look in his eyes.

"I thought so too."

Chapter 39

One of the horses tossed its head, breaking the odd intensity of the moment, and Carys flushed and looked away.

"You know, the collective noun for a group of ravens is an *unkindness* of ravens, but I think we should change it to a *rescue* of ravens. Huginn and Muninn saved the day."

"They did indeed."

They rode on for another half mile, then Tristan slowed the horses to a walk. "I want to see whatever's in that cage."

Carys pointed to a pair of stone markers ahead. "That's Davies land. That track leads back to the stables. You can turn in there."

Tristan did so, and after a short distance Trellech's crenellated towers appeared on the horizon. Carys felt a warm tingle of relief. *Home.* Lights from the party still shone brightly at most of the windows.

Tristan steered the cart beneath an enormous oak tree

and leapt down, and she wrinkled her nose at the familiar
smell of bear droppings and hay as he pulled back the metal
latch and swung open the cage door. He climbed up, heedless of the dirt, and she followed.

The trapdoor opened with a squeal to reveal a large black
metal box within.

"You can do the honors," Tristan offered.

Carys reached down and flipped open the lid. The trunk
was neatly divided into sections, each one filled with small
white cotton drawstring bags. One had come open—probably
the one Howe had inspected—and she sucked in a breath
at the glitter of golden coins that spilled from the neck. She
tipped the contents out into her palm.

"My God! I've never seen so much money in one place!
It's like a pirate's treasure!"

Tristan inspected the contents of another bag. "This isn't
just English gold. Look, that's a French louis d'or, and this is
a twenty-franc piece. This one's from Austria."

"How much do you think is here?"

He lifted the top shelf to reveal further divided shelves
beneath. "Hard to say, but if that's all gold too—then at least
ten thousand pounds. Bloody hell!"

He stood, almost hitting his head on the wooden roof of
the cage. Seeing him in there, his broad shoulders silhou-
etted against the bars, Carys felt another rush of pity for the
vicious bear. Such a huge animal would be utterly miserable
in there with so little space to move.

She dropped the coins she held back into the box and shut
the lid. "Say what you like about magic, Tristan Montgomery, but this is the work of the pookas. That fairy fire led us
to both danger *and* riches tonight."

He sent her a look that could have rivaled the Sahara for dryness. "Yes. Magic. That's what it was. Of course."

A piercing shriek and a burst of light interrupted Carys's defense, and she clapped her hand to her heart in fright. "Oh!" she breathed, as another explosion lit up the sky above the house. "They've started the fireworks."

She jumped from the cart to watch the display. "It must be midnight. We have to get back to the house."

Tristan climbed down and refastened the cage door. "How are we going to explain this to your brothers?"

The elation that had warmed her disappeared, replaced by a wave of anxiety. "Oh, God, I hadn't thought of that."

So much had happened in such a short space of time she could scarcely believe it herself. Even with the gold as proof, the night's adventures had raised more questions than answers.

"We need to unload this at the house, then send people to get the bear back into his cage," she said. "And we'll need to tell the authorities what we've found."

Tristan nodded. "Do you think there's even the smallest hope of us getting into the house unseen?"

"The stables are full of extra carriages." She glanced down at their muddy, disheveled clothing. "With a bit of luck we'll be mistaken for groomsmen."

"Another dream come true." Tristan let out a hollow laugh. "I *knew* attending a Davies party would end in disaster. It gives me no pleasure to be proved right."

Carys rolled her eyes. "Oh, rubbish. It gives you *immense* pleasure to be proved right."

Tristan's hand streaked out. He caught her wrist and spun her into his chest, and her heart swooped in sudden excitement at the gleam in his eye.

"I'll tell you what would give me immense pleasure," he growled.

"What?" She held her breath, hoping for a kiss.

"Spanking your pert behind." He matched actions to words, swatting playfully at the seat of her breeches, and she whirled away with a crow of outrage.

"Now get up on that cart," he ordered with a chuckle. "We've got some explaining to do."

Feeling rather deflated, Carys resumed her seat and they set off toward the house, illuminated at irregular intervals by Gryff and Maddie's impressive fireworks.

"I want to make sure Buttercup really is in his cage, and that Howe wasn't lying," she said. "Oh, goodness. I'd forgotten about Howe! We left him in the road. Should we send someone back to get him?"

"He's probably come round by now. And if he hasn't, his two circus friends will find him."

"If they do, they'll know they've been tricked."

"True. In which case, I expect all three of them will leave the area very swiftly. I can't imagine they'll want to explain to Lord Holland how they lost his money." He paused, thinking. "I suppose if they *don't* find Howe, then the circus folk will be out all night searching for the bear. They'll go to the village in the morning, expecting to find this wagon. They'll only realize they've been duped when it's not there."

"Either way," Carys said, "Howe knows we're on to him. He might go to the circus to warn them."

Tristan snorted. "Unlikely. There's no honor among thieves. He won't care about anyone's skin but his own. I bet he's already halfway to London."

"Let's hope so. But I do feel sorry for Victoria. What's she going to do if he disappears?"

"Crack open a bottle of champagne, probably," Tristan said drily.

They avoided the crowded stable block, and drove the cart around the back of Buttercup's enclosure. After a brief search, and much to her relief, Carys found the bear fast asleep beneath a tent of branches, with an empty stoneware cider flagon on the ground next to him. Even the flashes and bangs of the fireworks failed to rouse him.

At her insistence, Tristan unloaded the heavy box of bullion and hid it just inside the entrance to the cage, covering it with a mound of fresh hay.

"There, Buttercup will make the perfect guardian until we decide what to do with it." Carys dusted off her hands in satisfaction. "Now we just need to get back into the house without being seen. I doubt any guests will be in the library at this hour. We can climb in through one of the windows along the west side."

"Just like a bloody Shakespeare farce," Tristan grumbled.

As they started back through the gardens Carys marveled at everything that had happened since they'd been interrupted by Howe. It had only been a few hours ago, but *everything* had changed. And not necessarily for the better.

Her heart began to pound as she remembered the tryst in the mud.

Oh, God, would Tristan feel that he'd been put in an impossible position by their recklessness?

Montgomery he might be, but he was an inherently decent man. Even if her brothers accepted the explanation of the bear chase and the smuggling as the reason for their absence, if anyone *else* at the party had noticed their disappearance there could still be trouble.

They couldn't make the truth public. Neither Howe nor Lord Holland deserved their discretion, but Carys would never salvage her own reputation if it meant ruining Victoria's standing in society in exchange.

She bit her lip as she and Tristan slipped around the darkened side of the house toward the library. Even if *nobody* suspected anything between herself and Tristan, she had a sinking feeling that Tristan himself might prove the problem.

Would he insist on offering for her, even at the expense of his own future plans, if she discovered she was pregnant?

She didn't dare glance over at him as he stalked beside her, but her heart squeezed in her chest as she forced herself to face the truth. She would like nothing better than to be married to him—but only if he wanted her with the same ardor she felt for him.

She could never accept him if he'd only proposed out of guilt. Their physical passion was undeniable, but it would fade to bitterness and resentment without a deeper attachment. Without love. Tristan deserved to be happy with the woman he *chose*, not one who'd been foisted on him because of some foolish indiscretion.

A solitary lamp had been left burning in the library, and Carys breathed a sigh of relief that they might yet be able to slip back to their rooms undetected. She tried the third window from the left; the catch had been broken ever since she could remember and she'd often used it to sneak back inside after some scrape or other.

The window slid upward with a satisfying swish.

As soon as this evening's debacle was over, she would tell Tristan their agreement was at an end. There would be no more trysts. If her monthly courses arrived as usual, then they had nothing to worry about. If they *didn't* arrive . . . well, she would cross that bridge when she came to it. Maybe she'd consider Ellington's offer yet again.

The lamp in the corner suddenly turned up, and she froze with one leg half in and half out of the window. Gryff's elegant frame was folded in one of the wing chairs that flanked the fireplace.

Oh, hell and damnation.

"Oh, do come in," Gryff drawled, and Carys cringed inwardly at the combination of fury and cynicism lacing his tone.

Since there was nothing for it, she scrambled in completely through the window, then stepped aside as Tristan did the same.

Gryff's mouth flattened into a tight line. "Bloody hell, Carys. We've been looking for you everywhere." His piercing gaze flicked to Tristan. "Montgomery. You'd better have a bloody good explanation for why you've been absent for *two whole hours* with my sister."

His gaze roved over the disheveled state of their clothing and Carys tried not to squirm in mortification. Dear God, Gryff hadn't looked at her with such scathing disapproval since she'd tied Morgan's feet together and pushed him into the moat almost a decade ago.

"Now Gryff," she said placatingly. "It's not how it looks."

Gryff's brows rose toward his hairline. "I sincerely hope not. Because it *looks* as though you and Montgomery have been rolling around in the mud. Together. Alone."

Chapter 40

Carys couldn't stop the guilty flush that singed her cheeks. Just when she thought things couldn't get any worse, the door to the library opened and both Rhys and Morgan slipped inside.

Morgan was dressed as Poseidon, complete with a wreath of coral and seaweed. Rhys had come as a Roman gladiator.

"Ah! You've found them!" Rhys took one look at her and his lips quirked into a delighted smile. "Good God, Carys. You haven't been pig wrestling again, have you?"

Morgan's mouth twisted into a wicked grin. "I'd say she's been wrestling something even *worse* than a pig: a Montgomery." He nodded at Tristan. "Evening, Tristan. You're looking . . . rustic."

Gryff ignored their levity. "Are you seriously going to try to tell me there's a perfectly innocent explanation for all this?" He waved his hand to encompass their mud-covered costumes. "A midnight archaeological dig, perhaps?"

Carys could feel her cheeks getting even hotter. She must look an absolute mess. Her hair was loose around her shoulders, her cravat was lost somewhere in the woods, and there wasn't a part of her that wasn't caked in mud.

She glanced over at Tristan. He'd fared no better. She could see the lining of his jacket poking through a rip beneath his arm. His hair was a mass of matted waves, and she was fairly sure she could make out the outline of her own small, muddy handprint on the front of his breeches, dangerously close to his crotch.

Oh, lord.

Gryff glared at her. "Tell me you haven't been making love out there in our gardens?"

She bit her lip, unable to deny it, except to say that, technically, it hadn't been *their* gardens.

Deflection was her only hope, in the same way a dress could divert attention from a small bust with clever detailing. She tried to look surprised. "Didn't you see Howe? He was supposed to give you a message."

"What message?" Gryff growled.

"That Buttercup had escaped. Tristan and I went to look for him. Only, it turns out that Howe was mistaken; it was the bear from the circus that was loose."

Rhys's mouth dropped open. "Howe sent you after *that* bear? Hellfire, Carys, you could have been killed! I'm going to wring his neck."

"No need," Carys said quickly. "Tristan's already . . . had a word with him."

"I hope by 'had a word with him' you mean 'punched his bloody teeth out,'" Morgan said darkly.

Tristan's lips twitched. "That's not too far from the truth."

"Good," all three brothers said, at exactly the same time.

Carys tried to hide her smile. They might be overprotective, but it was nice to be so loved.

"We need to tell you about the circus bear," she went on. "Tristan and I trapped him in a pit over at Tristan's new house. His cage is out there by Buttercup's enclosure."

Gryff raked a hand through his hair. "How on earth—? God, Carys, you do get into some scrapes. Where are the men from the circus? Why aren't *they* dealing with this?"

"That's a long story," Tristan said evenly. "And before we tell it, someone needs to go and put the bear back in his cage before someone gets hurt."

"I'll go," Morgan offered. "I could do with a bit of excitement."

"I'll go too," Rhys said, smirking at Morgan. "In case you get eaten."

"Thank you," Gryff said.

Morgan sent Carys another sly glance. "But don't think you're going to get away with not telling us the rest of this story, miss." His eyes glimmered with amusement. "I can't wait to hear what you've been up to with our dear friend Tristan here."

"Go!" Gryff growled impatiently.

"Fine. But I demand a full accounting when we get back."

Carys nodded, and when the two of them had left Tristan stepped forward until he stood in front of Gryff's chair. "I need a moment alone with Carys."

Gryff got to his feet, and the two men faced each other

like boxers about to kiss gloves at the start of a bout. They
were both tall, almost the same size, and Carys could practically feel the antipathy and mistrust crackling in the air
between them.

"I think you've had more than enough moments alone
with her this evening," Gryff said softly. He turned his head
and trapped her with an accusing stare. "You didn't answer
my question, Carys." He flicked his icy gaze back to Tristan.
"So as head of this household, I'm going to ask *you*, Montgomery. Can you swear you haven't dishonored my sister?"

Carys took a step forward. "Don't be ridiculous, Gryff!
Everyone knows Tristan and I can't stand each other."

Gryff's brows lifted in cynical disbelief. "Oh, come on.
I'm not blind. Nor am I stupid. I've seen the way you two
look at each other. The air practically catches fire whenever
you're in the same room." He leaned closer to Tristan, who
did an admirable job of standing his ground. "Have you
slept with my sister?"

Carys's heart was in her throat. What would Tristan say?
He was so stupidly honorable, he wouldn't even lie to save
his own hide. He opened his mouth, and she closed her eyes,
but a sudden commotion in the hallway interrupted them.

The library door swung open and Howe burst in, with
Lucas, one of the underfootmen, clinging to his sleeve in an
effort to hold him back.

"Damn you, let go of me, you cur!" Howe growled.

"My apologies, my lord," Lucas panted. "I tried to tell
him it was a private room, but he wouldn't listen."

Gryff sent him a nod. "Thank you, Lucas. You may release him. I happen to want a word with Mister Howe."

The underfootman relaxed his grip and Howe shrugged

him off with a snarl of disdain. He strode farther into the room as the servant closed the door.

Gryff glared at him, but Howe's lips curled into an ugly sneer. One side of his jaw was swollen and his left eye was turning a livid shade of purple where Tristan had hit him. Carys bit back a satisfied smile.

"To what do we owe this pleasure?" Gryff drawled. "Because I've heard a rather alarming report about you this evening, Howe."

Howe glared at Carys and Tristan. "Whatever they've told you, it's all lies, to hide the truth."

"And what truth is that?" Gryff asked.

"That your little sister is a whore."

Carys gasped as Gryff's brows lowered in fury. Shame and disbelief caught her by the throat. This scene—or one very like it—had featured as one of her worst nightmares for years. She'd never wanted her brothers to find out about her shameful past with Howe, and certainly not like *this*, like some dreadful gothic melodrama.

"Explain yourself." Gryff's voice was dangerously low.

"She's not a virgin."

Gryff's lips twitched. "I think I'd already arrived at that conclusion myself," he said, with a trace of irony. "But that's between myself and Montgomery. What's it to do with you?"

Carys's stomach somersaulted at this fresh agony of misunderstanding. Gryff clearly thought Howe was insinuating she'd slept with Tristan, not himself. She prayed Howe wouldn't elaborate, that he wouldn't reveal the full extent of her downfall, but he shot her an evil, taunting glance.

"What's it got to do with me?" he jeered. "Oh, plenty. Shall I tell him, Carys? Or will you?"

Tristan stepped in front of her. "Don't say another word, Howe." His voice throbbed with suppressed violence. "Or I'll finish what I started in the lane."

"You can't touch me," Howe scoffed. "Not without ruining her. If you tell anyone what you saw tonight, I'll take her down with me." His lips curled into a jubilant sneer. "Her reputation's my insurance."

Carys's nails pressed into her palms as she clenched her fists. God, Howe was nauseating, using her as a human shield.

Tristan took a threatening step toward him, but Howe shook his head in warning.

"I'll tell everyone I had her first. Who'll marry her then?" He slashed her a smug look. "It's the truth, isn't it, Carys, love? Although I have to say, your performance wasn't much to boast about. Very lackluster, as I recall."

Carys heard Gryff's shocked inhalation and prayed for the floor to swallow her up. It was bad enough that he suspected she'd dishonored herself with Tristan, but now he knew about Howe too.

Oh, God.

In the bristling silence she tensed, fully expecting Gryff to explode, but it was Tristan who surged forward. In three quick strides he grabbed Howe by the neck and propelled him backward into the bookcase behind him with an audible crash.

Howe let out a yell of alarm and clawed at the hand at his throat, but Tristan shoved him even harder, pushing against him with his entire weight. Howe's face began to turn red as he gasped for air.

"You bastard." Tristan gave Howe a violent shake, like a

terrier with a rat. Howe's head thumped against the book-shelves.

Tristan loosened his grip a fraction, and Howe managed to let out a hoarse laugh.

"My God, don't say you've fallen for her wiles too? I thought you had better taste, Montgomery. She's a tart. She'll lift her skirts for anyone." He swiveled his bulging eyes toward Gryff. "She's been hoodwinking you, and the entire *ton*, for years."

Tristan's jacket strained over the muscles in his back as he shoved Howe again. A couple of leather volumes thumped to the floor.

"Her name will never pass your lips!" he growled. "If I hear even a whisper that she's not a virgin I'll know exactly where the rumor came from. I will find you and *hurt you*, Howe. Extensively. Do you understand? There are worse things than death, you bastard. You'll be praying for it when I get through with you."

The absolute certainty in Tristan's voice sent a shiver down Carys's spine. She had no doubt that he would do exactly as he'd threatened.

Howe, it seemed, was coming to the same conclusion. He blanched, his eyes wide.

Tristan leaned in even closer, so his lips were almost level with Howe's ear. "And you're wrong about her never finding a husband. She's going to be my wife."

Carys's mouth dropped open in shock, but Tristan gave Howe another shove for emphasis.

"You hear that? I'm going to marry her, and I don't care how many men she's slept with. If anyone questions her virginity, I will swear on my mother's grave that she came to our marriage untouched. It'll be your word against mine. Who do you think they'll believe?"

"You'd lie for her?" Howe spluttered, incredulous.

"I'd die for her," Tristan said coldly. "And I'd kill for her too. Believe it."

Howe seemed to deflate as all the fight left him. "I believe you!" he gasped. "I swear."

Tristan removed his hand from Howe's throat and stepped back. The other man slid down the bookcase until he sat sprawled on the floor.

Gryff stepped up to stand at Tristan's side in a silent show of masculine solidarity.

"Well, that was enlightening," he drawled.

Chapter 41

She's going to be my wife.

Tristan's furious pronouncement echoed in Carys's ears and she shook her head, stunned. She opened her mouth to say something—anything—to salvage the situation, but Tristan wasn't finished with Howe. He gazed down at him, his expression one of utter disdain.

"You know, even if we don't reveal your involvement with Holland, you're still ruined."

Howe squinted up at him from the floor. "What do you mean?"

Tristan straightened his cuffs in a gesture so instinctive—and so completely ineffective considering the disarray of the rest of his outfit—that Carys felt a ball of emotion clog her throat.

"I mean financially." He stepped back until he stood next to Carys. His shoulder brushed hers. "Ever since I found out that you'd been blackmailing Carys, I've been buying up your vowels at the clubs. I've nearly a thousand pounds' worth."

Carys's chest tightened even more at this new information.

Tristan had been doing that for her?

Howe's face turned a mottled shade of pink. He struggled to his feet and tried to flatten down his disordered neckcloth. "I'll pay you. I'll—"

"You'll leave England. For good," Tristan said coldly.

Howe made an odd, spluttering noise. "But—"

"You and George Brummell can visit France together. He needs to avoid his creditors too."

"You're banishing me?" Howe gaped.

"I'm saving you from a very long stay in debtors' prison, or worse. Think of it as a nice long holiday. I'm sure your wife will send you an allowance of a hundred pounds a year."

"A hundred pounds? I can't live on that!"

"You won't live at all if you stay here," Tristan said sweetly. "If you're not out of the country within the week, I'll have you arrested for treason. Go on. You can take a packet from Bristol to Calais."

"But we're at war with France!" Howe whined. "Bonaparte is in Paris! An Englishman won't be welcome there."

Carys glared at him. "Well, go farther afield, then. To Portugal. Or Egypt. I don't care. So long as I never have to see you again. And I know Victoria will be just as glad to see the back of you too."

"Bravo!" Gryff drawled. He caught Howe's elbow and steered him inexorably to the door. "Lucas?" he called. "See to it that Lord Howe is escorted off the property within the hour."

"He can borrow my carriage," Tristan said with a wicked laugh. "I believe it will be familiar to him."

Howe sent him a look of pure loathing, which Tristan countered with a sarcastic smile. "Off you go. Safe travels."

As the door closed behind a protesting Howe, Carys turned to Gryff.

"We're not really engaged—" She gestured between herself and Tristan. "He just said that to annoy Howe."

"Yes, we are," Tristan countered. He sent Gryff a look that was both a plea and a demand. "I'd like a moment with your sister, Davies."

Gryff shook his head and Carys thought he was going to refuse, but instead he stepped forward and enfolded her in a hug. She was so surprised it took her a second to return the embrace, but when she did he tightened his grip and pressed his cheek to her hair.

"Is what Howe said about you and him true?" he murmured. "Did you really lie with him?"

Carys nodded, her face buried in the folds of his coat. Admitting it was easier when she didn't have to look at him. "Yes."

She felt, as much as heard, his growl. It vibrated in his chest, a sound of anguish and fury. "Christ, Carys. When? How long ago?"

"Almost two years," she mumbled. "My first season. You were away in Portugal."

His arms tightened. "That bastard. Oh, sweetheart, I'm so sorry. But why didn't you tell me? I would have ripped him limb from limb."

A shaky laugh escaped her. "That's exactly why; you would have ripped him limb from limb. Or shot him in a duel. There would have been an enormous scandal. I couldn't bear to bring such disgrace on you all."

Gryff eased his hold and leaned back to look at her face, still keeping hold of her elbows. "You shouldn't have had to deal with it alone." He tilted his chin toward Tristan. "And from what *he* says, Howe's been blackmailing you too."

Her face heated, but she nodded. She might as well make a clean breast of everything.

"Yes."

Gryff's jaw clenched tight as he digested that information, and then he slanted another glance at Tristan. "I don't know what's been going on between the two of you, Montgomery," he said. "Should I thank you for buying up Howe's debts? Or shoot you for seducing my sister?"

Carys caught his sleeve. "Oh, no. You can't blame Tristan. The seducing was all my idea."

"It bloody well wasn't!" Tristan growled.

"It doesn't matter whose idea it was," Gryff said. "The fact of the matter is, you're ruined."

"Not if she marries me," Tristan insisted.

Gryff looked down at her. "Are you really engaged to him?"

"No."

"Yes." Tristan countered.

Gryff shook his head, exasperated. "Good God. Can no one give me a straight answer? Carys, do you *want* to be married to him?"

Heat scalded her cheeks as she fought not to perjure herself. "Not if he's only offering to protect my reputation. If I wanted a marriage like that I could just marry Lord Ellington. And besides, there's no need for us to marry. I'm not ruined publicly. Howe won't say anything. He's leaving the country."

"True, but you're still ruined *privately*," Gryff said. "It wouldn't matter if you were a man, nobody would care, but I'm afraid society holds women to a higher standard. Any potential husband will expect you to be chaste."

"Not *every* potential husband!" Tristan growled. "I don't care if she's slept with an entire cavalry regiment."

Gryff released Carys and studied Tristan as if he were a strange new species. "Why are you so keen to marry her, Montgomery? If it's merely to salve your sense of honor, then let me relieve you of that burden. Carys doesn't have to marry anyone unless she wants to."

"He *doesn't* want to marry me," Carys said miserably. "He said it himself. At the fair."

She turned to face Tristan in time to see his brows draw down in a fearsome frown.

"I did say that," he admitted. "But it wasn't true. Not then, and not now."

His blue gaze caught hers and her stomach flipped. He looked fierce and ever so slightly furious. Cool, collected Tristan was nowhere to be seen.

"I want to marry you because I bloody well can't live without you."

Carys stilled. "What?"

"I *love* you," Tristan said. "I can't imagine marrying anyone else *but* you."

"Oh, bloody hell," Gryff muttered.

Carys opened her mouth, but Gryff shook his head.

"Stop right there. I'm leaving. Tristan, you have your moment alone." He turned on his heel, marched to the door, and closed it behind him with a click.

Chapter 42

The silence that followed Gryff's exit was so heavy Carys was sure she could hear her heart pounding against her ribs. She glanced up at Tristan and found him gazing down at her with a look that made her hot and cold at once.

"You're only asking me because I might be pregnant," she said.

"No, I'm not."

He reached up and cupped her face, sliding his thumb over her chin and across her cheek in a devastating caress. Her skin tingled.

"Would it be so bad?" he asked softly. "Being married to me?"

She could hardly breathe. "Yes. I mean, no. But you don't want me. You want some perfect society hostess, like Lavinia Purser."

He let out a low chuckle. "I thought I did, but this week

has made me realize I need the exact opposite of that." His expression sobered and his eyes darkened with emotion. "I need *you*, Carys. I was so scared when that bear was chasing us. I thought I'd lose you. Or that I'd die without ever telling you how I feel."

He brought his other hand up to cup her face, cradling her as if she was the most precious thing in the world—and not a scandalous, mud-spattered hoyden.

"I love you. I've loved you for years, even when I couldn't admit it to myself. Why do you think the walls in my bedroom are green?"

A glow of happiness was welling up inside her, spreading to every limb, but she was still afraid to hope. "Why?"

"Because I imagined you there. Always."

Her throat felt hot and painfully tight. "Truly?"

"Truly. I want you by my side, to dazzle and charm everyone who comes into your orbit. I've seen you do it a thousand times."

"Only to make you jealous," she admitted.

He let out a strangled laugh. "Well, it worked. I've hated every man who laughed at your jokes, every idiot who's sighed over your figure. The day you wore that bloody handkerchief dress was the worst day of my life."

She managed a coy smile. "You didn't like it?"

"I loved it and hated it in equal measure."

"Why?"

He gave a wry, self-mocking smile. "I wanted to show you off to everyone, and hide you away at the same time—to keep you from prying eyes like a dragon hoarding treasure. I know that makes no sense. I wanted all your kisses. All your smiles. I still do."

She gave him one of those smiles. "The day we made our pact was one of the *best* days of my life," she said. "I got everything I'd ever wanted. You."

She stepped forward and slid her hands up over his chest until she could feel his heart beating beneath her palms. "I tried to tell myself it was just an exercise—that I could give you my body but not my heart—but I have *never* been impartial to you."

The tension in his body eased a fraction. "Then marry me. Live with me. Let me be your favorite enemy."

She bit back a smile. "You haven't technically proposed, you know."

He sank to his knees and caught her hands. "Carys Davies. Will you marry me?"

"You're a *Montgomery*. What will people say?" she teased.

"They'd say Maddie already married your brother and the sky didn't fall in. And since when do *you* care about what people say? You're the queen of scandal and setting new trends. This will be your crowning achievement."

She opened her mouth to answer, but he sent her a mock-warning glare. "If you *don't* marry me, you'll become an eccentric old maid, like my aunts."

"I like your aunts."

"The feeling is mutual. In fact, they like you far better than they like me. They'll be delighted if you join the family." He squeezed her fingers. "I promise you free rein in the gardens. You can make them as wild and as romantic as you like." He stood and tugged her closer. "I need your wildness. Please say yes."

Carys slid her hands up his chest and grasped his lapels.

"Yes. I love you. Yes."

Tristan's arms tightened around her and his mouth swooped down on hers. With a laugh she threw her arms around his neck and returned his kiss with all the glowing ardor in her heart. Their tongues tangled in a glorious battle for supremacy and she closed her eyes, abandoning herself to sensation.

In one swift move, never taking his lips from hers, he bent and lifted her up. She wrapped her legs around his hips and he groaned as his hands slid down to cup her bottom. He crushed her to him and she tangled her fingers in his hair, loving the intensity of his need.

"God, I love you in breeches!" he growled.

He turned and pressed her back against the bookcase, trapping her there with the glorious weight of his body. She ground against him, her blood turning to molten fire as she felt the bold evidence of his desire. She kissed him again, deeper, urging him on, hooking her ankles behind his back to anchor herself in place.

He dragged his lips from hers and pressed kisses along her jaw. "We can't. Not here. Your brother will be waiting for us."

Carys gently bit his lower lip. "He can wait. Make love to me."

Tristan nodded, his gaze slightly unfocused. "Yes." He shifted his weight and she slid down his body to stand on the floor. Her legs felt a little wobbly.

"Stay right there." He strode to the door, turned the key in the lock, and hastened back to her. "Now—"

He'd just picked her up in his arms again when an insistent fist pounded on the door. Gryff's voice echoed through the wood.

"Montgomery! I heard that! If you're not out of this room in three minutes, you'd bloody well be sending an engagement announcement to *The Times*, or I'll be seeing you at dawn with my pistols."

Carys bit back a mortified laugh. "Gryff, go away!"

"Are you marrying him?" Gryff demanded.

"Yes!"

There was a pregnant pause, and then Gryff growled, "Bloody hell. That'll be *another* Montgomery in the family."

Carys smiled up at Tristan. "You started it!" she shouted to Gryff. "You married Maddie."

"Maddie's *nice*," Gryff countered. "And anyway, she's a Davies now."

Carys smoothed her hand through Tristan's hair. "Tristan's nice," she defended, her eyes glowing with mirth. "At least, *I* think so."

"Spare me," Gryff groaned. "I'm going to bed. Montgomery, take care of her, or I'll shoot you. Brother-in-law or no."

Tristan's eyes met hers. "You have my word," he called out.

"Good."

Gryff's footsteps stomped away, and Tristan kissed her again. "You have my word," he repeated, more quietly, a promise and a vow.

Carys laughed and kissed him back. "Well, you have my heart. So we're equal. Now show me how wicked you can be."

Epilogue

July 1815.

Carys glanced up from feeding Huginn and Muninn to see her husband of three days striding across the grass.

The day after his proposal, Tristan had made the very un-Tristanlike pronouncement that he wouldn't wait to have the banns posted for three consecutive weeks at the parish church. He'd ridden up to London and petitioned the Archbishop of Canterbury, Charles Manners-Sutton, for a Special License. It had cost him not just the five pounds for the license, but the promise to design a Greek-inspired temple in the archbishop's garden too. Both men had been delighted with the arrangement.

Carys and Tristan had been married in the library at Trellech at eleven o'clock in the morning, with only a handful of guests in attendance.

Gryff, Rhys, and Morgan had all displayed varying degrees of pride, disapproval, and mistrust. Maddie and her cousin Harriet had both beamed with pleasure. Tristan's aunts, Constance and Prudence, had both sniffed delicately at their scented handkerchiefs and wiped happy tears from their eyes, while Nanny Maude had sent Carys a wicked congratulatory wink. Frances and James, both of whom had traveled down from London, had gazed soulfully at each other across the room; James had also proposed, but the two of them had decided to observe the formalities and wait the traditional three weeks to be wed.

Carys had carried a small posy of violets and lily of the valley. Harriet, much to her chagrin, had been the one to catch it.

It had been a race to get even a few rooms of their new home furnished in such a short space of time and many were still completely bare, but Carys was looking forward to filling the place with both furniture and love.

Her heart gave a little flutter as she admired Tristan's long legs and broad shoulders. He carried a roll of paper in one hand, and she blushed at the memory of exactly what he'd been doing with those marvelous hands only a few hours before.

The green master bedroom had been the first room to be furnished.

"I have something for you," he said as he reached her.

"What's this, plans?"

He nodded and dropped to the picnic rug beside her. "Yes. New ones for the garden, as you suggested. With the perfect balance of wildness and restraint."

"Like us." She grinned.

He unrolled the sheets and used four small stones to secure the corners.

"What's this?" Carys pointed to a series of irregular shapes a little way from the house. She leaned closer to read the faint notes that had been penciled inside each one.

"Enclosures for your animals. Even bigger than the ones at Trellech." He grinned at her expression of surprise.

"I thought you'd want them all to *stay* at Trellech."

He shrugged. "Gryff and Maddie don't want all of them. And besides, Buttercup is definitely your bear. As is Brenin."

Carys smiled. Brenin was the name they'd given to the bear they'd rescued from the traveling circus. The owner had gladly handed him over to her care when he'd been captured by the authorities the morning after she and Tristan had intercepted Lord Holland's shipment of gold.

Lord Holland was currently in Newgate awaiting trial for trying to aid Britain's enemies, but the circus owner had escaped his armed escort—undoubtedly due to some dubious contacts and a liberal application of bribes—and had disappeared.

Christopher Howe, according to Victoria, had taken a boat to Calais, and had last been heard of heading toward Paris.

Carys studied the plans, her heart full with the thoughtfulness of Tristan's gesture. If ever she'd needed proof of his love for her, this garden was it. The tiny saplings they'd planted would take years to mature. Just like their marriage, they would need tending and care, but they would grow stronger and more beautiful every year.

She leaned back and pressed her fingers into the warm grass and watched the two ravens bicker over a twig. Roots and wings: Tristan had given her the perfect combination.

"I don't see a peacock enclosure," she said. "Does that mean Geoffrey will be staying at Trellech?"

Tristan nodded. "Absolutely. I am *not* having that dreadful creature here. I value my hearing. And my sanity."

"Morgan will be so disappointed." Carys chuckled.

He slanted her a teasing glance. "Looking forward to setting tongues wagging with our return to London next week? Ready to be unveiled as Carys Montgomery?"

"I can't wait. I've ordered the most spectacular gown. People aren't going to know what to gossip about first." She sent him an anxious glance. "You know I'll always be a devilish Davies at heart, though, don't you? Are you sure *you're* ready for me to start muddying your name with my scandalous ways?"

Tristan caught her chin and pulled her forward for a kiss that turned from chaste to scorching in a heartbeat. The paper crumpled beneath his elbow as they sank to the rug, and the two ravens rose, cawing, into the sky.

He smiled against her mouth. "I wouldn't have you any other way."